$26.00

10-2016

Crepe Factor

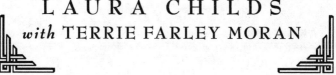

LAURA CHILDS
with TERRIE FARLEY MORAN

BERKLEY PRIME CRIME
New York

BERKLEY PRIME CRIME
Published by Berkley
An imprint of Penguin Random House LLC
375 Hudson Street, New York, New York 10014

Copyright © 2016 by Gerry Schmitt
Excerpt from *Egg Drop Dead* by Laura Childs copyright © 2016 by Gerry Schmitt
Penguin Random House supports copyright. Copyright fuels creativity, encourages
diverse voices, promotes free speech, and creates a vibrant culture. Thank you for buying
an authorized edition of this book and for complying with copyright laws by not
reproducing, scanning, or distributing any part of it in any form without permission.
You are supporting writers and allowing Penguin Random House to continue to
publish books for every reader.

BERKLEY is a registered trademark and BERKLEY PRIME CRIME and the B colophon
are trademarks of Penguin Random House LLC.

Library of Congress Cataloging-in-Publication Data

Names: Childs, Laura, author. | Moran, Terrie Farley, author.
Title: Crepe factor / by Laura Childs with Terrie Farley Moran.
Description: First edition. | New York : Berkley Prime Crime, 2016. | Series:
A scrapbooking mystery ; 14
Identifiers: LCCN 2016016134 (print) | LCCN 2016021602 (ebook) | ISBN
9780425266700 (hardback) | ISBN 9781101617571 (ebook)
Subjects: LCSH: Bertrand, Carmela (Fictitious character)—Fiction. | Women
detectives—Louisiana—New Orleans—Fiction. |
Murder—Investigation—Fiction. | Scrapbooking—Fiction. | BISAC: FICTION
/ Mystery & Detective / Women Sleuths. | FICTION / Mystery & Detective /
General. | GSAFD: Mystery fiction.
Classification: LCC PS3603.H56 C74 2016 (print) | LCC PS3603.H56 (ebook) |
DDC 813/.6—dc23
LC record available at https://lccn.loc.gov/2016016134

First Edition: October 2016

Printed in the United States of America
1 3 5 7 9 10 8 6 4 2

Cover art by Dan Craig
Cover design by Kate Anderson

Acknowledgments

Heartfelt thanks to Terrie Farley Moran, who contributed her energy, humor, and writing to this book. And to the usual suspects—Sam, Tom, Amanda, Bob, Jennie, Dan, and all the fine folks at Berkley who handle design, publicity, copywriting, bookstore sales, and gift sales. An extra special thank-you to all the scrapbook shop owners, bookstore folks, librarians, reviewers, magazine writers, websites, radio stations, bloggers, scrappers, and crafters who have enjoyed the adventures of the Memory Mine gang and who help me keep it all going.

And to you, dear readers, I promise many more mysteries featuring Carmela, Ava, Gabby, Tandy, Baby, Boo, Poobah, Babcock, and the rest of my crazy New Orleans cast. As well as a few surprises!

CREPE FACTOR

Chapter 1

RED rockets arced into an indigo-blue sky and exploded in a thousand points of incandescent light. The crowd at the Winter Market (already lubricated from tossing back multiple geaux cups of fine liquor) murmured a collective, appreciative "ooh" as the flat waters of the Mississippi River reflected mirror images of the colorful bursts.

"This is my favorite time of year," Carmela Bertrand said. "Right before we head into the holidays, when the weather's cooled down and you can feel the French Quarter literally pulsing with electricity."

"You sure you're not just having a hot flash?" Ava asked.

Carmela grinned and shook her head. "How old do you think I am, anyway?"

"A year younger than me," Ava sighed. "Isn't it amazing

how the old *tempus* can *fugit*? It's like living in a game show
with a permanent lightning round."

Carmela had cool blue eyes, hair that was short, choppy, and
streaked with honey, and a radiant complexion that was due in
part to the industrial-strength humidity of New Orleans. She
was smart, practical, and possessed a nimble mind that fairly
burned with curiosity. (Yes, the kind of curiosity that killed the
proverbial cat.)

Ava, on the other hand, was her dark twin. Masses of raven
hair, lush lips, heart-shaped face, and eyes slightly canted to
give her an almost catlike appearance. Tonight, her leather
slacks appeared to be airbrushed on and her red silk top was
cut so low that her generous décolleté seemed like an offering
to the gods. Even though she was a few ticks over the age of
thirty herself, she dressed the same as when she was a perky,
eighteen-year-old beauty queen candidate from Wetumpka,
Alabama.

"This turned out to be fun," Ava said as she stopped at
a jewelry booth to admire a small gold skull necklace. "I'm
glad we came."

"Instead of sitting at home, watching Netflix, and eating
ourselves into a fudge-and-kettle-corn stupor?"

"Speak for yourself," Ava said. "You're the one with the
tough cop, nose-to-the-grindstone boyfriend who toils non-
stop for all us sinners and ungrateful taxpayers. Whereas I
could have been swanning around some exotic five-star restaurant with my dear sweet Roman Numeral if I'd crooked
my little finger at him." Roman Numeral was Ava's pet
name for Harrison Harper Wilkes III, her latest conquest in
a long list of conquests that practically rivaled those of Alex-
ander the Great.

It was early December and Carmela and Ava were taking
in the excitement and raucous fun of the Winter Market.

This outdoor celebration of art, jewelry, crafts, foods, and vintage clothing had been set up adjacent to the French Market, its string of flapping canvas booths and gaudy electric lights backing up directly to the dark Mississippi. Hordes of bead-wearing, hard-drinking revelers streamed through the marketplace, while Christmas carolers, stilt-walkers, fortune-tellers, and the occasional fire-eater also mingled in to enliven the celebration.

"Mmn," Ava said. Eyes open wide, she gestured frantically with her glass of wine, looking as if she'd just swallowed a bug. "Wine. More."

"Why are you suddenly talking as if you just deplaned from a foreign country?" Carmela asked.

Ava tilted her cup back and gulped a final hit. "Because my throat was caught in drink-swallow-belch mode," she explained. She fluttered a hand against her chest, let loose a genteel burp, and said, "There. Better."

"Maybe for you," Carmela said. "So . . . what? You want another glass of wine? Maybe something spiced?" She steered her friend toward one of a dozen wine vendors.

"Couldn't hurt."

"Whatcha got?" Carmela asked the wine vendor, a middle-aged man with a heroic handlebar mustache and a red sweatshirt that said KISS ME I'M CAJUN.

"Spiced wine, mulled wine, and chilled red wine," the vendor told her.

"Two spiced wines, please," Carmela said.

"What's the difference between mulled and spiced?" Ava asked.

The vendor shrugged. "The spiced wine has spices and the mulled wine has mulls."

"Clearly you're not the vintner," Carmela said. "Or if you are, we're in big trouble."

"Nah, I just work here," the guy said. He shrugged again. "Hey, what are you gonna do?"

"How about pouring us a couple of geaux cups?" Carmela said.

Ava held up a hand. "Just plain red wine for me. Merlot if you've got it."

As Carmela and Ava sipped their wine, they wandered past booths selling pottery, photographs, beaded bracelets, hand-tooled leather belts, and T-shirts emblazoned with the words *BIG EASY*.

"Quigg's gumbo booth should be down here somewhere," Carmela said.

"He's here?" Ava said. "Why's that?" They continued to push through the crowd, past a row of food booths that offered po-boys, roast beef sandwiches, fried oysters, and shaved ice.

"Probably because selling food always proves to be lucrative at these events, as well as incredibly popular."

"You sure about that?" Ava asked. "Because I think I see one of Quigg's customers right now and the guy looks like he's ready to pop a blood vessel."

Carmela frowned. "What?" Across the way, a booth selling antique music boxes and bronze dogs had caught her eye. Then she turned her attention back to Ava.

"You see," Ava said, pointing, "Quigg's really throwing shade at that guy. Giving him a piece of his mind."

Carmela switched her attention to the mini drama that was being played out some twenty feet away from them.

"Are you *serious*?" Quigg's voice rang out. "You actually think you're doing the public a *favor*?" Quigg Brevard, the owner of Mumbo Gumbo, Bon Tiempe Restaurant, and St. Tammany Vineyard, was in the middle of a shouting match. A serious shouting match. His normally handsome face was pulled into a snarl, his olive complexion darkened to reflect his anger. Two of his employees cowered behind him in a booth strung with lights and papered with colorful menus.

The closer Carmela and Ava got to the turmoil, the more aggressive both parties got.

"You're a hack," Quigg screamed. "You have zero credibility in this town."

"And you're a fool," the man shouted back at him. "A pretender. An *insult* to decent restaurateurs." The man was forty-something, around Quigg's age, but completely opposite in stature. This verbal opponent, who darted in to deliver insults, was thin and wiry compared to Quigg's broad-shouldered, athletic build.

"You wouldn't know a decent eggs Sardou if it jumped up and bit you in the ass," Quigg shouted at him.

At that, the man snatched up a large bowl of steaming shrimp gumbo, cocked back his arm, and hurled it into the booth. Quigg ducked just in the nick of time, but the gumbo smacked hard against the back wall. *Whap!* Gumbo spattered the entire booth, dripping globs of roux, okra, and shrimp, and obliterating the red and green sign that listed the various kinds of gumbo. Crab, shrimp, and oyster, to be exact.

"Ouch," Ava said. "This is takin' on the appearance of a street brawl."

Quick as a snapping turtle, Quigg leaned across the counter and grabbed the man by his collar. "Get out of here!" he thundered. "Before I rip your fool head off."

The man windmilled his arms and jerked himself out of reach. "You'll be sorry," he snarled, waving a clenched fist at Quigg. "You're gonna pay for this."

"I hope you choke on a chicken bone!" Quigg yelled as the guy spun away.

"Quigg," Carmela called out. She wore a tentative, hope-fully soothing smile on her face. They were friends, after all. They'd even dated a couple of years ago.

"What!" Quigg screamed, not even bothering to look at her.

"Whoa. Quigg." Carmela walked up to the counter of his booth and held up a hand as if to create an invisible force field against his anger and bad vibes. "Take it down a notch. It's me, Carmela."

"And me, too," Ava said, managing a lopsided smile.

"What's going on?" Carmela asked. "Why were you bang-ing away on that guy? Did he wreck your car? Embezzle money from you?"

"Ach." Quigg snorted and flapped a hand derisively, still looking sublimely upset. "That was Martin Lash."

Ava glanced in the direction of the departed Lash, who had since melted into the crowd. "Who dat?" she asked.

"You girls know who he is," Quigg said in a dispirited tone. "He's the jerk who writes for that stupid food website, Glutton for Punishment."

"Oh, him," Ava said. "Yeah, I have heard of him. *Vieux Carré Magazine* called him 'the spicy new voice of foodies everywhere.'"

"And let me guess . . ." Carmela lifted a perfectly waxed brow. The pieces were tumbling into place for her. "Martin Lash gave one of your restaurants a very bad review."

Quigg's swarthy complexion darkened another couple of shades. "I wouldn't call it a review so much as he excoriated me."

"Say what?" Ava said.

"He wrote a nasty review," Carmela explained.

Ava frowned. "Well, that's uncharitable. Especially for a guy who gets to feed his face for free all over town."

"Lash is a blowhard with an ego bigger than a Macy's Thanksgiving Day balloon," Quigg said. "Which is exactly what I was trying to drill into his pea brain when you ladies came along and broke my concentration."

"It sounded more like you were threatening him," Ava said.

"So what was the upshot of all your hostilities?" Carmela asked. "Will Lash change his review? Maybe give you another chance?"

"He laughed in my face when I suggested that," Quigg said. "He told me that Mumbo Gumbo deserved a *negative* two stars." Mumbo Gumbo was Quigg's pride and joy French Quarter restaurant. So Carmela could understand why Quigg was upset. Correction: change *upset* to *infuriated*.

"There's nothing you can do?" Carmela asked. "There's no recourse at all?"

"Short of blasting him off the Internet I don't know what I can possibly do," Quigg sighed.

"Apologize?" Carmela said.

"Never," Quigg said.

"So the bad review just stays there forever?" Ava asked. "Swirling through cyberspace along with Kim Kardashian's selfies?"

"I suppose so," Quigg said. Now he just looked depressed.

"Maybe it's not that bad," Carmela said. She was trying to find an upside to this, a silver lining. "People don't pay all that much attention to reviews, do they?"

"Tourists do," Quigg said.

Carmela grimaced. New Orleans was a tourist town. Nine and a half million people flocked to New Orleans each year to partake of fine food, grand architecture, free-flowing booze, outlandish behavior, and haunted cemeteries.

"And whenever we hand out comment cards in the restaurants," Quigg said, "customers always mention the reviews they've read."

Carmela decided to quit while she was ahead. Aside from

hacking the Glutton for Punishment website, she didn't have any sparkling ideas to offer Quigg.

"We certainly wouldn't mind a couple bowls of your gumbo," Ava said. "*We* know how delicious it is."

"You're very sweet," Quigg said, but he was smiling at Carmela as he said it, looking a little wistful. "How you doin'?" he asked, leaning toward her, dropping his voice to a conspiratorial tone. "You still dating that cop?"

"Detective first grade," Carmela said. When she and Quigg had dated, nothing seemed to spark. Their relationship had been lukewarm at best. Now, every time Quigg saw her, he seemed to salivate over what he couldn't have. Carmela didn't know if all men were like that or just Quigg. Well, clearly her ex-husband, Shamus, wasn't. Whenever they crossed paths Shamus acted like a vampire fleeing a bouquet of garlic.

"We'll tell everyone to come to your booth," Ava said. "So they can taste for themselves how good your food is." She looked at the backdrop that was splotched and still dripping with gumbo. "That's if they can read your menu."

"Sure," Quigg said. "Whatever." He turned to one of his employees and sighed. "Mario, see what you can do about this mess."

"IS QUIGG ALWAYS SUCH A HOTHEAD?" AVA ASKED.

"I don't think I've ever seen him that angry before," Carmela said.

"New Orleans does that to you. After a while it messes with your mind and brings out your inner crazy. This city should come with a warning label." Ava held up her plastic cup. "Hang on a minute. I want to top off my Merlot." She wiggled her way to another wine booth and let them pour a stream of Chablis into her half-full cup.

"Really?" Carmela said. "And what does that get you?"

Ava gazed into her drink. "Pink stuff." She took a sip. "And it's pretty dang good, too. Mixed with the Merlot it tastes like . . . Chablot."

"Just don't spill that gunk on your suede boots. Or get sick and oopsy all over them. Remember what happened last time you mixed your liquor?"

"That was an extremely rare and isolated case of Wild Turkey not seeing eye to eye with French champagne," Ava said. "That wouldn't happen again in a million years."

"Hah."

"Say now," Ava purred, her eyes locking on to another booth, where candles flickered and black leather and silver chains gleamed. "What delicious little goodies do we have here?"

Carmela glanced into the booth. It was filled with leather corsets, garter belts, and lace-up boots. And was that a whip she saw dangling overhead? Oh my.

"A bondage lover's dream," Ava declared, fingering a leather garment. "I wonder if they have this corset in my size?"

The frizzy-haired woman working the booth smiled at Ava. "What are you, about a six or eight?"

"On a good day, yes," Ava said.

"This corset would fit you beautifully, then," the woman said. "And we also have it in red leather with gold studs."

Ava held up the black corset for Carmela to see. "What do you think?"

"For me, personally, I would go with the red," Carmela said.

"Be serious."

"Okay. For me, personally, I would skip the whole thing. Who wants all that leather cinched tight around your waist? I prefer to suck in my fat the old-fashioned way. By holding my breath."

"I'm going to try it on," Ava said.

"Of course you are."

"Just duck behind this curtain," the woman said, shoving a purple paisley shawl aside. "Maybe try it on right over your blouse."

Ava disappeared inside while Carmela waited. Candles flickered, leather gleamed, and Carmela felt more and more uncomfortable. "You almost ready?" she called out.

Suddenly, the entire booth began to shift and shake. Carmela wondered what on earth was going on back there? It couldn't be *that* tough to squeeze into a corset, could it? "Ava?" she called out.

Ava and the booth's owner peeped out from behind the curtain just as another enormous vibration rocked the booth.

"Ava, get out here!" Carmela called. Something felt very wrong.

Ava popped out, looking frightened. "What?" she yelped. She had the corset on around her. "Was somebody trying to rip open the back flap and get a peek at my chichis?"

This time the canvas booth trembled harder, as if the earth were about to open up and swallow it. Canvas flapped and rippled, an aluminum pole snapped, flaming candles wobbled and then toppled over, spewing rivulets of hot wax everywhere.

"Oh!" the booth owner cried as the booth jerked and spasmed.

"What's going on?" Ava asked, her eyes wide as saucers.

"Something's happening behind it," Carmela said. For some reason, there'd been a break in the crowd and they were the only ones around. That seemed to make the night feel darker, the flicker of lights more menacing.

Ava jerked straight up like a prairie dog on point. "It

sounds like somebody's tenderizing meat out back. Smacking a side of beef with a wooden mallet."

Carmela listened for a split second. "More like somebody's fist is connecting hard with somebody's face."

"You mean, like a fight? We should call a cop." Ava looked both fearful and distracted. "How come there's never one around when you need . . . ?"

Carmela pulled out her cell phone, ready to hit 911. But just as her finger was poised above the keypad, all hell broke loose. The tent jerked and shivered as if an F5 tornado were bearing down upon it. Then it teetered forward precariously, the overhead string of lights popping like cheap cheeseburgers on a grill. The table tipped forward and all the leather goods slipped to the ground.

"Dear Lord, what's happening?" Ava cried.

That's when a god-awful scream pierced the air. It rose up, tortured and shrill, like the death knell of a banshee.

Ava stumbled over to Carmela and grabbed her friend's arm in a viselike grip. "Was that scream even human?"

Carmela was just as stunned. "I gotta call . . ."

Another scream rent the air just as the tent collapsed completely, folding in on itself with a crash that sounded like the end of time.

"Holy crap!" Ava shrieked. She lifted a hand and pointed as a figure stumbled out of the darkness toward them.

Carmela and Ava stared, disbelieving, as Martin Lash staggered into the dim light. He was gasping for air and lurching wildly. Worse than that, a huge serving fork protruded directly from his carotid artery.

Feet clomping woodenly, eyes dark pools of pain, looking stiff and half dead, like the Frankenstein monster, Lash advanced on them.

"Holy shit!" Ava cried. "It's that blogger guy, Lash!"

Lash stared at them, eyes glazed and burning red, practically unseeing. Then his mouth formed a perfect O and he let out a low, threatening hiss like a dying vampire.

Stunned, practically scared out of their undies, Carmela and Ava backpedaled away.

"Help!" Ava squawked. But they were both too astonished by Lash's macabre dance of death to turn away completely.

Lash managed one more awkward, clumpy step, as if his dying brain was operating solely on autopilot. He hesitated, the giant fork in his gullet quivering and jiggling wildly. Rivulets of bright red blood spurted from his neck, creating blossoms of red down the front of his shirt. He stared at them blankly for a few more seconds, then flung his arms straight out to his sides. "Graaah!" he warbled as he slowly tipped back on his heels.

Carmela and Ava watched in horror as Martin Lash, blogger non grata, keeled over backward and landed hard on the pavement. Splat.

Seconds went by.

"You think he's dead?" Ava whispered.

Carmela tiptoed forward a couple of steps, caught the metallic glint of the giant fork still stuck in Lash's gullet, and nodded. "He's done for."

Chapter 2

IN spite of the dead body lying practically at her feet, the frizzy-haired booth owner spun around wildly like a gyroscope that was out of control.

"This is crazy!" she shrilled, arms flung out, wobbling on her high-heeled leather boots. "My beautiful leather goods . . . my booth!" She went into orbit again and pointed at Ava. "You there. Remove that corset. It doesn't fit you anyway." Then she went back to kvetching. "Last year it rained and everything turned into a soggy mess. This year it's raining dead men!"

"Well, jeez," Ava grumbled as she picked at the laces. "It wasn't that flattering anyway."

"That," Carmela said, "is the least of our problems."

Two minutes later, they were surrounded by a cadre of uniformed officers. Apparently, cooler heads had prevailed somewhere and a 911 call had gone out. Now two officers stood over the dead man, pretty much scratching their heads. Right on the heels of those officers came a raucous gang of looky-loos, predictably anxious to get their grisly kicks by looking at a dead guy.

"Get back. Everybody back," one of the uniformed officers hollered. His name tag said *BAILEY* and he was red-faced and huffing from the exertion, rings of sweat forming under his arms. When the crowd was sufficiently cowed, Officer Bailey glanced back at the dead man and then asked, "Are there any witnesses?"

Carmela raised a tentative hand. "My friend and I. We saw him stagger out."

"Him," Bailey said. "It sounds as if you know who he is?"

"I think his name is Martin Lash," Carmela said.

"Wait right there," Bailey said as the crowd pressed forward again. "You'll need to speak with one of the detectives."

The name Martin Lash did it, of course. The name was repeated, whispered, and then passed along again. The rumor that Lash had been stabbed—probably murdered—ran through the Winter Market like wildfire.

Carmela and Ava waited, surrounded by jostling crowds, until they heard the noisy, high-pitched bleat of an ambulance. Then another uniformed officer joined Officer Bailey as they tried to keep everyone at bay while the shiny white ambulance backed in slowly, the driver trying his best not to roll over anyone's toes.

Carmela and Ava watched, fascinated, as a gurney was unloaded and two EMTs rushed to the aid of Martin Lash. They worked quickly and efficiently, administering oxygen, doing chest compressions, even yanking out the giant meat fork. But short of a Lazarus-type miracle, nothing seemed to be working.

"That poor sucker's dead," Ava said.

"Don't be so hasty," Carmela warned.

"No, the rumor is that he's really dead," a voice behind them said. They turned around to find Quigg Brevard anxiously watching the frantic activity.

"Happy now?" Carmela asked him. She hadn't much cared for Quigg's matter-of-fact tone of voice. Rumors were just that: rumors. Maybe Martin Lash still had a fighting chance.

"Of course I'm not happy," Quigg snapped back at her. "Don't be ridiculous."

Carmela turned her attention back to the scene of the crime. The police seemed to be genuinely puzzled and all talking at once. And even as the EMTs continued to work over the body, the frizzy-haired woman scrabbled around shoving leather bustiers into cardboard boxes, the mustachioed wine vendor moved in closer, and some guy wandered through the crowd, selling kettle corn to fascinated onlookers for ten dollars a bag, twice the going rate.

Officer Bailey came up to Carmela and said, "Just a few more minutes, ma'am. The detective is on his way."

"Is he dead?" Ava asked. She pointed toward the body on the ground.

Bailey seemed unhappy. "It looks that way."

"Do you know who will be . . . ?" Carmela began. But the officer had already turned away. No matter. Carmela had already caught sight of a familiar blue BMW cruising toward the scene. She nudged Ava. "Guess who got the callout?" She looked around for Quigg, but he was gone.

"Huh?" Ava said. She could barely pull her eyes away from the EMTs and the craziness of the crowd.

Carmela turned her attention back to Babcock. He'd parked his car and was striding toward the murder scene now, looking rather serious and take-charge.

Tall and lanky, Edgar Babcock moved like a big cat with

a reserve of coiled energy. Even though it was late in the day, Carmela could imagine the scent of Dial soap, Paco Rabanne, and a nicely starched shirt as he hurried along. Babcock's ginger-colored hair was cropped short and his blue eyes were pinpricks of intensity. Interestingly enough, he was also a serious clotheshorse, always dressing extremely well. Tonight he wore a wool tweed jacket, dark slacks, and leather slip-on loafers that Carmela guessed were from Prada. It was no surprise that he was up for deputy chief.

Carmela touched two fingers to her heart. "Thank goodness," she said. "If anybody can figure this out, Babcock can."

"Absolutely," Ava said. "Because he's not only got the smarts, he's tenacious."

"A pit bull," Carmela agreed.

But right now Babcock had a scowl on his face and was waving his arms.

"Push them back," he yelled at Officer Bailey. "Get everyone out of here. I want at least a twenty-five-foot perimeter."

"Will do," Bailey shouted back.

But the onlookers were slow to move.

Babcock shook his head and repeated his order. He was losing patience.

Finally, Bailey and four other uniformed officers gained some control over the crowd, and the circle around the body began to widen. Then Bailey leaned in and said something to Babcock. Babcock nodded, glanced around, and started scanning the crowd. When his eyes landed on Carmela they widened in surprise.

Uh-oh, Carmela thought. But she lifted a hand and gave him a brief finger-flutter wave anyway.

Babcock looked toward the heavens, shook his head, and turned back to Officer Bailey.

"We might have a problem," Carmela said.

"What? Us?" Ava said. "Nah. I doubt it."

Carmela watched Babcock carefully as the crowd slowly dispersed and, one by one, he began questioning a number of vendors. From the blank looks on their faces, it was pretty clear that most of them hadn't seen or heard anything out of the ordinary. The frizzy-haired leather lady was no help at all.

"All I know is that he knocked down my booth." She jabbed a finger angrily toward the very dead Martin Lash. "Never seen him before, never hope to again."

Babcock questioned a few more vendors, but it wasn't until he talked to the music box vendor that he hit pay dirt.

"Yeah, he was yelling his head off and arguing," the music box vendor said. He was short and stocky with a hawk nose and a shock of dark hair. He looked like an extra in a wiseguys movie.

"There was an argument?" Babcock asked. This was the first he'd heard.

The music box vendor nodded. "Between the guy that got stabbed and the gumbo guy, yeah."

Babcock gave a slow, reptilian blink. "Gumbo guy?"

Uh-oh, Carmela thought.

"Quigg something," said the music box vendor.

"Quigg Brevard?" Babcock's eyes flickered over toward Quigg's booth, where a major cleanup was under way.

The vendor nodded. "Yeah, that's the guy."

That was also when Carmela stepped forward.

"Excuse me," Carmela said. "I also witnessed that particular exchange. And it wasn't . . . such a big deal."

The music box vendor rocked back on his heels. "That ain't what I saw, lady."

"What exactly did you see?" Babcock asked him.

"I . . ." Carmela started.

But Babcock held up a hand. "Please. Let the man finish. I'll get to you in a minute."

"From what I saw they had a pretty serious argument," the vendor said. "Lots of yelling, a few nasty cuss words."

"So you wouldn't exactly categorize it as friendly?" Babcock asked. "A friendly disagreement?"

"On a scale of one to ten," the vendor said, "it was about a fifteen. Ten being a meltdown at Chernobyl."

Carmela threw up her hands. "Oh, come on."

Babcock ignored her. He turned to Officer Bailey and said, "We need to get Brevard over here."

"Really?" Carmela said. She was suddenly very scared for Quigg, worried that he could take the fall for this.

Thirty seconds later, Quigg was standing with them, looking none too happy. But as soon as he recognized Detective Babcock, he hastened to explain. "Hey, Babcock, you know me. I wouldn't smack a mosquito at dawn nor dusk. I heard a rumor that Martin Lash got killed but I never had a problem with the man."

Then Quigg noticed Carmela watching him closely. "Look, so maybe I did have a few words with Lash earlier tonight." He spread his hands wide and shrugged his shoulders. "I own restaurants, he writes restaurant reviews. Sometimes we don't always see eye to eye, you know? But there was nothing physical between us. I mean, okay, he threw a bowl of gumbo at me and then went slinking off like a coward." He pretended to wipe a blob of food from his pristine apron. "But there's no hard feelings. Really."

"That's not what I hear," Babcock said.

Quigg leaned forward. "What do you hear?"

"For one thing, you just spilled your guts and told me

plenty," Babcock said, but in a moderate, reasonable tone of voice. "Apparently, Martin Lash wrote a review that you didn't agree with and then the two of you had a very nasty argument." He glanced around. "In front of several witnesses. Next thing we all know, Martin Lash turns up dead."

"He's good," Ava muttered.

"Shh," Carmela hissed. Babcock *was* good. And Quigg wasn't doing much to help his own case.

"You want to explain your argument?" Babcock asked. "Elaborate on what happened?"

Quigg glowered at him. "Explain why some hack writer insulted *me*? Are you serious? Martin Lash probably insulted every food vendor here. Why don't you go talk to them?"

"I already did," Babcock said. "But the evidence keeps circling back to you."

"Evidence?" Quigg shouted. "There is no evidence."

"We have several eyewitnesses," Babcock said.

"Maybe of the argument," Carmela suddenly interjected. "But not of the murder. Ava and I were there. We didn't see anybody else."

"And just why are you here again?" Babcock asked Carmela.

"To have fun?" she said in a small voice, just as the shiny black crime scene van bumped across the grass toward Martin Lash's dead body.

"Of course," Babcock said. He turned back to Quigg Brevard. "We're going to need you to come in and give us a statement. Expect to be with us for a while because I'm guessing that more than words passed between you and Lash . . ."

Quigg suddenly bristled.

Babcock continued on. "And I do want to hear the entire story."

"Sure. Whatever," Quigg said.

"As for you," Babcock said, turning to Carmela. "We need to have a very serious talk as well."

"Sure," Carmela said. *Gulp.*

IT TOOK ANOTHER HOUR FOR CARMELA AND AVA to finally get out of there, and by that time they were so jacked up they needed something to help them relax.

"A glass of wine," Carmela said as she stuck her key in the door. Her garden apartment was located just across a quaint little courtyard from Juju Voodoo, Ava's voodoo shop. Ava lived upstairs in a teeny-tiny apartment that was painted Pepto pink with lots of leopard-print design touches.

"Sounds perfect," Ava said.

But as the door opened, two wiggling, waggling dogs flung themselves at the two women.

"Down, babies, down," Carmela pleaded. But Boo, her fawn-colored Shar-Pei, was already smothering her with kisses. And Poobah, a spotted rescue dog, pawed excitedly at Ava.

"Watch the leather," Ava warned. "The shoes you can gnaw but the leather is sacrosanct."

"Poobah!" Carmela shouted. "Get down."

Poobah ducked his head and gave them both a crazy, crooked doggy smile, his tongue hanging out like a pale pink ribbon.

"He really is cute," Ava said. "For a Heinz 57 dog."

"Shh," Carmela joked. "Poobah still dreams of making it to Westminster."

Carmela cracked open a bottle of rosé then and they sat in her living room, digesting the evening, if not all the greasy and sugary food they'd consumed.

"Eh," Ava said. She flopped down across the leather sofa.

"I never thought a trip to the Winter Market could turn out so dreadful."

"It's one for the record books," Carmela agreed. She'd lit a candle, kicked off her shoes, and flaked out on her chaise lounge. Now, for the first time tonight, she felt like she was able to relax. Babcock had grilled her like a hunk of halibut over a bed of hot coals. Demanding to know why she and Ava had been at the Winter Market. Wanting to know how much of the argument between Quigg and Martin Lash she'd overheard. Carmela had been . . . cautious. She liked Quigg, she really did. And sometimes Quigg could be his own worst enemy. So, yes, maybe she'd been a little bit protective of him. Who wouldn't be if some crappy music box vendor was pointing his fat finger at their friend? Talking about a complete meltdown. Oh please.

"You know what?" Ava said.

"What?"

"I think I've got kettle corn stuck in my fillings."

"I'm not surprised, you ate enough of it."

"I'll probably have to pour a gallon of hydrogen peroxide into my teeth-whitening tray tonight."

"What's that gonna do?"

"Break up the chunks of caramel that are glazed onto my teeth?"

"That's a nice thought," Carmela said. She gazed about her apartment dreamily. It was a comfy, cozy place that had been her first refuge when she'd gotten divorced from Shamus. But now she'd turned it into the kind of genteel, elegant, slightly frayed home that born-and-bred New Orleans residents adored. A leather sofa, slightly nicked and scratched from dog paws. Persian carpet. Dark, crackle-glazed oil paintings. Thick velvet draperies that lent a slightly decadent feel. Yup, this was home, all right, and Carmela reveled in the fact that she'd created it all by herself.

"I hate to bring this up," Ava said.

"Then don't."

"But I'm not sure I've seen anything as gross as Martin Lash staggering toward us with that huge fork stuck in his neck."

"It was pretty awful," Carmela agreed.

"And the really bad thing is . . ."

"Yes?"

"Well, Quigg is kind of an obvious suspect," Ava said.

Ava's words dug deep into Carmela, creating a sick feeling in the pit of her stomach. "I know Quigg's a hothead sometimes. But, believe me, he didn't have anything to do with this."

"Are you sure about that, *cher*?" Ava held up a hand. "I mean, really sure?"

"Yes, I think so."

Ava pulled herself upright and reached for the wine bottle. Poured herself another drink. Her dark eyes drilled into Carmela. "You think or you know?"

"I know. Quigg blows hot and cold but he's no killer," Carmela said. At least she hoped he wasn't. Because if Quigg momentarily lost his temper and *did* kill Martin Lash, then he was in a world of trouble.

"That's good," Ava said. "That you're so sure of him. That you'd stand behind him like that."

Carmela arched a brow. "Ava, where are you going with this?"

Ava stretched languidly. Whenever she was going to present Carmela with a moral dilemma she stretched languidly, trying to look innocent. It was like a "tell" in poker.

"I was thinking that maybe you should help Quigg," Ava said. "Give him a little assist." There was a pregnant pause. "Because you're good at this Nancy Drew stuff."

"Are you crazy? You know I dated Quigg. *Babcock* knows I dated Quigg. So helping him would just open up a big fat can of worms." Boo, who was lying right near Carmela's feet, lifted her head and stared at her.

Ava stared at her, too, her brown eyes looking almost pleading in the flickering candlelight.

"No," Carmela said. "I want nothing to do with this case. Babcock doesn't trust Quigg anywhere near me, and if I nose around this murder case, Babcock probably won't trust me, either."

They sat for a few moments, Boo's front paws twitching a couple times as she dropped into sleep again.

"Nothing is worth risking my relationship with Babcock," Carmela said. "Nothing."

Ava fluttered a hand. "Not even saving a man from death row?"

Silence took over the room.

Chapter 3

SHAFTS of sunshine punched through early-morning rain clouds as Carmela pushed open the door to Memory Mine. The minute she stepped inside her little scrapbooking shop a sense of homey peacefulness enveloped her. It was the exact feeling she'd strived for when she first opened the shop on Governor Nicholls Street in the French Quarter a few years ago. The quaint space, deeper than it was wide, with brick walls and pegged wooden floors, had been an antique shop in an earlier incarnation. Now it was stuffed full of scrapbook paper, leather-bound albums, rubber stamps, ink pads, stencils, packets of ephemera, ribbon, cardstock, memory boxes, and all manner of gift wrap.

"Gabby?" Carmela called out. No answer. But the door had been unlocked and the lights were turned on so Carmela knew that Gabby Mercer-Morris, her dependable assistant, was somewhere on the premises.

And here she was now.

Wearing a chic caramel-colored sweater set and matching pencil skirt, Gabby came tiptoeing out of the back office in her Tory Burch flats, balancing a stack of scrapbooking paper, each color banded with its own wrapper.

Gabby spotted Carmela standing at the front counter and wasted no time. "Good morning, Carmela. Would you believe we've already had three calls and it's barely nine o'clock? There's a mother and daughter coming in shortly and they're hot to make wedding scrapbooks." Gabby ticked their requests off on her fingers. "The daughter wants a Mr. and Mrs. book, a bouquet book, a ceremony book, and of course she wants to create smaller books for all her bridesmaids." She paused to catch her breath. "So I'm glad you're here, what with all our regular customers coming in to stock up on holiday décor. Oh, and I left a copy of the *Times-Picayune* on your desk." Her brown eyes shone with intensity. "Apparently, a horrible murder took place at the Winter Market last night." She dropped her load of paper on the back table, the one they'd dubbed Craft Central. "Just when were you planning to tell me about *that*?"

Carmela smiled faintly. The newspaper had plopped down on her own doorstep at five o'clock this morning and she'd raced out to grab it, startling the paperboy, who wasn't used to seeing a frazzle-haired women in a filmy peignoir peeping out at him. Or maybe he was.

"How about now?" she said to Gabby.

Gabby put a hand on her hip, her brownish-blond bob nodding in agreement. "Well, I guess." Gabby was gentle natured and demure, a perfect complement to her quintessential preppy style.

"Do we have time to grab a couple cups of tea first?"

"It's already steeping. Cranberry Spice from that little shop you like so much in Charleston. It's one of their holiday house blends."

"Sounds perfect."

Gabby fetched two cups of tea in bone china teacups and brought them to the front counter. Along with the newspaper.

"This is so civilized," Carmela said. "And the teacups are a major upgrade from our usual clunky mugs that vendors give us for free."

"I bought a few cups and saucers at Pink Elephant Antiques just down the street. I figured if we were going to brew a proper cuppa we should probably have proper teacups." She took a sip. "So . . . the murder. Are you going to share all the grisly little details before we're inundated with customers?"

"Do you want me to?"

"Well, not the really bad stuff," Gabby said.

"The whole thing went down pretty much according to the newspaper story. The Winter Market, throngs of partiers, and one dead guy with a serving fork stuck in his throat."

Gabby grimaced and then tapped a finger against the newspaper. "There has to be more to it than that."

"I was getting around to that particular aspect. But what I'm going to tell you is just between the two of us, okay?"

Gabby suddenly looked nervous. "Sure. I guess."

"Right before the murder Quigg Brevard and Martin Lash were involved in a terrible shouting match."

"What?"

"Ava and I witnessed the whole thing. In fact, their argument got so heated that Lash grabbed a bowl of shrimp gumbo and flung it into Quigg's booth."

Gabby's brows shot up. "My Lordy."

"Of course we figured that was the end of it. They'd both had their Mount St. Helens explosion and the matter was over. So Ava and I kind of wandered off and started browsing the craft booths. Then, just as Ava was trying on this weird leather corset thing, Lash came staggering out from behind the booth, looking like an extra from *The Walking Dead.*"

"With the fork stuck in his throat," Gabby said.

"Yes, ma'am."

Gabby shook her head. "So horrible. So grisly."

"And then everything went boom, and about a zillion cops showed up, Babcock included."

"Did you tell him about the red-hot argument? Between Quigg and Lash?"

"I didn't have to. Some other helpful tattletale jumped in and took care of that."

"So what . . . now Quigg's a suspect?"

"Numero uno, Grade A prime."

Gabby frowned. "Quigg's got a big personality. I mean . . . he can be a little blustery. But you and I both know he wouldn't hurt a fly."

"Funny, that's exactly what I told the police. But they chose not to listen to me." Carmela shrugged. "I guess I'm not a re- liable character witness."

"So now Quigg's found himself in serious trouble," Gabby said. She whispered these last words as the front door suddenly banged open and smacked the wall.

Hello there, Carmela thought to herself. *Who are you?*

A middle-aged woman in a pink suit caromed through the door, pulling along a young woman dressed in bright blue yoga pants and a matching top. The middle-aged woman looked around speculatively as if she were the critic for *Southern Living* magazine, while the young woman remained hunched over her iPhone, poking at the screen.

"I'm Emily Jackson," the woman announced loudly. "This is my daughter Melanie. We're looking for Gabby?"

Gabby lifted a hand. "That's me."

"We called earlier about the wedding scrapbooks?"

"Of course," Gabby said. "Welcome to Memory Mine."

"We're kind of in a rush," the woman said.

"Good thing I've been thinking about your project, then," Gabby replied. "In fact, I've already pulled a few albums to help you get started. If you'll just step this way . . ." She swept an arm out and smiled at the younger woman. "Melanie? I take it you are the lady of the hour, the bride-to-be?"

"Yes'm," Melanie murmured without looking up from her phone. Which earned her a well-delivered jab in the ribs from Mom.

"Put that thing away," her mother hissed. "Pay attention."

The two women disappeared into the back of the store with Gabby, while Carmela slid behind the counter. She was there for six seconds at best before two more ladies came rushing in. They were dressed in identical jogging suits, one mint green, one charcoal gray.

Gray Suit said, "We need some nice rich paper suitable for Reveillon dinner place cards."

The lady in green clapped her hands. "It's going to be rather exciting. We've got family coming from all over the state."

"Even our great-aunt Delia from way out in Sugartown," the lady in gray said.

"Then you must have a very special menu planned," Carmela said.

"Turtle soup," Green Suit responded. "I told sister I don't give a whit about the other four courses, but we simply must have turtle soup. Daddy, bless his sweet heart, would roll over in his crypt if we served anything besides turtle soup for our first course."

Carmela led them back to her paper stacks and showed them a cardstock in the palest celadon green. "This could easily be trimmed into place cards," she told them. "And, if you want a festive accent, you could add a tiny holly leaf in the corner."

More clapping. "I like that. What do you think, Sister?"

Fortunately, Sister agreed.

Carmela packaged up the celadon paper, a rubber stamp of a holly leaf, and a red ink pad. Once the sisters had left, the store enjoyed a steady flurry of customers. One lady asked for colored raffia and brown kraft paper gift bags, one was searching for batik paper, another wanted to make holiday cards. Carmela pulled bags and paper, offered crafty suggestions, and (oh, happy day!) rang up sales.

When things finally settled down to a dull roar, with more customers browsing rather than asking for help, Gabby wandered back to the counter to join Carmela.

"How goes it with your bridal crew?" Carmela nodded toward the back table.

Gabby rolled her eyes. "They're still sniping about color schemes. I'm going to let them duke it out for themselves."

"Sometimes that's all you can do."

Gabby picked up a packet of brass brads and fingered it. "You know, I've been thinking about the Martin Lash thing. And I realized that I kind of know him."

Carmela leaned forward, wanting to know more. "Seriously? How's that?"

"I met Lash in an odd sort of way. You know, besides being a food critic, Lash is . . . was . . . the executive director of a small nonprofit group called the Environmental Justice League. They're very passionate about preserving Louisiana's swamps and bayous."

"Okay, I guess I did read something about that in the

newspaper article." Carmela wondered where this conversation was going.

"Well, that very same group once rudely accosted my husband when we were at a charity dinner," Gabby said. Her husband, Stuart Mercer-Morris, owned something like five different car dealerships and often referred to himself as the Toyota King of New Orleans.

"Accosted Stuart how?" Carmela asked

"Lash and his Environmental Justice League members were all worked up about how environmentally insensitive Stuart's cars were, so they picketed the dinner and started haranguing him about what awful vehicles they were."

"Didn't they realize Stuart just *sells* the cars, he doesn't manufacture them?"

"They didn't much care," Gabby said. "They were a lot more interested in making a big stink. And getting on the ten o'clock news."

"And this incident happened fairly recently?"

"A couple of months ago."

"That's a fairly interesting story," Carmela said. "I mean, if Lash has a history of verbal abuse and bad behavior, this is something Babcock should know about."

Gabby nodded. "That's exactly what I was thinking."

"I mean, if he's known for being a hothead . . ."

"Oh, Gabby!" a plaintive voice called from the back of the store.

Gabby touched a hand to her forehead in a dramatic, what-can-you-do? gesture. "I'll be right there, ladies."

JUST WHEN BUSINESS WAS HOPPING AND CAR-mela didn't think another scrapbooker could squeeze their way into her shop, Quigg came sauntering in. He was dressed in a slim-fitting charcoal gray suit that showed off his narrow hips and broad shoulders to perfect advantage. His tailored white shirt was open at the neck, giving his outfit a casual, European vibe.

Never able to help himself, Quigg did a quick scan of the ladies, his eyes lingering on the bride-to-be as well as on an extremely attractive woman who wore a supple black leather jacket and tight blue jeans. Of course, he wasn't unaware of his own good looks when the lady in black leather smiled back at him.

Just look at that tomcat, Carmela thought. *He's preening. Completely aware of the devastating effect he has on women. In fact, he works at it. Cultivates it.*

The self-knowledge that he was attractive to women was one of Quigg's most irritating traits. It had bugged Carmela endlessly when she'd dated him. Even when he'd escorted her to the world-famous Antoine's for a romantic, candlelight dinner for two, she'd never felt she had his full attention.

Once Quigg had checked out the women in the shop, he turned his attention back to Carmela.

"Carmela," he growled.

"Quigg," Carmela said back. *What does he want? Is he here to bring disaster and suspicion down upon my head, too?*

"I need to talk to you." Quigg moved much closer to her than necessary, invading her personal space, as was his habit with women.

Carmela hesitated. She had a funny feeling that she knew what he might want. And probably should have just tossed him back out on the street. Instead, against her better judgment, she crooked her little finger at him, indicating that he should follow her back to her office. She figured she'd be more in control of their conversation there.

It was only when Carmela plopped down in her leather

chair that she realized what a bad decision she'd made. Quigg sat down in the guest chair and squiggled it up close to her until they were touching knees. Now she felt down-right uncomfortable. After all, he was handsome, hunky, and they used to date. There'd even been a few tiny sparks when they'd kissed. Of course that had been a few years ago, pre-Babcock.

"I need your help," Quigg said with barely a preamble.

"How's that?" Carmela asked pleasantly when she was really thinking, *Oh shit. Here it comes.*

"As you can probably guess, I'm in big trouble. That rather public argument I had with Martin Lash last night did me no good at all."

"Okay."

"And of course you know that your tough-guy boyfriend, Detective Babcock, interviewed all the vendors from the booths surrounding mine. None of them put in a good word for me."

"Okay," Carmela said again, practically holding her breath.

"Anyway, about an hour ago, Babcock informed me that he'd collected a number of statements that corroborated the verbal disagreement Lash and I had."

"Verbal disagreement?" Carmela said. "That sounds fairly benign. When the truth of the matter is you two were screaming at each other like a couple of crazed harpies."

Quigg lifted a shoulder. "Whatever."

"Wait a minute," Carmela said. "Are you blaming me because Babcock is doing his job?"

Quigg leaned forward in his chair. "Not exactly. But I think you could have used your influence to help defuse the situation."

Carmela felt her temper flare. "Oh no, Quigg. You are so wrong. Your situation is your situation and the smartest thing I can do is stay out of it."

Quigg slowly reached over and took Carmela's hand. "But, darlin', I need your help."

Carmela cringed inwardly as she pulled back her hand. "No, you really don't."

"Carmela." Quigg focused his hazel eyes on her. Eyes that, a few years ago, might have won her heart if he'd tried a little harder, put a little more effort into the relationship.

"No," she said again.

"You know me, Carmela. You know that I'd never murder another human being. Never in a million years."

He had her there. Carmela knew for a fact that Quigg was a good and decent person. His chefs and waitstaff all adored him, and his companies donated generously to New Orleans charities. Once, when her beloved Children's Art Association had been strapped for cash, he had given her five thousand dollars (as an anonymous gift, no less) to buy art supplies for a bunch of at-risk kids.

"Carmela," Quigg said. "We've known each other for a good long time. You're the one person I trust who can help me."

"I wish you wouldn't say that."

"But it's true." Quigg gazed soulfully into Carmela's eyes, making her feel even more uncomfortable. "We had something special once. I know I blew my chance with you. But you've always remained gracious, always stayed a friend."

"Quigg, the New Orleans Police Department has the case well in hand. Let them solve it. *Trust* them to solve it."

Quigg's dark eyes drilled into her. "That's the problem. They think they *have* solved it. They've set their sights on me. And considering that altercation I had with Lash, I'm not in the best position to defend myself."

"So hire a lawyer."

Quigg squeezed his eyes closed and then opened them. "I need someone to poke around and figure out who the real killer is. I need someone who has experience in finding a killer, before I get completely railroaded." He paused. "Carmela, I need *you*."

Carmela gazed at him. Quigg was pushing all the right buttons. He was giving her sincerity and desperation as well as a modicum of flattery. She was reluctant to help him, but felt a little torn as well. For all his flirtatiousness, Quigg was a sweet guy, an innocent guy. And he seemed so . . . worried. Should she help him? Could she help him?

Quigg seemed to read her mental calculations. "Please?" he breathed.

Carmela took a few moments to make up her mind. Then she said, "I'll make you a deal. I'll try to find out what I can, but only on one condition."

"Name it."

She leaned forward to drive home her point. "You dare not tell Babcock a thing about this. Whatever I do to help will remain our little secret."

"My lips are sealed. And I promise you won't regret this, Carmela."

She was regretting it already. "We can only hope."

WHEN QUIGG FINALLY LEFT AMIDST A FLURRY of interested smiles and glances, Carmela breathed a sigh of relief. She'd made some promises to Quigg, yes. Promises that might be a trifle far-fetched. But with any luck at all, Babcock would be out there beating the bushes, working his expertise, aggressively hunting for the real killer. And once he closed the case, he'd never be the wiser that she had agreed to help Quigg.

Somehow, even with all that rationalization, the feeling of dread in Carmela's heart didn't ease. Oh well. She slipped behind the counter, picked up a roll of gold gossamer ribbon, and then grabbed for the phone when it rang.

"Memory Mine," Carmela said. "How may I help you?"

"I'm just checking to see how you survived last night," came a warm baritone voice.

Oh no, it was . . .

Carmela let out a yelp. "Babcock!"

Chapter 4

"WHY do you sound so surprised?" Babcock asked.

"You just caught me off guard," Carmela blurted out. Truth be known, she was suddenly in a blind panic over his call. Coming on the heels of Quigg's visit, it felt like Babcock might be tuned in to her vibrations. As if he could peer into her prefrontal cortex and know exactly what mischief she was up to.

"I'm just checking to see if we're still on for tonight."

"Yes. Of course we are," Carmela said. They were supposed to attend a fancy Reveillon dinner at the Hotel Montague with Ava and Roman Numeral. "Why? Has something come up?" *Like, please, have you solved the Martin Lash murder so I don't have to keep my promise to help Quigg?*

"The problem right now is I'm being pulled in a million different directions," Babcock said. "The mayor and Downtown

Council are totally freaked out over last night's murder. Going into the holiday season they're terrified it might scare away the tourists."

"They're always worried something's going to scare away the tourists," Carmela said. "And the tourists still come. We could have an invasion of zombie alligators from outer space and the tourists would still come to drink our liquor and wander through our cemeteries."

That made Babcock chuckle.

"So what exactly are you saying?" Carmela asked. "That you're trying to duck out of our date? That you can't give me two lousy hours tonight?"

"Carmela . . ."

"Because I've been looking forward to this for weeks." *And now that I think about it, I need to pick your clever little brain and see if you've made any progress in solving this case.*

"I give up, Carmela. You win. I'll be there."

"Thank you." She paused. "So . . . the Martin Lash case. How's that coming along . . . really?"

Babcock made a sound between a grunt and a groan. "Terrible."

That was the opening Carmela needed.

"I have some information that could be pertinent, perhaps even helpful."

"What's that?" Now Babcock sounded guarded.

"Have you ever heard of the Environmental Justice League?"

"No. But I'm guessing you're talking about one of those green groups. Clean up the river, wind farms, solar heating, something like that?"

"Sort of," Carmela said. "The Environmental Justice League is a small, nonprofit group that fights to keep the environment pristine. Their particular interest is swampland and bayous."

Babcock was less than interested. "Lots of that going around. So what's so special about this group?"

Carmela smiled to herself. She was a step ahead of him. "Martin Lash was their executive director."

There were a few moments of silence and then Babcock said, "Really?" He said it like he didn't believe her.

But Carmela was rolling now. "So I was thinking . . . couldn't that have been a motive for Lash's murder? People get pretty upset about environmental issues. Ever since the BP oil spill there have been lots of heated battles between folks who support the environment and folks who think industry and jobs should come first. If someone thought the Environmental Justice League was threatening their livelihood, well, things could have gone off the rails."

She could practically feel Babcock mulling over this new information and was determined not to say another word until he spoke.

"How do you know about this?" he asked.

"Gabby told me. Apparently Martin Lash accosted her husband a while back. He threatened to smash windows in his showroom or something bizarre like that because Stuart sold cars that Lash considered to be gas-guzzlers."

"So you're telling me that Stuart Mercer-Morris might have done Lash in?" There was a hint of irreverence in Babcock's voice.

"No, of course not," Carmela said. "You know Stuart, he considers chess a violent game. But it could be somebody of that ilk. A member of the business community who's been threatened by Lash and his merry band of environmentalists. From what I understand, Lash was a pushy, confrontational type of guy."

"Not anymore he's not."

Carmela didn't say anything. Babcock had a point.

Babcock continued. "Your old boyfriend Quigg Brevard has quite a nasty temper, too, from what I understand."

"He's not my old boyfriend."

"Then what is he?"

Carmela had to think about that for a moment. "An acquaintance?"

"Hah!" Babcock said. And promptly hung up.

CARMELA SET THE PHONE DOWN. HER MIND WAS spinning and she wondered if Babcock had even taken her seriously. Even if he hadn't, she felt like she was standing in the eye of a hurricane. She'd promised to help Quigg, but Babcock would go completely batshit if he thought she was meddling. Even worse, Babcock had always been a little jealous (okay, a *lot* jealous) about her dating Quigg, even though it had been a few years ago. So what was a girl to do?

Well . . . it probably wouldn't rip the fabric of the universe too badly if she did a teensy bit of poking into the Environmental Justice League, would it?

Carmela's fingers flew across the keys of the front desk computer as she ran a quick Internet search. And what she discovered surprised her.

Lawsuits!

From several news stories, she discovered that the Environmental Justice League was embroiled in over a dozen lawsuits. There was one with a group of real estate developers who wanted to fill in a small amount of wetlands, another with a commercial alligator farm, and yet another with an oil and gas exploration company.

Carmela was hitting the Print icon so rapidly that she was afraid the printer would jam. Still, she kept gathering her clutch of evidence.

"What on earth are you doing?" Gabby asked. She was peering across the counter at Carmela. "Printing patterns or something?"

Carmela gathered up her sheets of paper and tamped them all together. "Let me tell you something, Stuart wasn't the only business that Martin Lash and his Environmental Justice League went after. These are all articles I found about lawsuits."

"Lawsuits against . . . people?" Gabby asked.

"Individuals, companies, an unincorporated city, you name it," Carmela said.

"So Lash was a litigious type of guy."

"Lash either had a brother-in-law who worked pro bono or he had an entire law firm on retainer. Because it looks like he was going after everybody to protect those wetlands."

Gabby indicated the papers Carmela clutched in her hand. "Are you going to pass this information on to Babcock?"

"I already told him that Martin Lash was the executive director of the Environmental Justice League. And that he threatened Stuart." She riffled the papers with her index finger. "So maybe I'll hold on to this information for a while longer. Let him conduct his own brand of investigation."

"And then you'll . . . ?" Gabby was suddenly interrupted by the *da-ding* of the bell over the front door. "Oh," she said as Jade Germaine strolled in.

"It's the lady in her coat of many colors," Carmela said, referring to the brightly colored floral velvet jacket that Jade was wearing.

"How do, ladies," Jade said as she brushed a corkscrew of blond hair off her forehead. She waved to Gabby and leaned in to give Carmela a hasty air kiss.

"What brings you in?" Carmela asked.

"My undying thanks," Jade said. She put a hand on her hip, leaned back, and said, "I can't thank you enough for that scrapbook you created for me. My Tea Party in a Box business has taken off with a bang. Whenever I do a presentation to a potential customer, they start turning the pages and barely make it to the middle of the book before they want to book a tea party."

Carmela grinned. "That's great, Jade. But in all honesty, you provide a spectacular service. If Gabby and I ever decided to host a tea party, we'd put all our trust in you."

"That's right," Gabby agreed. "You're the tea expert. You're the one who can match the right Darjeeling to a poppy seed scone."

"But you ladies are the ones who gave my scrapbook the design spark," Jade said. "You encouraged me to stick with one type of paper so all my photos would stand out better. And they do. Every table setting, every teapot, every dessert looks fabulous on that Champagne Cream paper you recommended. And the gray silk shantung cover gets raves. No wonder my business is flourishing."

Gabby patted Jade's shoulder. "Don't you think your hard work had something to do with it?"

"I suppose," Jade said. "But now that I've hit the mother lode, I want to share some of my success."

"What do you mean?" Carmela asked.

Jade poked a finger at Carmela. "I'm hosting a tea party for the Evangeline Women's Club this Thursday and I want you to come."

"Me?" Carmela squeaked. "I don't know. That club is awfully fancy."

"Not just fancy," Gabby said. "Stuffy, too. Stuart's momma is on their board of directors and you know what a stickler for etiquette she is."

Jade waved a hand. "Not to worry, Carmela, you'll make a positively brilliant guest." She headed for the door and then turned to deliver her final words. "And I won't take no for an answer!"

The door was barely shut when Carmela turned to face Gabby, who was clapping excitedly.

"This is such an honor, Carmela. Just think, if you make a good impression, you could be invited to join the Evangeline Women's Club. They're like the crème de la crème of New Orleans women."

"Help."

Gabby cocked an eye at her. "Help? What's that supposed to mean?"

"I've never been to a fancy tea party before," Carmela admitted. "Not even once."

"Oh, come on. You've been to scads of upscale cocktail parties. Afternoon tea is pretty much the same thing. You wear a cute suit, a nice choker of pearls . . ."

"But there's a ton of etiquette involved in a tea party, isn't there? All that breaking of scones and sipping of tea and lifting your pinky finger."

"Carmela, under penalty of law, do not lift your pinky finger."

"Even if it's quivering nervously?"

"Why are you so worried?" Gabby asked. "Really?"

"Here's the thing," Carmela said. "Stuart's momma isn't the only stuffy woman on their board."

"What are you talking about?"

"Shamus's big sister, Glory Meechum? She sits on the board of the Evangeline Women's Club, too."

Gabby grimaced. "You mean the great stone face?"

"That's right," Carmela said. "The one Shamus used to call 'She Who Must Be Obeyed.'"

"Used to? What does he call her now?"

"Now that Glory's in complete control of Crescent City

Bank and all the Meechums' investments and real estate holdings, he calls her his sweet adorable big sis."

Gabby poked a finger at her mouth. "Gag me."

"You got that right."

MIDAFTERNOON, CARMELA AND GABBY CALLED it a day and hung a *CLOSED* sign on Memory Mine's front door. They were both attending the Hotel Montague's Reveillon dinner tonight, along with half of New Orleans, and really looking forward to it. The dinner was a very big deal—the first of many Reveillon dinners that would be held in the weeks leading up to Christmas and New Year's. Fancy and formal, with multiple courses, Reveillon dinners were a revived holiday tradition that hearkened back to the elegant dinners served after midnight Mass a century ago.

"I'm going home now to go get pretty," Gabby sang out. "I'll lock the front door."

"See you tonight," Carmela called back. She folded her computer printouts and stuck them in her purse, rolled the phone over to her answering service, and then slipped on her black leather bomber jacket.

Two minutes later, Carmela was out the door and bouncing down Royal Street. As she passed dozens of upscale art and antique galleries, all gathered shoulder to shoulder on this fanciful street, she decided to make a quick stop at Juju Voodoo. After all, her curiosity-killed-the-cat BFF just might be interested in the information she'd dug up on Martin Lash. And how it might help in what she'd decided to call her "shadow" investigation.

Chapter 5

THE façade of Juju Voodoo was in full holiday dress. A string of purple twinkle lights dangled along the edge of the uneven shake roof, purple wreaths decorated with tiny potion bottles hung in the window, and Day of the Dead figures sported fuzzy red scarves and Santa hats. Ava's trademark red and blue neon sign—an open palm with head, heart, and life lines—glowed from a curiously shaped window that looked almost like a sleepy eye.

Carmela pushed open the door and stepped inside.

"Ava?"

It took her eyes a few moments to adjust to the dim lighting that Ava insisted was part of Juju Voodoo's charming atmosphere. Votive candles flickered, a pair of red bat eyes glowed from up in the rafters, the flames of tall saint candles swayed in the slight breeze. The air was warm and perfumed with the scents of frangipani, jasmine, and passionflower.

Like a burlesque performer popping out of an enormous cake to thrill her onlookers, Ava suddenly burst through the purple velvet curtains at the back of the shop.

"*Cher*," she purred, heading for Carmela like a languorous jungle cat. "I thought that might be you."

Ava was dressed to kill in a V-neck leopard top, skintight black leather pants, and spike heels that were so high she was forced to take baby steps. Her masses of dark hair were pulled into a messy topknot, and long, dangly gold earrings brushed her delicately chiseled face.

"How are you faring after the unspeakable horror of last night?" Ava asked. "Me"—she touched a hand to her generous display of décolleté—"I didn't sleep a wink."

"Even after drinking six glasses of wine?" Carmela asked. "Or was it seven?"

Ava thought for a moment. "Perhaps I did catch a few z's after all." She fluttered both hands dramatically. "But the dreams I had would curl your hair!" She glanced sharply at Carmela's short bob. "Well, maybe not *your* hair."

"Thanks a lot."

"Still, I had terrible visions of Martin Lash lurching out of the darkness with that horrible huge fork quivering in his neck." Ava staggered across the floor, stiff-legged, perfectly pantomiming Lash's walk.

"Thank you for that lovely reenactment," Carmela said. "It's so much fun to dredge up bad memories."

"Oh, you." Ava bent forward and gave Carmela a quick peck on the cheek.

"But I'm guessing the murder hasn't soured you on going to the big dinner tonight?"

Ava's eyes glowed expectantly. "Not in the least. I'm looking forward to this evening. It isn't often a gal gets to parade around in a sexy, slinky gown."

"For you, that would just be on the even-numbered days," Carmela said. She was well aware that Ava's walk-in closet looked like the wardrobe department for *Moulin Rouge!*

Ava picked up what looked like a gingerbread man from the counter and handed it to Carmela. "Have a look at one of my new ornaments."

"Charming," Carmela said. It was a soft sculpture gingerbread toy with its mouth sewn shut and red cross-stitches marking the eyes, hands, and feet. "I take it this is holiday merchandise . . . voodoo style?"

"I have a few customers who appreciate . . . shall we say . . . certain oddities."

"Speaking of which, I've got something right up your alley."

"Do tell."

"Some information I dug up about Martin Lash. Research, I guess you'd call it."

Ava walked to the door and flipped the lock closed. "Why don't we go into the reading room and take a look." She led the way past display cases filled with amulets, talismans, and sparkling rings. A new display of candles featured images of the voodoo queen, Marie Laveau, while velvet scarves hand-painted with mysterious symbols hung from a wooden rack.

Carmela sat down at the small table in Ava's octagon-shaped reading room. This was where clients came for psychic consultations and tarot readings. The room managed to be both plush and spooky at the same time. Heavy green drapes covered the walls, music moaned from the speakers, and two backlit stained glass windows depicting beatific angels and lambs gave the room a spiritual glow.

"So," Ava said, her fingertips fairly dancing against the green velvet tabletop, "whatcha got?"

Carmela pulled her papers out of her bag and spread them across the table, aware that she was almost mimicking a tarot card spread. "I've been doing a little research on Martin Lash. Turns out he was also the executive director of a group called the Environmental Justice League."

Ava pushed a hank of hair off her cheek. "What's that exactly?"

"Besides writing nasty restaurant reviews, Martin Lash headed a nonprofit environmental group that loved to sue all sorts of people and companies that they perceived as infringing upon Louisiana's swamps and bayous."

"Isn't that what our Department of Natural Resources is for?"

"I suppose. But Lash and his group were what you'd call self-appointed environmental watchdogs."

"And they actually took people to court?" Ava asked.

Carmela fanned out a half dozen pieces of paper. "They sure did. Look . . . here are newspaper articles concerning a few of the cases and, in some instances, court records."

Ava poked through the papers. "This is kind of amazing. It looks as if most of the people Lash went after were major players. I mean . . . real estate developers and even an oil exploration company." She thought for a minute. "Maybe Lash made more than a few enemies along the way, huh? People who wanted him out of the way? Or dead?"

"I think that's exactly what happened," Carmela said excitedly. "But it wasn't just the big boys that Lash was after. He actually filed suit against several individual hunters and trappers. He accused them of violating public lands like the Bayou Sauvage Wildlife Refuge."

48 LAURA CHILDS

"And it all has to do with the bayous," Ava said. "Lash really had a thing for bayous."

"We all love the bayous," Carmela said. "And we're especially mindful of how fragile they are after parts of them were destroyed by Hurricane Katrina and the oil spill. But Lash was positively rabid about protecting them. About keeping *everybody* out."

"And now he's gone. Murdered." Ava tapped an index finger against one of the papers. "Could have been at the hand of one of these very guys."

"That's exactly what I think," Carmela said. "Lash must have been despised by a whole bunch of people."

"Everyone's been assuming that Quigg was the big hothead," Ava said. "But it's looking more and more as if Martin Lash was the one who was positively fizzing with anger and aggression."

"Lash didn't seem to like anything or anybody," Carmela said. "As a restaurant critic he mercilessly attacked local chefs, as executive director of the Environmental Justice League he went after any possible or perceived threats to the environment."

"Are you going to run this by Babcock?"

"I wasn't going to." Carmela began gathering up her papers. "But now that I've taken a second look at all this . . . um, what would you call this stuff?"

"Evidence."

Carmela sat back in her chair. "I guess it really is evidence. Of a sort."

"But you're not going to tell Babcock about this *tonight* are you?" Ava fluttered her eyelashes. "You're not going to ruin what promises to be a magical evening?"

"No, Ava, I promise I'll hold off."

"Good girl. Because right now I need to focus all my energy on deciding what to wear."

"You told me you were going to wear the gold dress with the bugle beads," Carmela said. "The one that makes you feel like Mariah Carey."

"Only twenty pounds lighter," Ava said. She sighed. "Yeah, the bugle beads. It's a cool dress. But that was before I revisited my black satin bias-cut dress."

"The one with the lace arms that makes you look like Spider-Woman?"

"That's the dress," Ava said. "The thing is, I really need to glam it up for tonight. I have Roman Numeral nibbling at the hook, now I just need to set it hard and reel him in."

"Holy smokes, Ava, you want to *marry* him?" In Carmela's mind, Ava was a serial dater. Definitely not the marrying kind.

Ava looked troubled. "Please don't say 'marry' like you're referring to the Ebola virus. You've known all along that marriage is my end game."

"But we're not at the end yet. We're not even in the second half. So there's still plenty of time left in the game."

"I hear you."

"And really, Ava. Roman Numeral?" Carmela had met Roman Numeral, aka Harrison Harper Wilkes III, a couple of times, and he'd never struck her as a sweep-the-ladies-off-their-feet kind of guy. He seemed more like a come-look-at-my-stamp-collection guy. Or a let's-listen-to-Kenny-G guy. Definitely not your romantic lady-killer.

But Ava assumed a dreamy expression as she talked about him. "I always find that the more numbers a man has after his name, the longer the lineage and the larger the trust fund."

"Ah. So there's beaucoup money involved."

"Let me put it this way. He drives a silver Jaguar XK

convertible and his folks have a tasty mansion just off St. Charles in the Garden District."

"In other words, he's another rich, indolent New Orleans Peter Pan–type guy with too much money and too much time on his hands."

A tiny line appeared between Ava's perfectly waxed brows. "I wish you wouldn't put it that way . . ."

"Are you sure you know what you're doing? He sounds an awful lot like Shamus and you know how well that turned out." Carmela rolled her eyes to add emphasis.

Ava shook her head. "But there's no comparison to the Shamus situation. For one thing, Shamus's battle-axe big sister was a huge problem for you. She was always in your face, always criticizing."

"You got that right," Carmela said. One of the benefits of her divorce, besides dumping Shamus and walking away with some choice real estate, was the fact that Glory Meechum was no longer in her life.

"The thing is, most of Roman Numeral's relatives have all moved to Houston, where their oil conglomerate is headquartered. So . . . poof! Holiday-only in-laws!"

"Okay, that's a plus. I'll give you that."

Ava continued. "Roman Numeral isn't exactly a lazy society boy, either. He wants to fulfill his destiny as a world-class photographer."

"But right now he's an *amateur* photographer."

"I'm positive he can improve his skill level. Sure, his photos might be a little blurry and soft focus right now. But if he really works at it . . ."

"*Work* being the operative word," Carmela said.

"Don't be a spoilsport," Ava said. "Roman Numeral is committed to improving his photography skills. Now I just have to help him realize that he's even more committed to me!"

*   *   *

CARMELA WAS STILL LAUGHING AS SHE SKIPPED across the courtyard to her apartment. Then, two seconds after she turned the key in the lock, Boo and Poobah rocketed toward her, jumping and barking joyfully.

"Kids, kids, enough already," Carmela told her crazed canines. She tossed her bag on the kitchen counter and grabbed two leather leashes. "Oh, you know what this is for?" she asked Boo, who was practically dancing on her hind legs. "I guess you do."

Then they were out the door, the dogs pulling ahead of her, almost yanking her down the sidewalk.

I feel like I'm waterskiing, Carmela thought as she was carried along, practically skidding around corners.

They charged down Toulouse Street, turned on St. Peter Street, and cruised past Jackson Square. It was crowded, as usual, with street musicians, artists, panhandlers, fortune-tellers, and T-shirt vendors.

Carmela listened to a bearded fiddler for a few minutes (Boo and Poobah being fairly attentive as well), then tossed two dollar bills into his open violin case. He nodded to her solemnly and smiled. Then it was back home without a moment to spare.

Once Carmela had poured out kibbles for the dogs, she focused her efforts on getting all dolled up for tonight. She wasn't hot on formal events, but Ava had loaned her a red velvet cocktail dress and promised that it would blow the socks off any man over the age of eighteen and under eighty.

Okay then. That leaves a sixty-two-year span of sockless men.

Carmela hit the shower, shampooed her hair, and then stood for a few minutes under the prickly spray. When the pipes started clanking and the water went from scalding to tepid, she jumped out.

Her hair was easy. She just towel-dried her short, honeyed bob, squirted in some gobs of gel, and hoped for the best. Clearing a spot in the fogged-up mirror, she decided her hair looked okay. A little crunchy maybe, but the gelled-artichoke styling gave her an interesting tough-gal look.

Makeup wasn't so easy. Carmela was a lipstick-and-mascara minimalist, so tonight would be a challenge. She mixed a little moisturizer into her foundation, patted it on gently, and then did her eyebrows. Staring in the mirror now, her strong, arched brows gave her unlined, un-eye-shadowed eyes the pale, lashless look of a rabbit. So much for that. A smudge of gray eye shadow went on, followed by dark eyeliner, and then two . . . wait, better make that three . . . coats of mascara.

Perfect.

Carmela slipped into her black satin lingerie and then stepped into the red velvet dress she'd borrowed from Ava. The heart-shaped bodice and tulip skirt cinched her perfectly. And the velvet . . . ah, the velvet . . . was as soft as a kitten's purr.

As carefully as if she were putting on Cinderella's glass slippers, Carmela stepped into a pair of black velvet heels. Okay, so they pinched her feet. Whatever. They also arched her back and boosted her height. She'd muddle through it.

Carmela lifted her chin, tucked in her tummy, and studied herself in the full-length mirror. *If this outfit doesn't grab Babcock's attention, nothing will.*

Chapter 6

THE Hotel Montague had rolled out the red carpet tonight. Which meant their curved driveway was thronged
with shiny black limousines disgorging a parade of society
types, society hopefuls, and pseudo celebrities. Gentlemen in
black tie escorted ladies who wore either flirty cocktail dresses
or long evening gowns. Many women were draped in fur
coats; most wore sparkly baubles of the celestial variety.

Carmela was enthralled. "Edgar, isn't this exciting? Isn't
this amazing? It feels almost like a movie premiere." She'd
jumped out of his blue BMW and was gaping at the liveried
attendants. And . . . was that a harpist over there? Yes, that
was indeed a lady harpist who was serenading guests with
the most angelic-sounding music right out here on the red
carpet.

"Don't park it in the garage," Babcock told the attendant. "I may need to make a fast getaway."

"Yes, sir," said the attendant.

"I knew this Reveillon dinner was going to be fantastic, but I had no idea everything would be so glam," Carmela marveled. Flashbulbs popped as they made their way down the red carpet.

Babcock shaded his eyes. "Why is the press here?"

"Because it's a holiday event," Carmela reminded him. "There'll be loads of pictures in the society pages."

"Not of us, I hope."

"No, not us," Carmela assured him as they made their way into the hotel lobby.

Garlanded evergreen boughs were draped around every brass banister, while enormous wreaths adorned the walls. What appeared to be almost one thousand poinsettia plants were arranged to look like a massive twenty-foot-high Christmas tree. With ringing bells and traditional songs, carolers dressed in Victorian garb welcomed guests.

Carmela gripped Babcock's arm as they walked up polished marble steps into the main part of the lobby. "Isn't this magical?"

Babcock ducked his head. "It's awfully crowded."

Carmela's smile didn't waver. "Then let's head out to the patio." She steered him through the crowd and out the tall double doors that led to the hotel's interior courtyard. Here it wasn't quite as crowded. A fountain pattered softly and potted palms looked even more moody when lit by flickering garden torches. Surrounded by the velvety darkness Babcock seemed to relax.

"Better," Babcock said, even though guests were spilling out here at an alarming rate.

A formally dressed waiter approached them with a tray

full of champagne flutes filled with golden bubbly elixir. "Care for a glass of champagne?" he asked them.

"Thank you," Carmela said. She accepted a glass of champagne, but was surprised when Babcock held up a hand to wave him off.

Babcock saw her quizzical look and said, "Work. I could get a call out at any moment. Murder doesn't party."

And neither do you, it looks like. Carmela sighed. And here she'd figured this event would be a little oasis of calm. That she wouldn't have to worry about dead bodies or crazed killers. Or suspects unjustly accused.

A second waiter approached them. "Care for an appetizer?" he asked.

Babcock peered at the silver tray the waiter was carrying. "What have you got there?"

"Toast points with caviar," the waiter said.

Carmela accepted a toast point and popped it in her mouth. Tiny black eggs burst as she bit down, releasing their subtle fishy delicacy. "This is delicious," she exclaimed. "Heavenly." Then she noticed that Babcock had passed on the caviar as well. Hmm, he was definitely going to require some loving attention to get into the party spirit.

Carmela snuggled closer to him. "Looking forward to the Reveillon dinner?" she asked. "Isn't this just a lovely place for it?"

Babcock laughed. "You say that every time we attend a fancy event. Whether it's at the museum or the arboretum or an upscale hotel. And I *do* notice, because if it wasn't for you, these are the exact kind of events I'd try to avoid."

Carmela stepped back from him. "Are you going to be a crab cake all night long?"

He smiled. "If I am, then can we go home?"

"Not on your life, bucko."

Carmela sipped her champagne and gazed out over the crowd. Something was going to have to change or they'd both have a miserable evening. But what could . . . ? She suddenly smiled. Ava and Roman Numeral were plowing their way through the crowd, headed straight for them.

"Ava!" Carmela called out. Ava was the perfect disrupter. Surely she could help jolly Babcock into a better mood, right?

Ava sashayed toward them like an undulating snake. Her hips rolled, her shoulders swayed, her black floor-length dress with its deep slash in front accentuated every luscious curve. She was trailed by a tall, fairly good-looking man with a neatly trimmed mustache and slightly receding hairline.

"You remember my dear sweet Harrison, don't you?" Ava trilled. "My *amour du jour*."

"Of course," Carmela said, giving Harrison her most airy of air kisses.

"Nice to see you." Babcock nodded.

"Look at this," Ava burbled. "The décor, the lights, the beautiful people. *Très élégant*."

"Two years at the Sorbonne and you've really got your French language skills down pat," Carmela joked. She noticed that Babcock had stepped away from their group and was fiddling with his phone. A text message? An e-mail? What was his problem, for cripes' sake?

Ava caught Carmela's eye and smiled. She'd noted how distracted Babcock was acting and was going to try engaging him. "Oh, Detective," she said in a teasing singsong voice. "This is supposed to be a party. Our happy time together. Why not stash your phone and give it a rest?"

Babcock smiled as he continued to focus on his phone.

"You know what?" Ava said. "I'll bet you didn't realize that Harrison was actually acquainted with last night's murder victim."

That little conversational gambit finally served to capture Babcock's attention. He looked up, mildly interested. "What?" he said. "How?"

Ava poked Harrison with an elbow. "Tell him, sweetie."

All eyes were focused on Harrison now.

"Perhaps the term *acquainted* might be a bit of an overstatement," he stammered. "I didn't really know the man *personally*."

"You can explain it better than that," Ava urged.

Harrison ran nervous fingers through his slicked-back, thinning hair. "The thing is, Martin Lash actually accosted me at one time."

"When was this?" Babcock asked.

"Where?" Carmela asked.

"I was down in the Baritaria bayou a few months ago," Harrison said. "Taking photos. So there I was in an absolutely gorgeous part of the bayou that I'd just discovered was a prime nesting spot for egrets and herons."

Carmela glanced sideways at Babcock, who was focused on Harrison but getting edgy just the same. She could practically hear him mentally willing Harrison to get to the point.

Harrison continued. "I'm just setting my f-stop when out of nowhere this crazy man comes rushing at me. He's dressed in khakis and one of those Smokey Bear hats, like some kind of game warden, and starts screaming at me, telling me I have no right to disturb the birds. He said he knew that I'd already been banned from the Jean Lafitte Preserve—which wasn't true at all—and told me I wasn't welcome anywhere in bayou country."

Babcock frowned. "How did you know this was Martin Lash?"

"That was easy. He knocked over my tripod—it was a Sachtler 0375, really high-end—and threw a pamphlet at me. I was so shocked I picked it up and saw it was from the

Environmental Justice League. Then I said, 'And who are you, the Green Lantern?' That's when he cursed at me and told me his name was Martin Lash and that if I knew better I'd stay out of the bayou."

"What did you do then?" Carmela asked.

Harrison shrugged. "What could I do? I packed up my equipment and left. I didn't fancy the notion of being alone in a bayou with a thousand birds and one deranged environmentalist."

"Quite a story, huh?" Ava said.

"Lash sounds like a person who excelled at making enemies," Carmela said.

"Enemies," Ava repeated. "A lot of enemies."

Babcock just looked thoughtful. Finally he glanced at Carmela and said, "Isn't that what your ex did for a while? Nature photography?"

"For a while," Carmela said. "Until Shamus decided that chasing young women and drinking old bourbon was a lot more fun."

"I suspect it probably is," Harrison said. He eased into a long, rolling chuckle until Ava poked him hard with an elbow and silenced him with a sharp look.

"Well," Babcock said, "we knew that Martin Lash was some kind of fanatical fruitcake. Extremely proprietary when it came to bayous and wetlands. Even though so much of it is public land."

"So you're saying he was a protector of sorts?" Carmela said.

"Even though nobody protected him," Ava said. "I mean, with a personality like an angry hornet, who would want to?"

"You're wrong about that," Babcock said. "Because *I'm* the one who's tasked with protecting his interests now. Even if it is after the fact."

Harrison looked interested. "So how are you doing? Has

anything shaken loose in the investigation yet? Do you have any solid leads or a suspect pool?"

Carmela knew full well that Babcock never liked to talk about his cases, but she had her own selfish reasons for being interested. "Yes, please tell us."

Babcock raised his hands in protest. "No, no, I don't dare reveal a single detail. I can't compromise the investigation."

"Come on, Babcock," Ava said. She put her thumb and forefinger together. "Just one teensy-weensy little hint? Please?"

Carmela took a step closer. Would Babcock let something slip? Anything at all?

"Tinfoil," Babcock said. "We found a small snippet of tinfoil in Lash's pocket."

Ava looked disappointed. "That's it? That's the clue?"

"That's it," Babcock said as his phone jingled. He pulled it out of his pocket, frowned again, and said, "Excuse me, I need to take this."

"Well, he's in a mood," Ava said to Carmela.

"He's been that way all day."

"Pressure from the job," Harrison said as another waiter passed by offering Gulf shrimp kabobs and pâté on crackers.

Carmela grabbed a shrimp canapé while Harrison opted for the pâté.

"Ava, my little flower," Harrison said when he noticed Ava hadn't helped herself to any food. "How come you're not eating?"

Ava grimaced. "If I take so much as a mouse nibble I'm liable to split my dress seams wide open. I don't know how I'm going to make it past the soup course tonight."

"Very carefully," Carmela said.

Harrison took Ava's hand and raised it to his lips. "Ah, but your figure is such a delight to the eye, my dear."

Carmela glanced around so she wouldn't break out in

hysterical laughter. "Have you seen Gabby and Stuart yet?" she asked.

"Ran into 'em in the lobby," Ava said. She was still gazing starry-eyed at Harrison, who was suddenly waving like mad at another couple. Then she turned to look, to see what all the fuss was about. "Harrison, who are those people?"

"The Jewels," Harrison said as a well-dressed couple suddenly swooped in.

"Harrison, it's been ages. Lovely to see you." An older man with gray caterpillar eyebrows and hooded brown eyes extended his right hand to Harrison while he beamed happily at the entire group. Then he turned to his wife, a pinched-faced, ultrathin woman with a white pixie haircut. "Didn't I say, not more than ten minutes ago, that we'd probably run into some old friends?"

The woman fingered a thick gold choker at the base of her skinny throat. "You most certainly did."

Harrison took over the introductions. "Carmela Bertrand and Ava Gruiex, may I present Harvey and Jenny Jewel, proprietors extraordinaire of the Jewel Caviar Company."

Ava was suitably impressed. "Ooh, I just adore fish eggs."

"You're from right here?" Carmela asked. "New Orleans?"

"That's right," Jenny Jewel said.

"I'm guessing you're a relatively new company," Carmela said. She'd never heard of them before.

Harvey smiled. "Did you enjoy the caviar you had on toast points earlier?"

"It was delicious," Carmela said.

"That was our caviar," Harvey said proudly.

"Well, this is fascinating," Carmela said. "I thought the caviar industry had been completely decimated. That all the beluga sturgeon in the Black and Caspian seas had been fished to extinction."

"They pretty much have," Harvey Jewel explained. "But that disaster was a long time coming, so some very clever people involved in aquaculture took matters into their own hands. Beluga sturgeons have been crossed with different types of sturgeon, such as shortnose and Atlantic sturgeon, to create hybrid fish that produce fabulous eggs. Now caviar is being farmed in a dozen different countries around the globe."

"That's amazing," Carmela said. "And where do you source your product from?"

"We buy bulk sturgeon caviar from a farm in Finland," Harvey Jewel said. "We ship the caviar here in refrigerated containers and package it ourselves in a repurposed shrimp factory that went bust after the BP oil spill."

"You probably use those teeny-tiny little jars," Ava said.

Harvey Jewel smiled. "Well, an ounce of caviar is still rather expensive."

"But there's a good-sized market for caviar?" Carmela asked.

Both Jenny and Harvey Jewel beamed.

"You have no idea," Harvey said, just as a bell tinkled to call everyone to dinner.

BABCOCK FINALLY JOINED THEIR GROUP JUST AS they were all sitting down at their table. Carmela was none too pleased with his behavior, but decided to give him a pass. His mind was occupied, after all.

"Look," Carmela said, reaching through a forest of wineglasses to pick up a small menu printed on elegant parchment paper. "They're serving duck gumbo as the first course. One of your favorites."

Babcock gave a noncommittal grunt.

"Excuse me?" Carmela said. She'd just about had her fill of Babcock's bad behavior.

"That call I just took?" Babcock said. "It was about your buddy."

"What are you talking about?"

Babcock lowered his voice. "Quigg Brevard somehow managed to have all of Martin Lash's reviews on the Glutton for Punishment website taken down."

Carmela was surprised. "He did? Really? Just like that?"

"Apparently he snapped his fingers and—poof!—the reviews simply disappeared." He took a sip of wine while he held her with his eyes. "You don't know anything about that, do you?"

The implication irritated Carmela. "No, of course not. And I can't imagine how Quigg managed to pull Lash's reviews down so quickly. Or figure out whose arm to twist."

"The guy's obviously got friends," Babcock said. "Business compadres who are willing to stick their necks out for him."

"Chill out, will you?" Carmela hissed. She was still miffed that Babcock continued to see Quigg as a suspect. The only suspect.

The rest of the dinner felt like a blur to Carmela. The food was fantastic, of course. A spicy duck gumbo; a colorful Noel salad topped with strawberries, cranberries, and walnuts; and an entrée of blackened redfish with pommes Anna. Desert was a delicious zuppa inglese, a creamy mélange of custard and sponge cake.

Carmela laughed, chatted, and made jokes as if nothing was amiss, but she was keenly focused on Babcock giving her what felt like a very cold shoulder. When dinner was finally over and couples began wandering into the bars and lounges for a nightcap, Babcock bolted a cup of black coffee and turned to her.

"I'm sorry, but I really have to leave," Babcock said. "Would you like me to take you home or can you catch a ride with your friends?"

Carmela gave him the chilliest stare her blue eyes could muster. "A lady always leaves with the gentleman who brought her."

Babcock stood up. "Then we'd better get going."

The ride home wasn't much better. Babcock made only noncommittal grunts to her idle, nervous chatter.

"Are you even listening to me?" Carmela asked.

"Of course I am."

"What did I just say?"

"Um, something about a concert?"

"Nice try."

"Carmela, I'm sorry. But I'm preoccupied. Can't you see that?"

"Yes, I can see that. In fact, everyone at the Reveillon dinner could see that."

He pulled his car to the curb and stopped. "Come on, it wasn't that bad."

She leaned across the front seat, gave him a perfunctory kiss, and reached for the door handle. "Edgar, it really was." And then she was out of the car and running through the porte cochere, headed for her apartment. Her heels clicked like castanets against the flagstones, her opera cape billowed out behind her.

What a disaster, Carmela thought. *What a waste of an evening. Better to have stayed in and snarfed an entire bag of Chips Ahoy! than to . . .*

A long shadow moved across the courtyard in front of her.

Carmela stopped in her tracks, eyes gone wide, heart suddenly fluttering in her chest like a wounded dove. *Someone's here? Waiting for me?*

Banana palms waved in the chilly breeze, the water in the

fountain splattered as it dripped from one level to the next. All familiar sounds that suddenly felt lonely and threatening.

Mustering her courage, Carmela called out, "Is someone here?" She was holding her breath, mentally girding herself for Martin Lash to stagger out and grab her like a returning corpse from *The Walking Dead.*

Instead, Quigg Brevard stepped out from the shadows.

"Holy crap!" Carmela cried. She lowered her beaded clutch from where it had been raised to use as a semi-deadly weapon. "You scared me to death."

Quigg held up his hands in an apologetic gesture. "Sorry, sorry. I didn't mean to frighten you."

"Well, you did." Carmela felt angry and cross and didn't care if he knew it. "What are you doing here, anyway? Besides lurking in the shadows?"

"I've been waiting to talk to you. I was hoping the boyfriend didn't come in for a nightcap."

She shook her head. "Little chance of that. Babcock's been totally preoccupied all night long. Trying to puzzle out Martin Lash's murder and, I suppose, clear your name."

"Somehow, I doubt that clearing my good name is his main mission in life," Quigg said. "I happen to know I'm still very high on his suspect list. Probably up there in the top two or three."

"And you're doing nothing to help yourself," Carmela said. "Babcock found out that you had Lash's Glutton for Punishment reviews taken down. He views it as questionable, suspicious behavior."

"Wrong," Quigg said. "It's simply smart business. I've got to distance myself from that idiot Lash as much as possible. His ravingly bad reviews could've killed me, especially where my new wines are concerned. I'm counting on this year's holiday sales to really cement my name in the wine industry."

"How can you think about business when you're suspected of murder?"

Quigg gave her one of his devastating smiles. "It's easy. I compartmentalize."

Somehow, the notion was appealing to Carmela. "I wish I could learn how to do that."

Quigg moved a step closer to her. "It just takes a little practice. Besides, I didn't kill Martin Lash. I'm innocent. And, my dear Carmela, you know that to be a fact."

Before Carmela could say a single word, before she even knew what was happening, Quigg leaned forward and wrapped his arms around her. She tilted her head back, about to lodge a formal protest. That's when his lips touched hers and, even though she knew it was the worst thing she could possibly do, she melted into his arms and kissed him back.

Oh no! Oh no! her mind screamed even as she wondered what had come over her and realized that she was quivering all the way down to her toes.

"You're an angel," Quigg whispered, his breath hot and urgent and tickling as his lips moved down to brush gently against her neck. Then he released his grip and slipped away into the darkness.

Like Lot's wife turned to salt, Carmela stood there staring into the darkness. *No*, she thought, still feeling the thrill of his lips pressed hard against hers. *I'm not an angel. And I definitely am in big trouble.*

Chapter 7

CARMELA and Ava strolled leisurely down Royal Street. It was just past noon on Sunday and tourists as well as locals were out in full force. The jostling crowds were enjoying the shaved ice vendors, rides in horse-drawn jitneys, and superlative window shopping. After all, only the finest sterling silver goblets, antique jewelry, and eighteenth-century oil paintings were on display in the upscale antique shops on Royal Street.

"Everyone's out so early this morning," Ava said. She wore a purple tweed jacket and pencil skirt with a black blouse that had tiny pearl buttons down the front. It didn't take a close inspection to see that Ava had neglected to close most of the buttons when she'd gotten dressed.

"Honey, it is early," Carmela said. "But it's early afternoon."

Ava stifled a yawn. "I guess it just feels like morning because I had such a late night. After the Reveillon dinner, Harrison and I went to Dr. Boogie's and knocked back a few more pops. Then we listened to some hot jazz . . . and went back to my place for . . . you know . . . yadda, yadda, yadda. How was your post-party? All snuggly and nice, too?"

Carmela shook her head. "Don't even ask."

"Please don't tell me that Babcock just dumped you at home like yesterday's California roll?"

Carmela was going to spill the beans to Ava about Quigg showing up, but since they'd just arrived at the pink stucco building that housed Brennan's Restaurant, she decided to save her tale of infamy for later. Right now she needed an eye-opening cocktail and a fortifying brunch entrée. Or maybe she'd throw caution to the wind and just skip right ahead to their flaming bananas Foster. Give in to the stark raving sugar junkie that lurked inside of her.

A well-coiffed maître d' greeted them in the entry. "Good afternoon, ladies."

"Huh," Ava shook her head. "If he says it's afternoon, then I guess it must be afternoon."

The smiling maître d' didn't lose a beat. He grabbed two menus and said, "I have immediate seating in the Chanteclair Room."

"Wonderful," Ava said. "And can we possibly get one of those little tables next to the glass wall overlooking the garden?" She batted her eyes for extra effect.

"Certainly, madame." He led them into a cheerful room with light green trellises adorning the walls and ceilings, then pulled out green cane chairs with coral seats and backs. Ava seated herself with one hand delicately outstretched as if she were a newly crowned queen.

A waiter dressed in black and white brightened by a pink sateen bow tie hurried over to their table. He presented them with an enormous wine menu.

"Perhaps you'd like to start with a bottle of wine?" the waiter asked. Brennan's was rumored to have a wine cellar containing fifty thousand bottles and it looked like every one of them must be listed.

"I'm thinking champagne," Carmela mused. She looked across the table at Ava. "What about you?"

"Like I'd ever say no to champagne?" Ava scanned the bubbly section. "What looks good? Besides everything."

"The last time I was here with Babcock, he ordered the Billecart-Salmon Brut Réserve."

"Sounds spendy."

"It is."

"So that's what we should have."

"Very good, ladies," said the waiter.

Carmela wasted no time in scanning the brunch menu. It was glorious, of course. Fried oysters, eggs Sardou, vanilla-scented French toast, and another half dozen of Brennan's famous brunch entrées.

"I wonder how Martin Lash would have reviewed this place?" Ava asked.

"Please," Carmela said. "Brennan's is a New Orleans in-stitution. Right up there with Commander's Palace and Antoine's. If Lash ever dared write a snarky review he prob-ably would have gotten himself lynched."

"As opposed to just stabbed. And by the way, what is Babcock doing about that? He certainly was in a sour mood last night."

Carmela's lips pulled tight.

"Oh no, has our own Dudley Do-Right been treating you badly?"

"More like just ignoring me."

"Because he's so preoccupied," Ava said.

"I suppose," Carmela said.

"And because he's fiercely jealous of Quigg."

"I really wish you wouldn't say that."

"But it's true." Ava smiled as the waiter brought their champagne, popped the cork, and deftly poured out two glasses. "So," she said when he was gone, "what's up? You look like a woman with a deep, dark secret."

"Secret?" Carmela said, her voice going slightly shrill.

"Ah, so I was right."

Carmela took a fortifying sip of champagne. "I suppose I *do* have something to tell you."

"I knew it."

"But you can't blab it to anybody."

"Who would I tell?" Ava asked.

"Um . . . everybody?"

"I wouldn't do that," Ava said.

"Then swear on something."

"Cross my heart and swear on my evil eye earrings." Ava leaned forward eagerly. "Okay, so tell me. Spill the beans, girlfriend."

"After Babcock dropped me off last night. After he pulled over to the curb, barely slowed the car, and practically pushed me out into the gutter . . . I was hurrying to my apartment . . ."

Ava gave an encouraging nod. "Yeeees."

"And . . . well . . . Quigg was kind of hiding in the courtyard waiting for me."

Ava grinned. "Look at you, hot momma. Juggling two guys at once. Back in the day I used to do that myself. You know, I'd line up two, maybe three dates in one night. Cocktail hour, then dinner, then a late-night rendezvous. Lately I've been trying to cut back."

"Ava, stop. This wasn't any kind of date. Quigg was just lurking there. Totally unbeknownst to me."

"He was just . . . waiting for you? Why, *cher*?"

"He wanted to talk about the murder. He was wondering if I'd found out anything new."

"But you haven't." Ava took a quick sip of wine. "Have you?"

"Not really. I had no real news for Quigg. Aside from the fact that Babcock is suspicious about how he waved a magic wand and had Martin Lash's reviews taken down from the Glutton for Punishment website."

Ava cocked her head. "That's all very interesting. But none of that explains why a man was standing at your front door in the wee hours of the morning." She wiggled her fingers. "So what really happened?"

Carmela had sipped just enough champagne to loosen her tongue. "I kissed him."

Ava gasped.

"I mean . . . he kissed me first. And then I just couldn't help myself."

"Girl, you are so walking a thin, red line."

"I know that!"

Ava dimpled. "So give me all the details."

"There are no details. It was just a simple kiss."

"Simple?" Ava smirked. "A kiss with a man like Quigg Brevard is never simple. You should know that."

"Which is why this whole thing is quite complicated."

"Of course it is," Ava said. "But the big question is, what are you going to do about it?"

"I have to do something?" Carmela asked. "What would I do? Jeez, Ava, all I want right now is for the kiss to have never happened."

"It's too late," Ava warned. "That kiss is out there in the ozone. It's like posting a bad selfie—it'll never go away."

"So what do you suggest I do?"

"You actually have several options. You can avoid Quigg for the rest of your natural-born days. You can confess your infidelity to Babcock and beg for forgiveness. Or you can live with this secret locked in your heart forever. Personally, the option I'd go for would be to kiss him again."

"Have you lost your mind?" Carmela cried, so loudly that a couple of people turned to stare. "Kiss him again?" She lowered her voice. "Babcock would kill us both. And because he's a smart detective who carries a gun, he would probably get away with murder." She picked up her menu and waggled a finger at the waiter. "Ah, forget it. Let's just order."

They did order. Eggs Benedict for Carmela and eggs Sardou for Ava. Then Carmela sat and stared into the garden for a few minutes, deep in thought.

"You okay?" Ava asked.

"I don't know what to do."

Ava picked up the bottle of champagne. "Have another drink, sweetie. Champagne makes everything better."

BY THE TIME THEIR FOOD ARRIVED, CARMELA was sufficiently calmed down.

"My entrée is perfection," Ava said. "Angels must have descended from heaven and whipped up this sauce."

"Then they must have gotten a hall pass good for the entire day, because my eggs Benedict is marvelous, too. But," Carmela admitted, "I'm already thinking ahead to dessert."

Ava aimed a fork at her. "Bananas Foster for two."

"You got that right," Carmela said. "There's nothing better than caramelized banana flambéed in rum."

"Except maybe Brennan's chocolate rum drink. That's my idea of perfection. Pigging out on chocolate while you get a nice buzz on." Ava smiled. "See how much better you're feeling now?"

"That's because I'm drinking. And overeating."

They settled down then, enjoying their brunch as the day stretched into late afternoon. When Carmela finally glanced at her watch and saw that it was almost four o'clock, she said, "Would you believe that Martin Lash's viewing starts in a couple of minutes?"

Ava was surprised. "They've got him fixed up already? They patched up that awful old grisly hole in his throat?"

"Apparently so," Carmela said. "The notice for his visitation appeared in the *Times-Picayune* this morning. Visitation today, memorial service on Tuesday."

"Those funeral directors sure work fast, huh?"

"I think they pretty much have to," Carmela said.

"And there's a valid reason why you're thinking about attending Lash's visitation? And I'm guessing you want to drag me along with you?"

"Chalk it up to curiosity."

Ava laughed. "Now that's something I can relate to."

TWENTY MINUTES LATER THEY WERE STANDING outside a wrought-iron fence, gazing in at a three-story white clapboard mansion. The windows were framed with black shutters while four Ionic columns fronted the building. A discreet brass sign with the words CASTLE FUNERAL HOME was affixed to the fence at eye level.

"This place looks kind of spooky," Ava said. "Do you think it's haunted?"

"Probably not," Carmela said.

"I read somewhere that New Orleans is the most haunted city in the United States."

"Nice try," Carmela said as they started up the steps to the front porch. "You're still coming in with me."

Just as they reached the double oak doors with stained glass inlays, the right door popped open and a liveried doorman leaned out. His graying temples and stiff bearing made him look just like Carson, the butler on *Downton Abbey*.

"Come in, ladies," the doorman said in cultured tones. "How may I direct you?"

"We're here for the Martin Lash visitation," Carmela said.

"Straight ahead," Carson said. "Kindly sign the guest book as you pass by."

"Will do," Ava said as they stepped into a large marble-tiled entry. The walls were painted a deep rose color, the woodwork was gilded, and a large crystal chandelier dangled overhead. A flurry of white doves and levitating cherubs were painted on the ceiling.

"So tasteful," Carmela said. "Yet so understated."

"I wonder who their decorator was?" Ava said. "The last archduke of the Austro-Hungarian Empire?"

"Let's just play nice and sign the guest book."

They stepped up to a polished wooden lectern that held an oversized leather book. The pages were a creamy ivory paper edged in gold. A faux quill pen was stuck in a faux inkwell.

"Are you going to sign your real name?" Ava whispered.

Carmela hesitated. "Maybe . . . not." She wasn't sure why not, except for the fact that coming here today fell into the murky realm of investigating. And she really didn't want anyone to know that she was investigating. Not yet, anyway.

"So I guess we just go in this way," Ava said. She wandered toward a doorway that was flanked by two enormous urns filled with white gladiolas.

"Wait a minute," Carmela said. She'd stopped to glance at a framed photo on the wall.

"Who's that?" Ava asked. "The owner?"

"I think . . . I think it's one of the clients. Take a look."

Ava peered at a portrait of a woman dressed in a 1950s-era cocktail dress. She was seated in a Danish modern easy chair, one hand resting casually on the armrest. At her side was a glass of wine and a plate of cheese and crackers. But there was something strange about the woman's expression. Something unnatural about her rigid posture. "Oh my Lord," Ava exclaimed. "She's dead!"

"I think she had herself embalmed sitting up," Carmela said. "So it appeared as if she were attending her own party."

"This is kind of a crazy place," Ava said. She looked a little befuddled. "It's also the first time I've even attended a visitation with a buzz on."

"There's a first time for everything," Carmela said.

But when they entered Slumber Room C with its plush gray carpet, dark plum walls, and two rows of chairs facing a casket, Ava dug in her heels.

"Oh no, not an open casket. I hate open caskets with those overhead pink lights beating down on the corpse. It always reminds me of the heat lamps at a bad all-you-can-eat buffet."

"They're just trying to perk up their client's pallor," Carmela reasoned.

"Still, I really *hate* looking at dead people."

Carmela tried to calm her down. "Pull it together, will you? You've seen dead people before. In fact, we saw Martin Lash's corpse at its absolute worst. He's bound to look better now that he's had the benefit of a mortician and a cosmetologist."

"You think?"

"He probably looks so good he could pose for a class picture. And for goodness' sake, button your shirt. Every man in the place is starting to stare at you."

Ava brightened considerably. "They are?" She carefully buttoned one button. "Okay, all decent." She lifted her chin and threw back her shoulders, causing her button to pop open again. "Let's go take a gander at the man of the hour."

Curious, a little nervous, they tiptoed up to the casket.

Chapter 8

MARTIN Lash was lying there in his bronze Slumber-luxe casket looking small, pale, and waxy. In other words, a typical stiff. He'd been carefully dressed in a black cutaway suit and starched white shirt with an old fashioned high collar and black-and-white-striped tie. His head, which looked a trifle lopsided to Carmela's eye, rested on a white ruffled pillow that looked like it had been plucked right off the settee of a New Orleans house of ill repute.

"It's pretty clever the way they've got Lash all gussied up like that," Ava said, studying him. "That old-fashioned collar hides a multitude of sins. Mainly, the big gawking hole in his throat where the meat fork gouged him."

Carmela let loose a shiver. "Please don't remind me."

But now that Ava had gotten started, she couldn't let it go. "How do you think they plugged up that hole, anyway?

A couple of tidy little stitches with heavy-duty thread? Some kind of magic sealing wax?"

"No idea. But I'm sure the funeral director didn't just pop over to Home Depot for a can of caulk."

"And what's with the boutonniere? His prom days are over."

"His life is over." Carmela glanced at the mourners who were milling about. Most were looking grim faced but a little lost, too. She and Ava clearly didn't know a single soul here and it didn't appear that Lash had a very big family. Or any family at all, except for the little lady who was sitting in a maroon velvet armchair sniffling into her lace handkerchief.

"Excuse me," Carmela said. She put a hand out and touched the arm of one of the ushers. "Is that the mother?"

The usher gave a sober nod. "Yes. That's Mrs. Armstrong Lash, the deceased's mother."

"Are we going to talk to her?" Ava asked. She was big-eyed and nervous as she stared at the little lady in the black knit suit and sensible low-heeled shoes. Carmela figured Ava didn't trust any woman who wore chunky heels.

"I think we should go over and express our condolences, yes," Carmela said.

Ava nudged her. "You go first."

Carmela crossed the plush carpet with a reluctant Ava in tow.

"Excuse me? Mrs. Lash?"

The woman looked up at them with red-rimmed eyes. "Yes?" she quavered. She had a round face, frizzy gray hair, and an incongruously pointed chin.

"We just wanted to express our condolences," Carmela said.

Mrs. Lash looked hopeful. "You were friends of Martin's?"

"We only just made his acquaintance recently," Carmela said.

"Very recently," Ava muttered.

Mrs. Lash reached out and grabbed Carmela's hand. Carmela flinched. The woman's hand felt old and smooth, like aged paper that was beginning to crumble.

"Thank you for coming," Mrs. Lash said. "It's nice to meet some of Martin's friends." She eyed Ava's short skirt and thigh-high boots and asked, somewhat nervously, "You were the girlfriend?"

"Me?" Ava cried. "Oh no. No way."

Mrs. Lash seemed relieved. "Do you ladies write for that food website? Or do you work at the Environmental Justice League?"

"Neither," Carmela said. "We were just acquaintances."

"And not even very good acquaintances," Ava added.

His mother offered a sad smile. "I can't thank you enough for coming."

"No problem," Ava said. She was itching to blow this pop stand.

"I hope you'll be able to attend Martin's memorial service this Tuesday," Mrs. Lash said.

"Uh . . . we hadn't heard about that," Carmela lied.

"It will be held at St. Roch Chapel," Mrs. Lash said. "One of Martin's very favorite places."

"Really?" Carmela said. St. Roch Chapel was a depressing little Gothic chapel with pairs of crutches hanging on the wall.

"Please try to make it," Mrs. Lash urged.

"Sure," Ava said, backing away. "We'll give it a shot."

"SHEESH," AVA SAID. "I FELT LIKE SOME KIND OF phony baloney, implying that we actually knew her son."

"I'd say you made it fairly clear that you didn't," Carmela said.

"I tried not to offend her. Because I . . ." Ava's eyes lit up. "Hold everything, *cher*, are they serving *drinks* over there?" Ava was this close to turning into a heat-seeking missile.

Carmela glanced across the room where a buffet table had been set up. Wine bottles glistened and there were large trays of food. "I guess. It looks like they're serving wine and appetizers."

Ava shook her hair back off her shoulders. "Now that is classy. I mean, who serves wine and cheese at a viewing?"

"A funeral parlor?" Carmela said. "Probably because they've got adequate refrigeration?"

"I'm going to pretend you didn't just say that and have myself a nice refreshing beverage," Ava said. She plowed through the crowd like a three-masted schooner cutting through the waves. "Now this is lovely," she said, grabbing a wineglass and batting her eyes at a man who had just picked up a bottle of Cabernet Sauvignon. "And so unexpected."

"May I pour you a glass of wine?" the man asked. He was dressed in a brown corduroy jacket and tan slacks and had longish brown-blond hair. A look Ava probably would have deemed "crunchy granola."

"Why, yes, you certainly may." Ava watched as he filled her glass, then extended her hand. "I'm Ava. And you are . . . ?"

"Josh Cotton," said the man.

"How do you know Martin Lash?" Carmela asked, edging in between the two of them. This was what she really wanted. A chance to question some of the mourners.

Cotton fixed her with a toothy smile. "I guess you could call me second-in-command at the Environmental Justice League. I'm the associate director."

"How lovely," Ava said.

"Except," Carmela said, "you're probably first in command now. There seems to be a wide-open vacancy at the top."

"You're right about that," Cotton said. "But I could never hope to fill Martin's shoes. He was absolutely passionate about preserving Louisiana's natural wonders and the creatures that live there."

"Like the alligators and cottonmouths," Ava said.

"You say he was passionate," Carmela said. "Some would say rabid."

Cotton laughed nervously. "I suppose he could have been characterized that way. And the truth of the matter is, I did struggle with Lash over policy."

"In what way?" Carmela asked.

"Well . . . I firmly believed that Lash's methods of harassment and confrontation concerning environmental issues were severely outmoded. A better way, a smarter way, to bring about change these days is through dialogue and compromise."

"And you're just the man to do that?" Carmela asked.

Cotton took a sip of wine. "I might be."

"I like a take-charge man," Ava said.

Cotton smiled at Ava. "Will you be attending the memorial service on Tuesday?"

Ava gave him a wink. "Could be. You never know."

"It's nice that Martin's mother chose to have the service here instead of in his hometown," Cotton said.

"Why is that?" Carmela asked. "Better yet, *where* is that?"

"Martin kept a small apartment here in New Orleans, but he really preferred living down in Triumph."

"That's pretty far south of here," Carmela said.

"Yes," Cotton said. "Martin really thrived when he was close to the natural world that he loved so much."

"I can just imagine," Ava said.

Cotton beamed at Ava. "Ava, I was wondering if you'd like to . . ."

"I'm sorry, but we were just leaving," Carmela said. She grabbed Ava's arm and pulled her away.

"What are you doing?" Ava hissed. But she went along anyway.

"Ava, that man could be a suspect in Lash's death."

"Huh?"

"What if he wanted to get rid of Lash so he could move into the top slot?"

"Doggone, I never thought of that."

"He also struck me as being a little weird," Carmela said.

Ava tapped her own teeth. "You mean because of his teeth? They are kind of big."

"No, it's the fact that he seems somewhat unconcerned about Lash's death and is already planning on how he'll handle the organization."

"Gotcha."

"Which is why we should probably take off."

Except the surprises just kept coming. Carmela and Ava were just about to exit Slumber Room C when they ran smack-dab into Carmela's ex-husband, Shamus Allan Meechum.

"Shamus!" Carmela whooped.

Shamus peered at her. "Carmela?" He didn't look thrilled to see her.

They stared at each other like a couple of frill-necked lizards, ready to do battle, until Ava intervened.

"Aren't you the surprise guest," Ava drawled.

"You, too, Miss Sassy Pants," Shamus said. At which point Ava broke into a fit of giggles.

That seemed to break the ice. Or at least the staring contest. Shamus smiled his devil-may-care grin and his handsome, boyish face lit up.

"Nice to see you gals," he said.

"Women," Carmela corrected. "Not gals."

"Whatever," Shamus said.

"We certainly didn't expect to see *you* here," Carmela said. She was curious. Why exactly was Shamus here, anyway?

"Oh well . . ." Shamus waved a hand dismissively. "The Crescent City Bank Foundation just awarded the Environmental Justice League a grant of fifty thousand dollars."

"What for?" Carmela asked.

"I don't know. I guess to help police the environment."

"You're handing out cash money?" Ava asked.

"Grants," Shamus corrected. "You realize that Crescent City Bank isn't just a commercial bank—we have a heart, too. We're mindful of the community."

"Sure you are," Carmela said. She figured his bank would slice out someone's kidney if there was a buck to be made.

"Which is why we gave out this particular grant," Shamus continued.

Ava twisted around and pointed toward the casket. "But you do realize that Martin Lash is dead."

"Yes, but his organization isn't," Shamus said. "We have every confidence that Josh Cotton will keep it going. Perhaps even more successfully than Lash did." He focused his gaze on Carmela. "But I'm curious, Carmela. What the hell are you doing here?"

"Funny you should ask," Ava said.

"I'm listening," Shamus said.

Carmela decided to give it to him straight. "We witnessed Martin Lash's murder the other night."

"What!" Shamus screeched.

"When he got forked," Ava said, helpfully.

"And that's why you're here? Because you saw the guy die?" Shamus asked. "If you ask me, that's macabre. It's sort of like ambulance chasing."

"Tell him the whole story," Ava said.

So Carmela told Shamus about the argument between Lash and Quigg Brevard and how Quigg was worried that the blame was going to be heaped on his shoulders.

"So she's investigating," Ava said.

"No, I'm not," Carmela said.

But Shamus wasn't buying it. He knew her too well. "What does your boyfriend have to say about your going to bat for Brevard?" he asked in a snarky voice.

Carmela ducked her head. "He doesn't know about it." She poked him hard in the chest. "And don't *you* go and tell him."

"Huh, and you once called me a coward."

"That's because you are, Shamus. You boogied out of our marriage without giving me any notice. Seriously, the post office got more notice than I did."

"You're something else, Carmela. Still a real pistol. Still filled with spunk."

Carmela crossed her arms. "I do what I want these days."

Shamus gave her a commiserating look. "I don't think you need to worry much about Quigg Brevard. That guy's a wussy. He couldn't murder anyone if his life depended on it." His face took on a gleeful look. "But you know who really hated . . ."

Shamus's mouth abruptly snapped shut and his eyes went buggy. He realized that he'd probably said too much already.

Carmela pounced on him like a rabid Socialist going after a member of the Tea Party. "Excuse me, *who* are you talking about? Where were you going with this?"

Shamus did everything but dig his big toe into the carpet. "Aw, I really shouldn't say any more."

"You really should," Carmela said. "In fact, now you have to."

"The cat's half out of the bag already," Ava said. "So you may as well let 'er rip."

"All right," Shamus said. "But you didn't hear this from me."

"Our lips are sealed," Ava said. "Lip glossed, too."

"Do you know who Allan Hurst is?" Shamus asked.

"Nooo," Carmela said. "Should I?"

"Is he a society guy?" Ava asked. "Does he drive a Bentley?"

"He probably drives an old beater," Shamus said. "No, Allan Hurst is the owner of Fat Lorenzo's restaurant over on Magazine Street."

"What kind of restaurant is it?" Ava asked.

"Italian," Shamus said. "But that's not the point."

"Then what is?" Carmela asked.

"The problem," Shamus said, "is that Hurst never really got Fat Lorenzo's off the ground because Martin Lash wrote a horrible review the very first week they opened."

"And let me guess," Carmela said. "Because of that hateful review customers stayed away in droves. Which means Hurst probably lost a ton of money."

Shamus nodded. "Did he ever. Hurst is still bitter about Lash's review. Still struggling to pay back a bank loan he signed for personally."

"And you know all this because . . . ?"

"Because I gave him the bank loan," Shamus said.

"If Hurst doesn't repay the loan, will you foreclose on his restaurant?"

Shamus gave a thin crocodile smile. "In a heartbeat."

BACK AT HOME CARMELA WAS READY TO COL-lapse. She'd eaten and drunk too much at brunch, the visitation was freaky, and seeing Shamus always gave her a sick headache.

What to do? Well, she could pull the shades and check out Netflix.

Except the phone was suddenly ringing.

What now? Please don't let it be Shamus calling to bug me about something insignificant.

But it was Quigg.

"Now what do you want?" Carmela asked. She could hear restaurant noises in the background and figured he must be downtown at Mumbo Gumbo.

"I was just wondering if you'd made any progress?" Quigg asked.

"You have to stop bugging me—you're driving me crazy."

Quigg's laugh was a short bark. "You're tough, Carmela. You can take it. Besides, my life is hanging by a thread right now. The police want to slap on a pair of handcuffs and throw away the keys. Send me to Angola prison or worse. You realize Louisiana still has the death penalty."

"But now it's lethal injection, not Gruesome Gertie," Carmela said. Gruesome Gertie was the name of the old wooden electric chair that had been used up until 1991.

"What a lovely thing to bring up, Carmela. Thank you so much for planting that image in my head. I'm sure I'll have wonderful dreams tonight."

"Quigg?"

"What?" Now he just sounded testy.

"Cool your jets. I just came from Martin Lash's visitation."

Quigg let loose a low whistle. "You *have* been working on my behalf."

"I'm not completely indolent."

"So who was there? What did you find out?"

Carmela gave him a quick report on Josh Cotton, who she figured was probably going to take over the organization.

"So there's motive right there," Quigg said. "Cotton wanted to get himself into the power position."

Then she told Quigg about Allan Hurst, the owner of Fat Lorenzo's.

"I heard about that. Hurst is another restaurant owner who got blindsided by Lash. He thought he was going to get a stellar review and instead he got creamed. The review came out, like, the day of his grand opening and really slammed the door on business. He never really got Fat Lorenzo's off the ground. I wouldn't be surprised if he had to close down pretty soon."

"What I need to know," Carmela said, "is if you have any information about Hurst personally? Is he the kind of guy who would retaliate? I mean, would he kill over a bad review?"

"I don't know. But somebody sure did a nasty job on Lash. Maybe it *was* Hurst. I heard that he was really angry and bitter."

"Maybe that's just wishful thinking on your part."

"Hey, I'll do anything to get out from under this black cloud."

"Please don't say that. It makes *you* sound like you might have retaliated."

"I wouldn't do that."

"Even though you're angry?"

"Hey, did you know that Martin Lash said that my wine was no better than pig swill? Can you image that? The grapes that I've nurtured and labored over for six years?"

"I have to go now," Carmela said.

"Hey . . . how about that kiss last night?"

"You can forget about that, buster! You caught me at a weak moment."

"Okay, okay, sorry. Just keep working on this Lash thing, will you? You're doing great."

Carmela hung up the phone and thought hard about Quigg. Her takeaway was that he was horribly angry. With that kind of temper, could Quigg have killed Lash? He'd been right there, after all. He'd certainly had the opportunity. Plus he'd been mad as a hornet and all jacked up . . .

She sighed and flopped back down on her leather couch. And why was she involved in this, really?

Why indeed?

Maybe because she could still feel the urgent way Quigg's lips had pressed against hers last night?

Oh dear.

Chapter 9

SUNSHINE streamed in the front windows of Memory Mine this Monday morning as Gabby gathered up packages of brightly colored crepe paper. Carmela was standing behind the front counter, studying an invoice that had arrived in the morning mail.

"Did you order five hundred rubber stamps of a cartoon spider crouched in a cobweb?" Carmela asked.

"Um . . . no, I did not. Did we get billed for that?"

"Yes." Carmela set the rogue invoice aside. It was either a mistake or some company was trying to slip an invoice past her, hoping to get paid. Happened all the time. Last week, an invoice for the magazine *Today's Reptile* had shown up.

"I'm going to start organizing all our paper and scissors," Gabby said. "So we're as prepared as possible for our crepe paper class."

"Every time we get ready for one of these classes I'm grateful for our previous tenants," Carmela said. "The ginormous table those antique dealers left behind is so perfect. We can seat—what?—something like a dozen people around it? Fourteen if we all scrunch? Heck, we could probably serve Christmas dinner there if we could squeeze a forty-pound turkey into the microwave."

"Those guys probably left it behind because they couldn't budge it," Gabby laughed. "It's a behemoth and weighs a ton. The really good thing is it's also dented and scratched so a few more scissor nicks don't make a bit of difference." She paused and pushed back a hank of hair. "So what else should I lay out? Oh well, I suppose it depends on what we'll be doing exactly." She gazed at Carmela with an inquisitive smile.

Carmela picked up a roll of brass wire. "I'm planning to demo crepe paper flowers, crepe paper wreaths, fringed streamers, and surprise balls."

"I guess there's a reason you advertised this class as a Crepe Paper Party. There'll be so much going on, lots of fun things to work on."

"And it really is fun, isn't it?" Carmela said. "Especially when our customers get all jazzed up about a particular craft. You see their eyes start to sparkle and can almost see the creative juices flowing."

"I love the interaction with customers," Gabby said. "Helping them see a project through. Plus every time somebody takes a class with us it kind of springboards them into the next project."

"Which is oh-so-good for sales."

"I'm guessing you have a few more classes planned?"

"Always," Carmela said. "I was planning to bring back our Paper Moon and Shadow Box classes right after the holidays."

"Just in time for Mardi Gras," Gabby smiled. "When

everybody goes hog wild with their invitations, scrapbooks, and party favors."

"The other thing . . ." Carmela stopped mid-sentence as the bell above the door *da-ding*ed. Then a visitor she certainly wasn't expecting—namely Babcock—pushed his way into her shop. *Talk about an unexpected visit.*

Gabby, as if sensing an impending crisis, quickly turned tail and disappeared into the back of the shop. So she was no help. No, Carmela knew she would just have to smile and face Babcock all by herself.

"Hey," Carmela said. "Surprise, surprise." She cringed inwardly, figuring her words sounded stupid. Or worse yet, indicated some degree of guilt—meaning she had something to hide. Which she sort of did.

Babcock pressed himself against the front counter and leaned in close to her. She could smell his dreamy aftershave and could almost feel the smoothness of his cheek pressed against hers. Nice. Much better than Quigg's.

Don't think about that now, she warned herself. *Don't start making comparisons.*

"I didn't hear from you yesterday," Babcock said in his low baritone.

Carmela flashed him a bright smile. Wait, was that too bright? Did showing too much teeth make her look goofy guilty?

"I went to brunch with Ava," Carmela said. "Then one thing led to another." There was simply no need to spill her guts about going to Martin Lash's visitation yesterday afternoon. No need at all.

"One thing led to another?" Babcock asked. "Led to what?"

Carmela wasn't going to go *there*, that's for sure. So she tucked her hands behind her back and crossed her fingers.

"Oh, we had brunch at Brennan's. And then we wandered around and visited a couple of art galleries."

"Uh-huh."

"Lots of new exhibitions," Carmela babbled on. "I guess everyone's all geared up for Christmas."

Babcock gave a distracted nod. His mind was definitely on something else besides art galleries. "I have a question for you."

Carmela's heart sank. This was it, the coup de grâce. He'd somehow discovered that she'd been to Martin Lash's visitation. And, really, she should have known. Should have realized that there'd be undercover cops hanging out there, looking for suspicious characters. And that once they'd spotted her, they'd report back to her boy toy du jour.

"Ask me anything," Carmela whispered, steeling herself for the crack of the bat and a line drive down center field. Right to the heart of the matter.

Babcock leaned in even closer as amusement danced in his sharp blue eyes.

Please don't torture me like this.

"Did you have the bananas Foster?" he asked.

Carmela blinked. "Whu . . . ?"

"You know very well what I'm talking about. The signature dessert at Brennan's."

Relief flooded Carmela's wonked-out brain. "The banan . . . why, yes!" she said brightly. "We did. And aren't you the clever detective to figure it out, a regular Sherlock Holmes. Of course we had bananas Foster. We practically went facedown in it. That's the whole point of going to Brennan's, after all."

Babcock cocked his head at her. "I figured as much. I also figured you were still pretty steamed at me. You know, because of Saturday night." He gave her an aw-shucks look. "I have to apologize for that, Carmela. I guess I wasn't a very good dinner companion."

Carmela waved a hand. "Oh, that." She felt so flooded with relief at not being caught in a web of lies that she was more than willing to give Babcock a pass. "That's all behind us. I realize you have a very demanding job and I understand that an investigation will sometimes interfere with . . . well, with us."

Interestingly enough, Babcock had just given her the perfect opening.

"So tell me," Carmela continued. "How *are* you coming with the Martin Lash investigation?"

"Carmela . . ." Babcock's voice carried a hint of warning.

Carmela kept up her innocent-until-proven-guilty act. "Don't get me wrong. I'm not trying to meddle. In fact, I wouldn't *dream* of it."

Oh, I so hope a bolt of lightning doesn't come down and strike me upside the head, Carmela thought.

"But I did have an idea," she managed to slip in.

"What exactly are you talking about?" Babcock asked.

"I've been thinking about Martin Lash's sideline. About how he wrote all those nasty restaurant reviews."

"Uh-huh." Babcock was watching her carefully. About as carefully as a mongoose observes a cobra.

"And I was wondering if you'd looked at *other* New Orleans restaurateurs who received horrible reviews from Lash."

Babcock shook his head. "Do you think we should?"

"It seems to me it might be a good angle to investigate."

"I'm not so sure about that. It would take a tremendous amount of manpower and would probably just lead to a bunch of dead ends. Not only that, we'd probably have a bunch of disgruntled restaurant owners beating on our heads."

Carmela nodded agreeably with him even as she wondered

if she should tell him about Allan Hurst and the horrible review he got for Fat Lorenzo's. No, this wasn't the time or place.
She would play her cards close to the vest for now. Maybe she'd
even look into this all by herself.

"Speaking of bad reviews," Babcock said, "your pal
Quigg Brevard is coming in to talk to us this afternoon."

"Really? I thought you were pretty much finished with
him. That you'd dismissed him as a possible suspect."

Babcock gave her a cool smile. "Sweetheart, I'm just getting started." Then his phone rang, startling both of them.
He glanced down, frowned, and said, "Gotta go." He gave
her a quick peck on the cheek. "Thanks for not holding a
grudge about Saturday night."

"See you later," she said, waving as he darted out the
door. *Thanks for not calling me out for a zillion trillion lies.*

A FEW MINUTES LATER, GABBY CREPT BACK UP
to the front desk. But before she had a chance to ask Carmela if she and Babcock were all lovey-dovey again (Gabby
being a huge champion of romance) their next-door neighbor came slaloming through the door.

The Countess Vanessa Saint-Marche was the owner of the
overpriced, overhyped jewelry shop Lucrezia.

"Carmela!" the countess cried out. "And Gabby!"

The countess was whippet thin, so tan she looked like a baseball glove, and big on theatrics. Today she was costumed in a
full-length leopard-print coat, her gobs of jewelry a walking
advertisement for her shop. The countess's gold dangling multi-
link earrings were so long they nearly collided with the thick
choker of gold and pearls that was wrapped around her neck.

"I just saw your handsome young detective leaving a
moment ago," the countess announced. She didn't just talk, she

announced. Her hands fluttered in circles, jangling the half dozen shiny bracelets that graced each wrist. "You shouldn't let a plum prize like him walk around all single and fancy-free." Now she held up a warning finger. "Some other woman could snap him up and then where would you be?" She cocked her head forward like an inquisitive bird. "Out in the cold, I suppose."

"Carmela and Babcock are just fine," Gabby said, rushing to defend her friend. "They're completely devoted to each other."

"Lovely, lovely," the countess said. "Which is why I'd adore getting that man into my shop to pick out an engagement ring."

"I don't think you should necessarily rush love," Carmela said.

The countess let loose dry chuckles as her skinny shoulders rose and fell. "Oh, my dear, *of course* you should. When you find the perfect man—or even an imperfect man, a scratch-and-dent type of fellow—you need to hurry up and lock that relationship down tight."

"Carmela's got it locked," Gabby said. "She really does."

"Then remember this," the countess said. "Lucrezia carries the most exquisite diamonds in all of New Orleans. Cushion cut, pear shaped, even old mine estate pieces. You send that fine detective of yours my way and I'll make sure he gets a good deal." She winked at Carmela. "And that *you* get yourself a killer diamond!"

"DO WE HAVE ANY ASPIRIN?" CARMELA ASKED. "Talking to that woman always gives me a splitting headache."

"Here," Gabby said. She reached behind the desk and pulled out a bottle, shook two out for Carmela. "Take two of these with a hit of Diet Coke. It's a surefire remedy."

"A surefire remedy would be if she closed her shop and moved out. I'm not sure she's even a legitimate countess. Her title—and her diamonds—could all be a complete fabrication."

"I read somewhere that you can buy a title," Gabby said. "Mostly titles like duke, earl, and viscount. And if your title is in the British Isles, you sometimes get a small plot of land—like eight inches by eight inches—to go along with it."

"Sounds more like a cemetery plot where you'd bury an urn," Carmela sniffed.

Gabby raised an eyebrow at Carmela and said, "You've got cemeteries on the brain? Yeah, you better hide out in your office for a while. You've got it bad."

"What have I got?" Carmela asked.

"The grumps."

CARMELA DID AS SHE WAS TOLD. WENT INTO HER office and chugged a good long slug of Diet Coke. When she felt fizzy bubbles rise up in her nose she quit and let loose a few good sneezes. Her sneezing fit finally over and done with, she took a spin around in her chair and studied some of the sketches she'd pinned to her wall. All ideas for projects: a booklet with a small pocket that would hold a tea bag, a wooden box that she would paint with copper and gold and stencil with an image of an old clipper ship, a small clutch purse made of super durable paper that would look great when it was stamped and embellished.

Lots of projects to do. Not so much time.

Carmela leaned back in her chair and massaged her temples. Just how long was she going to be able to cope with Babcock's suspicions about Quigg? How long could she deal with Quigg coming on to her?

She knew her life was devolving into a circus. And not

the fun kind, either. More like the kind where all sorts of wacky clowns spilled out of a tiny little car and into her life.

Staring at her computer screen, Carmela skipped her fingertips lightly across the keyboard. What about this Allan Hurst and his restaurant? What *was* the deal with that?

Babcock had told her that all of Martin Lash's reviews had been purged from the Glutton for Punishment website, so that wouldn't be any help.

So where could she find the Fat Lorenzo's review? How was a girl supposed to get any research done?

Carmela clicked along and twenty seconds later she was on Yelp. And found that a helpful someone had posted a quote taken directly from Martin Lash's review of Fat Lorenzo's. She scanned it quickly.

> *Don't worry about getting Fat at Fat Lorenzo's. The food is inedible. Start with a salad. I promise you wilted greens, mushy tomatoes, and mushrooms that were artfully diced to cut away the mold. Entrées? Unless you enjoy gelatinous pasta, rubbery calamari, and shoe-leather chicken, skip this course entirely. As for dessert, if tepid coffee and cheesecake the texture of curdled grits are your faves, then you're in luck. With so many intriguing restaurants in New Orleans, why waste a moment—or a dollar—at Fat Lorenzo's? Take my word, this Fattie won't be around for long.*

Yipes! Talk about a vicious, venomous review. And that was only part of it. Carmela could understand why customers had stayed away in droves. Lash made Fat Lorenzo's sound like eating there was tantamount to catching the bubonic plague. She could almost understand—but not justify—Lash's murder. Allan Hurst, the owner, must have been hysterical when Lash's review came out. And now, according to

Shamus, Hurst had zero customers and was carrying a mountain of debt. Revenge did seem to loom large!

Next, Carmela ran a search on Allan Hurst. She didn't find much, just an archived article from the business section of the *Times-Picayune*. It was your basic bare-bones announcement about the restaurant planning to open within a few months. The press release was accompanied by a small, grainy photo of Hurst.

Carmela studied the black-and-white photo. Hurst looked deer-in-the-headlights surprised, eyes wide open, brows beetled, like maybe he'd taken a not-so-good selfie in his shaving mirror.

And now his business, probably his life's dream, was in ruins. Was Allan Hurst the type of hothead who'd grab a meat fork from his own kitchen, tail Martin Lash to the Winter Market, and then stab him in the neck?

Carmela wasn't sure. It was hard to tell all that from a tiny black-and-white photo.

"Carmela?"

Carmela spun away from her computer. "Are our crafters here already?" she asked Gabby. Had she fallen down the rabbit hole and been consumed with this whole Martin Lash thing for the last couple of hours?

But no. Gabby was just asking about lunch.

"If you want to mind the front counter," Gabby said, "I'll run down to Pirate's Alley Deli and grab a couple of po-boys for lunch."

"Great. Thank you." Carmela stood up. "Wait. And get me another Diet Coke, too."

Gabby smiled. "The caffeinated kind?"

"Can you think of anything else that jacks you up so nicely?"

Gabby shook her head. "Nothing that's legal anyway."

Chapter 10

CARMELA was still nibbling the last delicious bites of her po-boy when she heard the front door bang open. She sat up straighter in her chair and dabbed at her lips. "Hello?"

"Hellooooo!" came a familiar yodel.

Tandy Bliss, Carmela thought to herself. When Tandy swept in you were assured of a serious tornadic event.

"Hey there, Gabby," Tandy bellowed again. "Where's Carmela? Did she forget we've got a class today?"

Carmela wiped her hands on her napkin, stuffed the remnants of her lunch in a brown paper bag, and dumped the detritus into her trash can. Then she grabbed her second Diet Coke and ran out to greet Tandy just as Gabby was reassuring her that the crepe paper class would indeed start in just a few minutes.

Elbows out, Tandy punched her fists on nearly nonexistent hips and turned to face Carmela. "Have you heard from Baby? She's supposed to be here and she's late." She tapped a toe. "Late again."

Carmela couldn't help but smile. Tandy's temperament was as fiery as her intensely hennaed red hair.

"Sweetie, she'll be here," Carmela said. "Relax. Take a breath."

Tandy was still spinning like a Texas dust devil. "She's not always prompt, you know. And this is *important*."

Before Carmela could hand Tandy a paper bag to keep her from hyperventilating, the door opened again and a blond-haired woman wearing a navy blue Chanel jacket over a sleek white blouse and perfectly pressed blue jeans strode into Memory Mine. With her artfully cut hair and still-flawless-yet-fifty face, she looked like the idealized version of a mature woman.

"There you are!" Tandy cried.

"Tandy, honestly," Baby said. "I could hear you screaming from all the way out on the sidewalk." Baby Fontaine was a Garden District socialite with a gentle demeanor and unerring common sense. She also had a finely tuned sense of humor.

"Because I was wondering where you were," Tandy said. "Time's a-wastin'."

"Not to worry," Carmela said, shepherding them back to the craft table. "You're all just fine on time. I'm guessing you'll probably be able to finish at least two or even three craft projects today."

"That's what I'm talkin' about," Tandy said as she plopped into a chair.

As Gabby started passing out rulers and scissors, the front door flew open again and two more ladies came in. The taller of the two, a silver-haired woman dressed in a wheat-colored cashmere sweater and khaki slacks, said "Is this right? The crepe paper class?"

"This is it," Carmela said. "Come on back."

"I'm Margery Landon," the woman said. "This is my sister Allison May."

Allison May, dressed in a black turtleneck and jeans, gave a finger wave when her name was mentioned.

Carmela introduced herself, then led them back and made introductions all around.

"I think we've got one more person coming," Gabby said.

"Josie?" Carmela said.

"That's right."

Josie Thibideaux, a young librarian who'd begun taking craft classes the previous summer, showed up some two minutes later.

When Carmela was sure that everyone was present and accounted for, she stood at the head of the table and held up a large wreath made entirely of poufy black crepe paper flowers. A black crow with beady red eyes was perched in the center of the wreath.

"Spooky," Tandy said, causing everyone to laugh.

"It is spooky," Carmela agreed. "I made this wreath a couple of months ago for Halloween. But when you use different-colored crepe paper flowers, this basic wreath can be adapted for almost any holiday. For Christmas, you could do red, green, silver, or whatever you'd like."

Gabby stepped in. "Since we're all going to create flowers just like Carmela did, you're going to need a template for the flower petals." She proceeded to hand out metal templates to everyone. "For each flower you need to cut about eight to ten petals."

"So you cut out all your petals and then squeeze them together at the bottom . . ." Tandy said.

"That's right," Carmela said. "And then you secure them in place with a twist of wire. Once that's done, you kind of bend and pull each petal, working it into a flower shape."

"Neat," Baby said as she started tracing and cutting. "I think I'm going to do a pale blue wreath and decorate it with some of those sparkly little white birds I saw at the front of the shop."

"Perfect," Carmela said.

The women all started working on their flower petals, except for Tandy. She wanted to make super huge flowers, so Gabby fixed her up with a slightly larger template.

Once the flowers were made, the next project on the agenda was a surprise ball. And to Carmela's surprise, everyone wanted to make one.

"I've got, like, a jillion nieces and nephews," Margery said. "So this might be just the thing for them."

"Explain, please," said Josie.

Carmela held up a small red rubber ball. "What you do is anchor a long strip of crepe paper to a ball and then start wrapping. As you wrap the strips, you insert little gifts, like tiny toys, charms, candy, or fortunes. Then when the ball is all wrapped up, you put a gold sticker on it and tie it with ribbon. It's great for the holidays—for kids or as party favors."

"Could I do all candy?" Josie wanted to know.

"Of course," Carmela said. "You can do anything your heart desires."

Thirty minutes later, the table was a riot of crepe paper flowers and surprise balls. In the meantime, Gabby was busy snipping hunks of wire into three-foot pieces and bending them into circles.

"Okay," Gabby said. "Set aside your surprise balls for a moment, it's time to grab your flowers and fashion your wreaths."

She passed out the wire and everyone slipped their flowers

on and anchored them in place. Then the ladies began searching the scrapbook shop for embellishments. Josie decided to create delicate pink bows for her wreath. Margery stamped angels onto cardstock and was busy cutting them out. Once her angels were cut into tags, she would color them using a copper-colored pen.

Baby, who was sitting next to Carmela, nudged her friend and said, "What's this I hear about you witnessing a murder the other night?"

Carmela wrinkled her nose and whispered, "Oh, you heard about that?"

"Well, it was a fairly nasty business, so the *Times-Picayune* served it up as a feature story," Baby said. "But my neighbor Deb Darling was actually *at* the Winter Market and told me that she saw you there. Apparently the police had roped off a spot and you were being questioned?"

"Because Ava and I witnessed the whole thing. Can you believe it? Some girls' night out, huh?"

"Must have been awful."

"It was hideous," Carmela said. "Like something out of a horror flick. But you know what? The truth of the matter is, Ava and I *didn't* really see the whole thing. We only saw that guy, Martin Lash, come staggering out from behind the row of tents."

"With a meat fork stuck in his throat," Baby said, a trifle aghast.

"Yup." Carmela took a slug of Coke. "And the worst part is . . ."

"There's a worst part?" Baby asked. "Besides just the really bad part?"

Carmela nodded. "Babcock thinks that Quigg Brevard did it."

"Your Quigg?"

"He's not really my Quigg," Carmela hastened to say.

"He used to be."

"No, no, not for a long time. That relationship is ancient history."

"Still," Baby said, "Quigg always struck me as pretty much of a pussycat." She smiled to herself. "Well, maybe a bit of a tomcat, because he always seemed to have an eye for the ladies. But I can't believe Quigg would ever outright murder someone."

"Tell that to Babcock," Carmela said. "He's suspicious because Martin Lash . . ."

"The dead guy," Baby said.

"The dead guy," Carmela said. "The dead guy gave Quigg's restaurants some really rotten reviews. And then Quigg got on his high horse and confronted Lash and the two of them had a knock-down, drag-out fight right in the middle of the Winter Market for everyone to see. I mean, *food* was thrown."

"No!" Baby said.

"And then not five minutes later, Martin Lash wound up with a meat fork stuck in his neck, spurting blood like the Trevi Fountain." Carmela touched a hand to her chest and took a deep breath. "And that's why Babcock is looking so hard—and disdainfully, I might add—at Quigg."

"So what's Quigg doing about it?" Baby asked. "I mean, has he hired an attorney to defend him? Or maybe even a private detective to help find the real killer?"

Carmela blinked at the "private detective" part.

"Oh no," Baby said. "He didn't."

"Of course he did."

"He really asked you to get involved?"

"More like pulled me into it," Carmela said. "He says I'm the only one he really trusts."

"And of course you have the ear of the lead detective."

"No, I don't," Carmela said. "Not for this. Babcock isn't telling me squat. I'm on my own. Out on a limb, you might say."

"Don't sell yourself short," Baby said in a low voice. "You're pretty good. You've managed to unravel more than a few crimes in your day."

"Which pretty much infuriates Babcock."

"You two have a tempestuous relationship, don't you?"

"It's cooling on ice right now. Since Babcock shut me out completely."

"And how do you feel about that?" Baby asked.

"Like I want to thumb my nose at him. Like I want to snoop around and figure things out for myself."

Baby reached over and patted Carmela's hand. "Then do it, honey. You're one smart cookie, don't you know?"

THE WREATHS TURNED OUT BEAUTIFULLY, THE surprise balls were charming, and Tandy's flowers morphed into six gigantic red and purple blooms. She ended up attaching them to long green pipe cleaners, so she could stick them into a large ceramic pot.

"That was so much fun," Gabby said, half yawning, as everyone trooped out the door, heartfelt thank-yous drifting back to them. "But I'm ready to go home."

"Then go," Carmela said. "Just . . . go. I'll roll the phones over to the answering service and lock up."

Gabby managed a crooked smile. "Yeah? But what about straightening up the craft table?"

"There's not that much to do. So just take off. Have a nice evening."

"Thank you, I will," Gabby said, pulling on her jacket.

Two minutes later, Carmela was all alone, wandering through her shop, straightening up a little, but deciding to leave most of it until morning.

Then the phone rang.

"Hello? Memory Mine." Carmela hoped it wasn't a customer wanting some last-minute favor. But it was Quigg. "How did it go today?" she asked him. She meant the questioning by the police.

"Terrible," Quigg said. "They're utterly convinced I'm a stone-cold killer."

"But you're not." At least she hoped he wasn't.

"Tell that to your boyfriend. He was ready to beat me bloody with a rubber hose. Carmela, you said you'd help me. I'm feeling frantic here."

"I'm trying, Quigg, I really am."

"Then please try harder. You don't know how close they came to actually detaining me today."

"But they didn't. They let you go, right? I mean, you *are* out?"

"Yeah, I'm over at Mumbo Gumbo. I've got bills to pay and customers to charm. Anyway, they asked the same old questions over and over again. Why was I arguing with Lash? Did I leave my booth? For how long? Over and over until my head was spinning."

"Maybe you passed their little test. Maybe they're finally finished with you."

"Only your boyfriend knows for sure, and he didn't look anywhere close to being satisfied. He looked frustrated and distracted."

Carmela knew that look. It meant Babcock wasn't done with Quigg. Not by a long shot.

"If you can pull anything out of your hat, Carmela . . ."

"I know," she said. "I hear you."

"Carmela, you mean everything to me . . ." Quigg's voice went hoarse as he choked up. And then, suddenly, he was gone. Hanging up the phone because he didn't want her to hear him breaking down.

Damn, Carmela thought. Quigg was really hurting. Really

scared. But what could she do? How could she ever hope to resolve this?

Her mind twirled at warp speed. Quigg needed her. Babcock wanted her to stay clear of the case.

But from everything Carmela knew about Martin Lash, he wasn't exactly a model citizen. If only he'd had the decency to get murdered several miles away. Maybe out there in the bayous he loved so much. But no, he had to collapse at her feet and die in front of her very eyes.

So what's a girl to do?

And then a thought struck her. Hmm. It was a long shot. It was slightly dangerous. But it might just shake something loose.

Chapter 11

"THANK you for riding shotgun," Carmela said to Ava. They were blasting down Highway 23 in her Mercedes, radio turned to B97 FM, headed for Martin Lash's house in Triumph, Louisiana.

Carmela didn't know what they might find there, didn't even know if they could figure a way in, but it was all she could come up with on short notice.

"Quigg sounded pretty desperate, huh?" Ava said.

"Like he's circling the drain."

"I must say you've certainly taken a keen interest in helping him."

"Probably because he asked."

"Oh, I'm sure he asked you very politely," Ava said. "Although Quigg's charm has always been in being impolite. Exerting his machismo and being a little bit . . . forward."

"Mm hm," Carmela said.

Ava glanced sideways at her. "Has he? Been forward, I mean? Aside from that single stolen kiss you told me about?"

"Not really. And I don't think we should talk about this anymore."

"Your cheeks are flushed pink and you're making a lemon face. I think Quigg is starting to get to you."

"We're not going to talk about this anymore." Carmela reached over and turned the radio up louder.

R. Kelly's sultry song "Down Low" filled the car. *Keep it on the down low. Nobody has to know . . .*

THEY PASSED THROUGH PORT SULPHUR AND EMpire, and then, some twenty minutes later, bumped across a narrow bridge, wooden planks rumbling beneath their tires, and rolled into the small, unincorporated community of Triumph.

"Jeez," Ava said, "the joint looks deserted. They really roll up the sidewalks here, don't they?"

"It's a pretty small town," Carmela said. "And it's late."

"Not *that* late." Ava pressed her nose to the window as they cruised down what was probably the main drag. "There's Booger's Bait Shop. And Manny's Pizza." She giggled. "I hope they never get their orders mixed up."

"Just keep your eyes peeled," Carmela said. "We're looking for Levee Road."

It wasn't all that difficult to find. Five minutes of driving around and a couple of wrong turns brought them across Highway 11 to Levee Road. From there they crawled along slowly for ten blocks or so, a few small homes popping up on their right, the Mississippi River turgid and dark to their left. Finally, they rolled to a stop in front of Martin Lash's house, the place looking dark, deserted, and lonely.

"You wouldn't call this an actual residence per se, would you?" Ava asked.

Carmela gazed at the ramshackle one-story wooden building that Martin Lash had called home sweet home. Thanks to pounding rain, searing heat, buckets of humidity, and the occasional hurricane, all paint had been blasted away and the exterior worn down to a dull gray. The sagging roof looked like it was covered with corrugated tin, a small porch hung off the front of the house, and the yard was basically an ugly patchwork of weeds and mud.

"There's lots of commercial fishing around here," Carmela said, "so maybe it's more of a camp shack." They climbed out of the car and stood on the side of the deserted roadway.

"I'd hate to be the Realtor who had to list this place," Ava said. "One-bedroom, one-bathroom dumperoo with a river view if you don't mind the rich, ripe odor of decomposing fish. Why do you think Lash lives way down here anyway? Correction, lived."

"It's probably what Josh Cotton said yesterday. Lash wanted to be close to the swamps and bayous."

"A regular nature boy," Ava said. "You think there are alligators crawling around here?"

"Sure there are. Well, not *here* here. But nearby."

Ava studied her nails. "So what's on the program now?"

But Carmela had already started for the house. "We're going to sneak inside and poke around," she said, her words drifting back to Ava.

But getting inside was easier said than done. When they approached the front door, they saw it had been fitted with a shiny Schlage padlock.

"Somebody's security-minded," Ava said. "Do you think we can pick that lock with a bobby pin?"

"I think that only works in B movies."

"Okay, then can we pry it off?"

"Doubtful," Carmela said. "Let's see what's going on around back."

They tiptoed around the shack, stumbling when they hit a few spongy areas.

"This is awful," Ava whispered. "I'm wearing my new Giglio Frederick reptile boots and don't want them to get ruined."

"Real reptile?"

"Vinyl reptile. Which is probably why my toes feel sweaty. Oh, hey, look. There's a back door." Ava grabbed the handle with both hands and rattled it. It barely moved. "This isn't working out very well. What's plan B?"

"There is no plan B." Carmela shrugged.

Ava put her hands on her hips. "There has to be a contingency plan, or at least some way to get in. Here, over here." She stumbled through a tangle of weeds. "Let's try this window. See that ratty old screen? It looks like it's practically rusted out. Come over here and give me a boost."

Carmela picked her way toward Ava, bent over, and laced her fingers together. "When I flip you up, try to grab ahold of those shutters. Then see if you can kick out that screen."

"Got it." Ava stepped into Carmela's hands, jumped up, grabbed onto a shutter that was partially hanging off, and gave a powerful kick. There was a clatter as the screen fell to the ground, then a loud pop and the sound of breaking glass.

"Oops," Ava said, her voice suddenly fading out, like a radio signal that had gone away.

"Be careful!" Carmela cried. But she was talking to dead air. Ava had already catapulted herself inside the shack. "Are you okay?" she hissed at the dark, gaping hole that, just seconds earlier, had been a functioning window.

Ava's voice drifted back. "I'm okay, but the whole dang

window popped out of the frame. Now there's broken glass all over the place."

"You didn't get cut, did you?"

"I think I'm okay." Ava's head and shoulders suddenly appeared. Then she stretched a hand out. "Come on, I'll reel you in."

Carmela grabbed Ava's hand as she scrabbled up the side of the house and was yanked through the window as slickly as Alice tumbling through the rabbit hole.

"Whoa, whoa," Ava gasped. She was sprawled on the floor and Carmela had landed on top of her. "You're crushing my chest—I can't breathe!"

Carmela hastily rolled off her. "Dear Lord, I didn't crack one of your ribs, did I?"

Ava placed both hands on her chest and felt around gingerly. "No, everything seems to be in place. Thank goodness I'm wearing my Lady Goddess Longline Bra. It holds me in pretty dang tight."

They stumbled to their feet and glanced around the dim interior.

"Now what?" Ava asked. She lifted her nose and gave a suspicious sniff. "It smells horrible in here. Like something died."

"It's probably just mice."

"But you don't know that for sure. What if it's the ghost of Martin Lash?" Ava's eyes grew big. "Maybe his spirit floated back here. The man died suddenly, so could be he's not at peace yet."

"You saw him yesterday and he looked peaceful enough lying in his overpriced casket. Besides, if your spirit could float anywhere it wanted to, would you come back to a dump like this?"

"Heck no," Ava said. "I'd probably ectoplasm my way into

a fancy mansion in the Garden District. Or find a Neiman Marcus store and go on a spiritual shopping spree."

"Okay then." Carmela looked around. The place *was* dark and spooky.

Every stick of furniture was covered with a white drop cloth so the room's perspective took on a strange, humpy look.

"Did you bring a flashlight?" Ava asked.

"I've got one. But I'm kind of afraid to turn it on. If somebody sees the light playing on the walls, they might alert the local constable."

"Who'd probably come swooping in here and arrest us," Ava finished.

"So for now we just poke around surreptitiously," Carmela said.

"What are we looking for?" Ava whispered.

"Not sure. I guess maybe something that might point the finger away from Quigg?"

"You mean like a clue? To solve a mystery?"

"Works for me."

Ava crept forward a few feet and promptly stumbled over a low, leather ottoman. "Oops, clumsy me. Say, what if there *isn't* a clue?" For all her bravado at breaking in, she was clearly having second thoughts.

"I don't know," Carmela said. "The thing is, Lash was murdered, right? In what was probably a crime of passion. So somebody must have seriously hated him. Maybe we can find something that sheds light on that. Maybe Lash was involved in some sort of criminal operation. Or maybe he was a secret drug dealer."

"Maybe he had a really nasty breakup with his girlfriend," Ava said.

"Somehow, I think it's got to be more pressing than that.

Anyone who forks someone in the throat has to be seething with rage."

"I've had boyfriends I could have killed," Ava said.

"No, you haven't. Not with that much fury." Carmela shuffled along. "Let's just keep looking."

The house had a combination living room/dining room/kitchen, a small bedroom, a bare-bones bathroom, and an even smaller second bedroom. That's where they found Martin Lash's computer.

"This is good," Carmela said. "Maybe there's something on his computer that will point us in the right direction."

Ava's bloodred nails flicked across the keyboard. Then she frowned. "Nothing's happening."

They hit keys, rebooted, fiddled with it, and still the computer remained mute.

"It's password protected," Carmela said. "So we need to think of a password."

"LASH," Ava said. But that didn't work.

They tried entering a few more passwords, finally resorting to BARITARIA, GLUTTON, and even NASTY REVIEW.

"Zilch," Ava said. "Maybe he's got something stashed in his desk?"

That required a little more light, so Carmela turned on her Maglite and began pulling out desk drawers like crazy.

"Here's a notebook," Carmela said. Although with its leather cover it looked more like a journal.

"What's it say?"

Carmela turned a few pages. There were notes that Lash had scrawled to himself. And even though it was difficult to read his back-slanted handwriting, Carmela could get the gist of it. "Look at what he wrote here."

"What?" Ava crowded in to see.

"It says here 'Josh Cotton has been going behind my back, lobbying the board of directors. Very dangerous.'"

"Whoa."

"That's not all," Carmela said. "Lash goes on to write 'Time to get rid of him?'"

"It's almost like he was plotting Josh Cotton's demise," Ava said.

"Almost, but not quite. Still, if Lash was going to get rid of Cotton, maybe Cotton found out and got to him first."

"Wow. And Cotton seemed so sweet when we talked to him yesterday. Like a regular, normal guy."

"Don't you know by now there are no normal guys?"

"*Cher*, when you say stuff like that it's like an arrow to my heart."

"Keep looking."

Ava pulled open the bottom drawer. "Here's a bunch of papers all stapled together in a blue folder."

"What is it? Let me see."

Ava showed it to her.

"Holy smokes, this is another lawsuit."

"Against Lash?"

"No," Carmela said as she scanned the papers quickly. "This is a lawsuit that Lash filed against someone named Trent Trueblood."

"What's a Trent Trueblood?"

"I have no idea—let me take a closer look." Carmela flipped through a half dozen pages. "Okay, so it looks like Trueblood is a real estate developer who was in the process of building a neighborhood of high-end town houses a little bit south of here near Boothville. A placed called, um, Parson's Point Townhomes. But before he could begin actual construction, Lash filed suit against him."

"You mean the Environmental Justice League did," Ava said.

"No, that's what's kind of strange. All the other lawsuits I found mention of were filed by the Environmental Justice League. But this is Martin Lash *personally* filing a lawsuit against Trueblood."

"Does that make a difference?"

"I don't know. But it's interesting. Very strange, actually."

"So what do you think?"

"This lawsuit also points to motive," Carmela said. "I mean, if I were a hotshot real estate developer who got stopped in his tracks by some random little ecology dude, I'd guess that would be a fairly powerful motivator to make him go away."

"Go away," Ava murmured. "As in 'disappear permanently.'"

Scritch. Scratch.

Ava straightened up like she'd been touched with a red-hot wire. "What was that?"

"I don't know."

Scritch.

"There it is again," Ava whispered.

Carmela held her breath and listened. It was coming from the side window. "It sounds like somebody's moving around outside. Trying to see in. Or *get* in."

"Holy shit," Ava whispered. "Are we gonna get popped by some cop for breaking and entering? I've already got two parking tickets that I haven't paid as well as a cat living in my apartment illegally."

"Shhh. There it is again." Carmela knew that if the intruder—if that's what this was—went around back he'd soon find that an entire window had been kicked in. And then their goose would really be cooked.

"You think one of the neighbors saw us and ratted us out?" Ava asked.

"I don't know," Carmela said. "It could be some deputy or town marshal who's making his night rounds."

"If it's a cop there could be searchlights and bloodhounds."

Carmela listened again as something clinked against the glass on the side window. "Or maybe it's a real burglar who knows Lash is dead and figures this place would be easy pickin's."

"This is crazy," Ava said. "We break in here and now some other yahoo is trying to break in on us? It's not fair."

"The important thing is we don't want to be arrested, because there isn't anybody in their right mind who'd spring for bail after a stunt like this."

"You don't think Babcock would help us?"

"Not the way things are right now."

"We gotta get out of here," Ava said. "And not get caught with any incriminating evidence."

"We need to grab that notebook and lawsuit!"

But Ava was a step ahead of her, gathering up the papers and stuffing them under her longline bra.

"There's room in there?" Carmela asked. Ava was stuffing papers like crazy.

"There is if I really suck in."

"Okay, the plan is we go out the same window we came in through."

"Right."

They bumped their way back down the hallway, crossed the living room (trying to avoid all the broken glass), and leaned out the window.

"We go on three," Carmela whispered. "One . . ."

Ava leapt through the window like a crazed gazelle, landed in a soggy patch of yard, and managed a decent tuck and roll.

"Two," Carmela said, flying out the window after her. She wasn't quite as graceful with her landing. She landed hard and muttered a surprised "Oof." Her foot struck hard against something metallic.

Ava grabbed Carmela's arm and yanked her to her feet. "Come on. Whoever was around front for sure heard that. We gotta get out of here!"

Then they were flying across the backyard, leaping over a drainage ditch, and stumbling across a spit of land and into someone else's backyard.

"Keep going," Carmela hissed. She could hear someone pounding after them now. Heavy boots crunched against gravel, phlegmy breathing sounded not more than twenty feet behind them. "We'll circle back for the car later!"

They were running for their lives, hanging on to each other, Ava trying to keep the stolen papers from slipping out of her corset and scattering in the wind.

"Holy crap," Carmela said, managing a quick look over her shoulder. "He's gaining on us!" It was dark so she couldn't see the face, but it looked like a guy wearing a flapping jacket.

"Run!" Ava screamed. And this time it was a loud, full-bore, foghorn shriek.

"This way!" Carmela cried. She grabbed Ava's elbow and pulled her in the direction of a small shack. "When I tell you to duck, I want you to duck," she said. "Wait for it . . . wait for it. Okay, now! Duck!"

Carmela and Ava both scrunched down and shimmied under a shoulder-high rope as they struggled to maintain their pace. At the last second, Carmela spun around and gave the rope a mighty twang. Instantly, leg traps, nutria pelts, and some other kind of stinky animal carcass began to sway violently. A few steps on, Carmela flung out an arm, this time knocking down a whole clutch of fishing gear. Oars tumbled, fishing poles went crashing, buoys clattered, everything creating a pick-up-sticks mess for whoever was chasing them.

Carmela's well-executed but impromptu plan worked. Their pursuer crashed directly into the traps, pelts, and fishing gear that she'd set in motion. Swearing mightily, he stumbled, fell down, tried to get back up, and then got hopelessly tangled.

"It worked!" Carmela whooped as they gained thirty yards on their pursuer. Then a good fifty yards. Still, they kept running.

"Are you okay?" Ava asked as they tore through a back alley.

"I think I've got a fishing hook stuck in my ear," Carmela said.

"Fishhook earrings are very in style right now."

They cut down Moen Street, dashed around a corner, and ran down a dark street. There was an insurance agency, a check cashing place, and a meat market. But nothing was open.

"There's a light up ahead," Ava said as they huffed along.

"I think it's a bar." Carmela recognized the telltale neon glow of an Abita Beer sign.

"We can duck in there incognito and relax with a cool, refreshing beverage," Ava cried.

"Perfect," Carmela agreed as they pulled open the door to Sparky's Tap and spun their way inside. "We'll just be completely low-key and blend in."

The words weren't out of her mouth as they skidded to a stop and took a look around. Besides the bartender, who was standing stop-action style with an open mouth and a white bar rag in one hand, every man in the place had turned toward the door and was staring directly at them!

Ava was the first to recover. "My goodness," she drawled. "Fifty men and only two of us. I'd say those are pretty decent odds."

Chapter 12

"LAST night you dragged me to a spooky old cabin," Ava grumped. "And here we are this morning—trucking our way into a gloomy old church."

"You should be the last one to complain," Carmela said as they tiptoed past the tilting gravestones and white marble mausoleums of St. Roch Cemetery. "You had a pretty good time at Sparky's. Dancing, flirting, cavorting . . ."

"I was not cavorting." Ava gave a mousy smile. "Well, maybe just a little bit."

"Between your cleavage and your eyelash batting, I'm surprised a couple of those good old boys didn't run out and trap a few nutria to make you a fur coat."

"There's still a chance of that," Ava said. "I passed out more than a few of my business cards. And weren't those boys nice to give us a ride back to the car?"

"I always did want to ride in the back of a pickup truck with five Cajuns who were belting out 'Le Bouquet de Mon Coeur,'" Carmela said.

Ava smiled. "And in pretty decent harmony."

Carmela stopped and gazed at the façade of St. Roch Chapel. "Look at this place. Who holds a memorial service here anyway? I mean, with all the gorgeous, historic churches in New Orleans, Martin Lash's momma had to pick this place?"

"I'm guessing she has a few screws loose," Ava said. "Not unlike her baby boy. Besides"—she grabbed Carmela's hand and tugged—"we don't have to attend this stupid service. We could turn tail right now and go to our respective businesses. Have ourselves a nice productive day."

"I know. But I'm still trying to ferret out a little more information. The quicker Lash's murder is solved, the quicker my life gets back to normal."

"Are you sure that's what you want? Normal, I mean? That would mean nuzzling with Quigg Brevard in the shadows is verboten."

"That little incident is going to remain buried in my deep, dark past," Carmela said. "I shouldn't have told you about it and I'd be happy if you never brought it up again."

They walked up the gravel path to the chapel, pulled open a heavy wooden door (complete with squeaky sound effects), and slipped inside. It was dark and gloomy, the kind of place where a crowd of frenzied medieval townies might have voted to burn some poor woman as a witch. Two red candles flickered on the altar and the few rows of pews that lined the place were completely empty.

"Looks like we won't have any trouble finding a seat," Ava said. "Do you think we're early?" She looked around. "And who on earth is that Gloomy Gus up there on the altar?"

"That, my dear, is a statue of St. Roch himself."

"His hat and cape look overly accessorized," Ava said. "Though I am sort of digging that cross-body bag. It does give his outfit a certain panache."

Carmela frowned. "We should take a look around. I get the feeling that maybe we're in the wrong place?"

"Do you think the service could be happening in one of the side chapels instead?" Ava asked.

But no. When they strolled into a side chapel, it looked pretty much the same as it did on creepy picture postcards that French Quarter gift shops sold to tourists. A dark little room stuffed floor to ceiling with crutches, old leather braces, false limbs, plaster anatomical parts, and fake eyeballs.

"This stuff is so dang strange," Ava said, peering at a metal neck brace. "Uncomfortable-looking, too."

"Ex votos," Carmela said.

"Ex-what-os?"

"The plaster arms and legs, the foot braces and statuettes, were left in supplication to St. Roch."

Ava screwed up her face. "But I thought he was the patron saint of plague victims."

"He was," Carmela said. "But I guess he was good at healing, too. What probably happened was his job description expanded, just like it has for a lot of us these days." She'd just picked up a low hum of voices coming from the main chapel. "Say now, I think the party might be getting started after all."

They strolled back into the main chapel, where Lash's mother was just being seated in the front pew along with another older lady. They were both dressed head to toe in black and sniffling discreetly into white lace hankies. Another dozen or so people were filing in and finding places.

"There's the guy with the teeth," Ava said.

"Josh Cotton," Carmela said. "Come on, we better hurry up and grab ourselves a spot."

They shuffled into the chapel and took their seats in the second to the last row. Carmela figured this might be the catbird seat from which to keep an eye on everything (really, everyone) that was important.

And it didn't take long. Two minutes later, a minister with thinning gray hair, wire-rimmed glasses, and a white cassock that barely covered his bulging belly took his place at the altar. Then there was a shriek of steel wheels as a utilitarian-looking metal coffin roller poked its nose through the doorway.

"I think the guest of honor has arrived," Ava whispered.

The coffin roller, bearing the bronze coffin of Martin Lash, was slowly pushed inside the chapel by one of the somber funeral directors from Castle Funeral Home. As it creaked and squeaked its way down the aisle toward the front of the church, four ushers in morning coats and striped pants followed behind, their pace slow and measured.

"Mmn," Ava said, casting an admiring glance at the men. "Fresh troops."

As the coffin approached the front altar, Martin Lash's mother let out a tremendous wail.

"Dear Lord," Ava said. "I'm surprised she didn't knock the fake feet off the wall. That lady is louder than thunder."

Carmela gave her a warning shush as the minister stepped up to the coffin and raised his hands.

"Good morning," the minister said with a sad smile. "I am Pastor Nicholas Gryer and I am pleased to welcome the friends and family of Martin Lash as we celebrate his life today."

Once again, a tragic howl issued from Mrs. Lash.

Two ushers bent down to lock the casket rollers in place and then they all took their seats. Carmela took this opportunity to look around the church. The final count in the chapel was about two dozen people, and the only ones she recognized were

Josh Cotton and Mrs. Lash. And she didn't know them particularly well. Still . . . she wondered if Lash's killer might be in attendance. She'd read somewhere that killers sometimes checked in and followed their victim's progress. But the somber faces on today's mourners betrayed no hint of glee or interest in what might possibly have been their handiwork.

Pastor Gryer was deep into a reading of the Twenty-third Psalm now. Carmela felt around on the pew, found a Bible, and scrambled to find the "I will fear no evil" part. Ava, on the other hand, was examining her nails as if trying to decide whether or not to freshen her manicure.

"We are all saddened by the loss of our dear Martin," the pastor intoned. "A fine man who has contributed so much to our community. He is mourned by his mother . . ."

As if on cue, Mrs. Lash interrupted with a cacophony of yelps that trailed off into sobs.

Pastor Gryer continued, ". . . his dear aunt Edith, and his many friends."

Ava glanced up. "His friends? There are barely enough people to fill this puny chapel."

The pastor brought his fingertips together and recited a prayer for the dead followed by a prayer for the grieving. He bowed his head and ended with, "May we all feel Your love in this hour of sadness." He paused for a moment and then said, "We all know what a giving, loving person Martin was. And today, his friend and fellow environmentalist, Josh Cotton, will say a few well-chosen words."

Josh Cotton stood up so quickly you could hear his knee joints pop. Then he moved swiftly to take his place in front of the statue of St. Roch. His body stiff and rigid, he stood with his hands at his sides, staring straight ahead. Finally, Cotton cleared his throat and began. "Martin Lash was my friend and colleague."

Mrs. Lash let out another cry as Cotton went on to dish up a few platitudes and praise Martin Lash as a driven and stalwart leader.

Carmela listened with half an ear. To her way of thinking Cotton was a little too passionate in his praise of the man he hoped to replace. Hadn't he mentioned making a few changes when they spoke with him at the visitation Sunday night? Sure he had. If he wanted to take control of the organization and run it according to his own standards, was he capable of killing Lash? Possibly. And if Cotton was power hungry, could he have smoke-screened the murder by making it look like Lash was killed by a local restaurateur? After all, Lash—with his sideline as food critic—had alienated a fair number of New Orleans restaurant owners. So it was certainly a logical assumption that an angry restaurant owner might have done him in. At least it was one theory that Babcock subscribed to. In Quigg's case, that is.

With suspicion over Josh Cotton percolating in her brain, Carmela found it difficult to focus. As she let her eyes wander about the dingy chapel, she noticed a man she hadn't seen earlier. Dark eyed, with a tumble of dark hair, he looked tight-lipped and grim as he slumped in the corner of the pew across the way.

Carmela flashed back to the grainy black-and-white photo she'd looked at just yesterday and recognized Allan Hurst, the owner of Fat Lorenzo's.

Now here was a man she definitely wanted to talk to.

The service droned on for another twenty minutes, with the end finally coming when the minister gave a final blessing and several people walked up to the casket and laid white roses on top of it.

Good, Carmela thought. Enough already. She was ready to go home.

As soon as the service was concluded, as soon as the ush-ers unlocked the coffin rollers and paraded the whole she-bang back down the aisle again, Carmela pushed out of her pew and rushed to the back of the chapel. And by the time Allan Hurst reached the door, Carmela was standing right there, blocking his way.

"Mr. Hurst. Good morning. I need to speak to you."

Hurst stopped in his tracks and peered at Carmela with curiosity. "Do I know you?"

Carmela offered a sweet smile. "Not exactly, but I have a few questions I'd like to ask you."

"I don't think so." Hurst started to slip by her, but Car-mela grabbed his arm.

"I'm looking into the murder of Martin Lash," Carmela said.

Hurst's eyes bulged out. Now she had his attention.

"Who are you?" he asked.

"My name is Carmela Bertrand."

"And you're investigating Martin Lash's murder?" He sounded wary. "Are you with the New Orleans Police De-partment?"

"No, I'm not. I own a scrapbooking shop."

Now Hurst really looked puzzled. "You own a . . . wait a minute. Nice try, lady. I'm guessing you're really a reporter. You look like one of those crazy Lois Lane types."

Carmela gripped his arm tighter. "I already told you. I'm investigating the death of Martin Lash. But only as a con-cerned citizen." She hoped her words sounded fairly neutral.

But Hurst was beginning to lose his cool. "Why would you possibly care about a reprehensible creature like Martin Lash?"

Carmela hesitated a split second and then decided to try the sympathy angle.

"I was at the Winter Market when Martin Lash was killed,"

Carmela said in a slightly sorrowful tone. "I saw him stagger out with a giant meat fork stuck in his neck and watched him drop dead at my feet. So, you see . . ." She blinked rapidly, trying to muster a few tears, but no dice. "I have a sort of vested interest," she finished quietly.

Hurst's reaction was explosive. "Lady," he said, "I would have been *delighted* to have Martin Lash drop dead at my feet. Why do you think I'm here anyway? To mourn him? Hah! I'm here to make sure that miserable excuse for a human being is dead as a doornail and that they're really going to drop the lid on him." With that, Hurst pushed his way past a stunned Carmela and hurried out of the chapel.

"He certainly has a strong opinion," Ava said. She'd been observing their exchange from the sidelines and now came over to join Carmela.

"But does an angry, sour personality mean that he's a murderer?" Carmela asked.

Ava squinted after Hurst. "Hard to tell." Then, "I wonder what the food's like at his restaurant?"

WHEN CARMELA AND AVA STEPPED OUTSIDE, they were taken aback by the grandeur of the funeral procession. Martin Lash's coffin was being loaded onto an honest-to-goodness horse-drawn funeral coach that was painted with a high-gloss black lacquer and edged with silver trim. A liveried driver sat up top of the coach and held the reins to four horses. Each black horse was outfitted in full funeral regalia, complete with black leather harnesses and tall feathery plumes on their heads. With clouds parting and sunbeams bouncing off the casket and coach, it looked like a scene straight out of *Grimm's Fairy Tales*.

"I feel like we've been teleported back to the days of the

Austro-Hungarian Empire," Ava said. "Bring on the noodle and strudel. Hook me up with a cute archduke."

Carmela shook her head. "I'm not sure I've ever seen such a spectacle before. Yeah, there've been funerals with jazz bands and professional dancers, even a few with rap music. But this . . . this has got to hit a ten on the old wack-o-meter."

"When it's my time to go I'd love a big crazy send-off like this."

"When you go, there'll probably be dancing skeletons, Ouija boards, and flickering saint candles."

"Or you could just scatter my ashes at Neiman Marcus." She thought for a moment. "Better rip up my credit card, though."

Carmela noticed Hurst walking toward his car, a red Mini Cooper. "I'd like to know more about that guy. Maybe even pay a visit to his restaurant, Fat Lorenzo's."

"Where's it located again?"

"Over on Magazine Street."

"Then why don't we hit his place tonight?" Ava suggested. "We can drop by our favorite resale shop, The Latest Wrinkle, and take a look at their new duds. Maybe try on a few over-priced but still stylish Chanel or Dior jackets and then mosey down the block and have dinner at Fat Lorenzo's. I can hope-fully find a new outfit and you can look for clues." She smiled serenely. "That way there's somethin' in it for everybody."

Chapter 13

WHEN Carmela finally arrived at Memory Mine, Gabby was on her hands and knees, stuck halfway inside the bow-shaped front window. She was surrounded by a tangle of red, green, and gold ribbon as she carefully arranged a display of scrapbook pages and velvet-covered albums. Carmela gave a quick wave from out on the street and Gabby responded with a lopsided smile.

Once inside the shop, Carmela found that Gabby had already reversed motion and backed her way out of the window.

"Hey there," Gabby said, scrambling to her feet and adjusting the pussycat bow on her white silk blouse. "You caught me right in the middle of doing a little housekeeping. How was the funeral?"

"Strange," Carmela said. "The mourners were just as eccentric as the surroundings."

"St. Roch *is* a pretty creepy place. All those weird teeth and eyeballs hanging on the walls and perched on little altars. Maybe that place brings out the worst in people. Maybe it's like the bad juju Ava is always warning us about."

"Yeah, maybe . . . but how are you doing? Or, rather, I should say *what* are you up to? Those albums look fantastic in the window, by the way. And I take it you have more planned for this updated display?"

"I thought the holidays called for some new inspiration," Gabby said. "So I made an executive decision to move things around and decided to add some of the crepe paper crafts we worked on yesterday."

"I like it. And how about throwing in some journals and memory boxes?" Carmela asked.

"Oh, those will go in, too. Don't worry. I'm going to pack as much creativity and charm into our little window display as is humanly possible."

Carmela picked up a package of colored beads and fingered it. "Gabby, you and Stuart get invited to lots of business-related social events. Have you ever come across a real estate developer by the name of Trent Trueblood?"

Gabby straightened up and smoothed her plaid skirt. "Trueblood? Yes, I do know that name."

"I'm guessing he's kind of a big deal around town." *And he was also named in a very strange lawsuit.*

"Give me a second." Gabby tapped an index finger against her front teeth. "Okay, I'm starting to remember this now. Trueblood was actually seated at our table when we attended the Chamber of Commerce Awards Dinner. He told me . . . well, actually, he kind of bragged about it . . . that he was developing Bridgewater Estates over near Lake Pontchartrain. You know, where that whole neighborhood was basically wiped out by Hurricane Katrina and then condemned by the city."

"Such a pity," Carmela said. "Now instead of a street filled with quaint Caribbean cottages and single homes there'll be cookie-cutter mega-mansions with fake white pillars. They'll turn that area into a neighborhood with no real character at all."

"Well, don't say *that* to him." Gabby tipped her head sideways at Carmela. "So why exactly are you asking about Mr. Trueblood?"

"Let's just say I found out that he was involved in a lawsuit with Martin Lash."

Gabby's face tightened. "Good heavens, every little detail you uncover about your Martin Lash character gets stranger and stranger."

"The thing is . . . Trueblood is also trying to build townhomes down in Boothville, and Martin Lash was vehemently opposed. As in lawsuit opposed."

"Wait a minute. So now you're saying that Trueblood might also be a suspect in Lash's death? Carmela, you've got to watch your step. Trueblood's a big-time wheeler-dealer. He hobnobs with people on the city council and with the zoning commission. I mean it, be careful."

"I will. I am."

"Bite your tongue," Gabby said. "Once again, you're rushing in where angels fear to tread. You should back away from this nasty Martin Lash business right now and let Babcock handle the investigating. He's the professional, after all." She paused. "He's the one with the gun."

"There's a huge problem. Babcock still thinks Quigg is the guilty party."

Gabby shook her head slowly. "Carmela, please don't ruin a beautiful relationship over this. Over your . . . defense of Quigg. Babcock loves you. He wants to marry you."

"Funny. He hasn't mentioned it lately."

Gabby gave a deep sigh. "Yes, he has. *You* just don't want to hear it."

CARMELA DUCKED INTO HER OFFICE, PLOPPED down in her purple leather chair, and powered up her computer. Bridgewater Estates had a high-concept website complete with symphonic music, 3D floor plans, videos, and (natch!) up-to-date information on financing.

On the Contact tab, Carmela found their telephone number and hastily punched it into her phone.

The receptionist answered with a sweet honeyed voice and welcoming manner. "Bridgewater Estates. This is Effie. How can I help y'all?" The same symphonic music from the website played faintly in the background.

"Yes," Carmela said. "I was just looking at your website and wanted to get a little more information about Bridgewater Estates."

"Uh-huh," Effie said. "I could send you a brochure if you'd like."

"I was actually thinking about stopping by your sales office."

"And you'd be most welcome to do so, honey. We're open today from one to four, so y'all can just drop by and take a look."

"Is there any chance of meeting the developer in person?" Carmela asked.

"Mr. Trueblood is usually in his office most afternoons," Effie said, a smile coloring her voice. "Though he is a busy man, so he does tend to pop in and out. But I'll tell him you're going to drop by and hope he sticks around. Best I can do."

"That sounds great. But do tell him that Carmela Bertrand will definitely be stopping by." Carmela hung up the phone just as a shadow lurked at her door. She turned, worried it might be Babcock, coming by to harangue her again, but it was Gabby.

"Carmela, I've got a lady here who needs some expert advice on holiday cards."

Carmela jumped up from her chair. "Then I guess that would be me."

"I really need help," the customer said. "I know I'm late getting started."

"Not a problem," Carmela said. She pulled cardstock, note cards, gold paper, and ribbon and set it all out on the back table. "What I would do is start with these precut note cards in midnight blue."

"Sounds good," said the woman.

"Then I'd layer on a scrap of gold paper that's kind of torn . . ." Carmela ripped a shred off. "Like this."

The woman nodded. "Okay."

"Then I'd adhere a sliver of ribbon, add a snippet of lace, and glue on this brass charm in the form of a star." Carmela picked up a paper punch. "Then I'd punch out a few more gold stars and sprinkle them around."

"I love it," the woman said. "And what about the inside?"

"Well, you could write your greeting using a metallic pen so it shows up against the dark blue, or you could glue in a small square of cream-colored paper."

The woman thought for a moment. "The cream paper. Definitely the cream."

"Well, there you go," Carmela said. She snuck a peek at the clock on the wall and decided it was time to get going.

THE BRIDGEWATER ESTATES SALES COMPLEX was set smack-dab in the middle of ten acres of tumbledown homes, most in the end stages of demolition. Bulldozers roared and scooped; large dump trucks waited in line to haul away the final remnants of people's lost lives.

The two model homes looked incongruous amidst such disarray. They were mega-sized and gaudy, with peaked rooflines and fake brick façades. The sales office that sat next to them was housed in an enormous double-wide trailer.

Carmela stepped inside the rather deluxe-looking trailer and gazed around. "Anybody home?"

A young woman with poufy blond hair and extra-long dark blue fingernails glanced up from a reception desk. "Hello there," she said, her smile stretching wide across her face.

"Effie?" Carmela said.

"That's right, sugar." Effie was wearing a tight black turtleneck, tight black pencil skirt, and sky-high stilettos. When she crossed her legs her skirt slid way above her knees. Carmela wondered if maybe she wasn't one of Ava's distant relatives.

Carmela touched a hand to her chest. "I'm Carmela Bertrand. I called earlier?"

"So you did. Let me start you off with one of our presentation kits." Effie grabbed a folder and began stuffing all sorts of photos, plans, and papers into it. Carmela wondered how she could function with such long, sharp nails. Talons, really.

"Your homes look gorgeous," Carmela lied.

"Prettiest new homes in the city," Effie said. "Fit for a queen." She smiled again and handed the folder to Carmela.

"Thanks." Carmela glanced around. "Before I check out the model homes, is Mr. Trueblood here?"

"You're in luck. He's still hanging around the office." Effie stood up, gave a kind of shimmy, and led Carmela into a second room where a large, architect's model occupied a Ping-Pong-sized table. Lit by overhead pinpoint spots it was dazzling. "This is what the whole complex will look like when it's finally completed," Effie said, waving a hand.

Carmela gazed at the model of Bridgewater Estates. It consisted of at least twenty mega-mansions, a central reflecting pool and recreation building, a tall spiked fence that ran all the way around the entire complex, and a gated entrance complete with uniformed guards.

Not very neighborly, she decided.

"Good afternoon, ma'am," a voice suddenly boomed in Carmela's ear.

Carmela looked up into the dark eyes of a man who was tall and rangy, with a pencil-thin mustache and slicked-back jet-black hair. He reminded her of an old-fashioned movie villain that you'd boo and hiss at. "Mr. Trueblood?" she said.

The man bobbed his head. "That's me, Trent Trueblood. Perhaps you've seen me on TV advertising True Blue Homes by Trueblood?"

"Perhaps I have." Carmela had no recollection of seeing his smiling face beaming out at her from the tube. "I'm Carmela Bertrand. Nice to meet you."

Trueblood stood over the model and spread his arms like a happy evangelist. "Isn't this spectacular? Each home is a minimum of five thousand square feet, with four or five bedrooms, chef's kitchen, five bathrooms, butler's pantry, exercise room, and state-of-the-art security system. We offer more size and luxury than most of the homes in the Garden District."

But without the class, heritage, and genteel atmosphere, Carmela thought.

Trueblood peered at her. "Do you have a large family? Are you interested in the four-bedroom Manchester model or our larger DeQuincy model that gives you five bedrooms with a bonus room over the four-car garage?"

"Actually, I'm more interested in your other development."

Trueblood didn't miss a beat. "Ah, you're referring to our Parson's Point Townhomes down near Boothville. Yes, we're about to begin construction in a matter of weeks."

"That's great news," Carmela said. "Because I'd heard those plans had been scratched."

Trueblood held up an index finger. "Not scratched, just put on hold for a while pending a few pesky details that needed to be ironed out. But I'm delighted to tell you that project is now proceeding full speed ahead."

"So no problems with zoning?"

"Absolutely not. My company obtained a special permit from the Department of Natural Resources to build on the Boothville site. We developed a town house concept that will have low to no impact on the surrounding environment." Trueblood rubbed his hands together in anticipation. "There will only be a dozen homes, constructed in the most ecologically sensitive way possible. And the entire community of Parson's Point will be surrounded by acreage that I've already purchased and donated to the Louisiana Department of Wildlife and Fisheries." He smiled. "It will offer country living . . . bayou living . . . at its absolute finest."

"Excuse me," Carmela said, "but I'm confused. Wasn't there a good deal of opposition to that project? Weren't environmental-impact statements called into question? Wasn't there"—she paused—"a lawsuit?"

Trueblood ran a hand over his well-pomaded hair. "There was an ill-advised lawsuit but it's gone now."

"Gone," Carmela said. "As in settled?"

"Dropped. And not only that, my company is planning to fund a research study in those very waters. Our press release on that just went out today." Trueblood smiled broadly. "Would you like to see a brochure for our Parson's Point Townhomes?"

"I think I would."

"Then let's have Effie get you one." Trueblood continued his sales patter as he led her back to Effie's desk. But Carmela had stopped listening. Instead, she was thinking about how Martin Lash's death had been extremely convenient for Trent Trueblood and his Parson's Point Townhomes. Maybe . . . possibly . . . the tens of millions of dollars he stood to make had given him the impetus and derring-do to plunge a kitchen fork into Lash's neck and solve that contentious lawsuit for good?

The notion chilled her. But it also gave her the incentive to keep digging.

Chapter 14

NEW Year's Eve was still weeks away, but the mannequins in the front window of The Latest Wrinkle were
all dolled up and ready to party like they'd time-tripped back
to the go-go '80s. One wore a clingy, low-cut black sequined
gown, the other wore a red fringed dress that barely reached
mid-thigh. Both mannequins had sparkly silver spiked heels
on their nonexistent feet.

"Isn't it amazing what those rich Garden District ladies
purge from their walk-in closets?" Ava squealed. "Perfectly
stunning dresses that they've grown tired of. And some of
them still have the price tags on." She pointed at the mannequins. "Just put me in either one of those sexy numbers
and I'll have Roman Numeral gasping for air."

"You already do," Carmela said mildly. "The man is crazy
for you."

Ava focused on the short red dress. "I certainly have the legs for that one. As for the black . . ." She inhaled deeply and jutted her cleavage forward. "You can't deny I've been gifted with the necessary assets."

"There's no denying," Carmela laughed.

"Then let's go inside, girlfriend, and see what else is on the racks."

LISETTE GALVAN SAW THEM COMING AND LIT UP with a smile. She struck an I'm-a-little-teapot pose, one hand on her hip, the other arm stretched and bent to the side, the better to pull Ava in for a hug.

"It's always a happy day when Miss Ava comes to call," Lisette crooned. "And twice as happy because you've brought Miss Carmela. Ladies, it has been way too long."

Lisette, whose short, round stature did resemble a Brown Betty teapot, gave Ava a hearty squeeze. "Fortunately, the store is quiet right now so I can say out loud that you are my favorite customer." She released Ava and moved to give Carmela a hug. "You're in the running, too, my dear. But Miss Ava sends me so much business I cannot help but adore her. Tell me, ladies, what fashion delights are we looking for today?"

"Something splashy and sexy," Ava said.

Lisette was pleased. "For holiday parties, of course. Why don't you dear ladies look around the store while I delve into our inventory of newly consigned items. I'll see if I can pull out something extra special for you."

Carmela wandered over to a three-tiered shelf draped in mauve-colored velvet that stood in front of an ornate Baroque mirror. She scanned knuckle duster rings and bangle bracelets, then picked out a long silver necklace with blue beads.

"I love that," Ava said, sidling in next to her. Then her hand went directly to a black velvet choker embroidered with tiny beads that formed a lilac flower motif. "And this is *très* Goth, don't you think?"

"Floral but with a dark vibe," Carmela said. "Pretty much perfect for you."

Then Lisette was with them and holding up two long, flowing skirts. "I know these aren't proper dresses per se, but these skirts are so gorgeous I wonder if you'll indulge me and try them on." She handed Ava a black taffeta ballroom skirt with a huge ruffle at the bottom and gave Carmela an ivory satin skirt that fell in elegant, loose folds. Then she shooed them into a large dressing room and pulled a plum velvet curtain across the entry.

Ava emerged first, twirling across the room like a flamenco dancer hopped up on speed, her black skirt swirling and flipping up to reveal an expanse of hot pink ruffle underneath. "I love this. It's snug over my hips but still fans out to let me kick up my heels."

"It's perfect," Lisette said. "Wear it with a tight black cashmere sweater and pile on a ton of pearls or else one gigantic statement necklace." She peered past Ava. "Carmela? How are you doing, dear?"

Carmela came out holding up the ivory skirt. "No way. It's slit too high for my conservative sensibilities. Like verging-on-porno high."

"Hah!" Ava cackled. "You could use a few come-hither outfits in your wardrobe. Keep that hot boyfriend of yours wanting more."

"I have another skirt in gray," Lisette said.

Carmela smiled. "Let's take a look."

That long skirt was perfect on Carmela. Lush, but not too revealing. Just right.

"The silver-gray color is made to wear with jewel tones,"

Lisette pointed out. "Maybe a midnight blue silk blouse or even a bright red silk T-shirt."

Carmela gave the thumbs-up sign. "Sold."

"You know," Lisette said in an almost conspiratorial tone. "Mrs. Peychaund, who's married to a state senator and lives in that ginormous mansion over on Harmony Street, brought in a half dozen Dior jackets a few days ago. I doubt they're more than two years old."

"Bring 'em out," Ava said. But when she tried on a pink and white tweed jacket, it was too big. "It fits me okay across the décolleté area," Ava said. "But look at the shoulders and hips."

"Too big," Carmela said.

"Too bad," Ava sighed.

"So . . . just the skirts?" Lisette asked.

"For now anyway," Ava said.

As Lisette was running their charge cards through, she said, "Has anybody told you about our upcoming fashion show?"

Ava's ears perked up. "Fashion show?"

Lisette gave a conspiratorial wink. "We're doing a Mardi Gras fashion show the first week of February."

"With models and everything?" Ava asked.

"We'll hire a few professionals, yes," Lisette said. "But we want to sprinkle in some real people, too." She glanced at Carmela and Ava. "Would you ladies be interested in modeling a couple of outfits?"

Ava's grin stretched all the way across her face. "Would we ever!"

FAT LORENZO'S WAS A SCANT THREE BLOCKS away. And when they pulled up in front of the restaurant—where there was plenty of parking probably due to a distinct lack of customers—they were pleasantly surprised.

"Look at this place," Ava said. "This is a lot more charming than I expected."

"What were you expecting?" Carmela asked.

"I don't know. Some little dingy shack painted with red and green stripes, I guess."

Housed in a rehabbed redbrick building, Fat Lorenzo's restaurant was fronted with black wrought-iron pillars and a polished wooden door studded with brass, and featured a side portico that held a scatter of outdoor tables and chairs.

Inside was even better. Hammered tin ceiling, black leather booths, brass lamps covered with green glass shades. The placed looked elegant and sedate, almost clubby.

Unfortunately, there was no one to greet them at the deserted host stand.

"It's hard to believe they're even open," Carmela said. There wasn't a soul in sight. Not even anyone at the bar—no mixologists or drinkers.

Just as Carmela decided she'd better go scouting, a woman in a dark gray suit came rushing out from the back. Her mahogany-colored hair billowed around her head as if she'd just been spun through a static machine. Her lips were pulled tight across her face.

"Good evening," the hostess said in a fairly cheerless tone. "Welcome to Fat Lorenzo's." Without waiting for an answer, she grabbed a large black book and led them to a small table in the middle of the deserted restaurant.

"Excuse me," Carmela said. "But could we sit in the booth over there?" She pointed to a cozy booth set against a brick wall where a riot of green plants tumbled down.

The hostess led them over to the booth and slapped down the menu. "You can sit anywhere you like," she droned. "We're not exactly busy."

"And you're not exactly cordial," Ava whispered once they'd

settled in. "What's with this place anyway? For having a location in one of the hippest parts of town, there sure isn't much buzz. No cute guys, not even any ugly guys." She glanced around. "No guys at all."

"There's not much of anything going on," Carmela said. "Apparently Martin Lash's scathing review really has kept customers away."

"Like using garlic and holy water to ward off vampires."

"Too bad, because this restaurant is really quite elegant. I mean, look at this brickwork and stained glass. Allan Hurst must have sunk a fortune into decorating this place."

"And then Martin Lash came along and stomped on his dream," Ava said. "After which somebody came along and stomped on Martin Lash." She paused. "Do you think Hurst could have grabbed a fork from his own kitchen and gouged Lash to death?"

"I don't know. He certainly could have. Considering the fact that Fat Lorenzo's is probably doomed, Hurst certainly had sufficient motive."

Ava's brow puckered. "But *several* people had motive."

"Therein lies the problem." Carmela opened the menu. "Wine," she said. "This isn't the dinner menu, it's the wine menu."

A waitress dressed in black slacks, white shirt, and long black apron hurried toward their table.

"Welcome to Fat Lorenzo's," the waitress said. "My name is Annie and we're delighted to have you join us tonight." Her bright smile made it sound as if she meant every word. Definitely a pleasant change from the dour attitude of the hostess.

Annie placed a single sheet of paper in front of each of them.

"Are these your specials?" Ava asked as she studied the five entrées that were listed.

"This is the menu, ma'am."

Ava picked up the paper and waved it. "This is it?" She flipped it over and saw that the back side was completely blank.

"We're still experimenting with our menu, trying to find our niche," Annie said carefully.

"And your clientele," Ava said.

Annie's smile suddenly sagged. "Our owner, Mr. Hurst, thinks nobody comes in because of some bad review he got the first day this place was open." She lowered her voice. "It's been like a curse. Something toxic hanging over our heads."

"Business can't be that bad," Carmela said. She really did try to find the good in things.

Annie brightened a little. "But you're here and it's still early. Last night our first dinner customers didn't arrive until nine o'clock."

"That's a long time to stand around and do nothing," Ava said.

"Tell me about it," Annie said.

Carmela studied her menu. "How's the food here?"

"Yeah," Ava said. "We don't want to get stomach poisoning or worms or anything."

"Ava!" Carmela said.

"I'm just sayin'."

"The food is actually very good," Annie said. "I eat it and I'm fit as a fiddle in a Cajun band." She whipped out her order pad and pencil. "Order something, see for yourself."

Ava ordered the salmon fettuccini because she decided the salmon was low-cal. Carmela opted for spaghetti and home-made sausage. Some ten minutes later, their food arrived with a complimentary glass of Chianti.

"I've got an in with the bartender," Annie confided.

"*Is* there a bartender?" Carmela said. "I figured he was a ghost."

"Or a skeleton," Ava said. "Since you seem to be running

on a skeleton crew." Then she got serious. "But really, why the free glass of vino?"

"To hopefully keep you coming back," Annie said.

"THIS FOOD IS DELICIOUS," AVA SAID TO CARMELA as she ate hungrily. "Why isn't this place packed to the rafters? Why aren't there a bunch of selfie-posting, hipster Millennials buzzing around here?"

"Probably on account of that snake Martin Lash," Carmela said. "I'll tell you one thing, Fat Lorenzo's didn't deserve a review so deadly it would kill business before it even got started. No wonder Allan Hurst despised Martin Lash. No wonder he was so vitriolic at the funeral this morning."

"So you think Hurst might be the killer?"

"As far as I'm concerned, it's a three-way tie between Allan Hurst, Josh Cotton, and Trent Trueblood. Any one of them could have pulled it off."

Ava held up a finger. "Wait a minute. Trent Trueblood? The lawsuit guy?"

So Carmela told Ava about how she'd visited Trueblood's sales office and poked around, asking questions about the Parson's Point Townhomes.

"And you think Trueblood is a viable suspect along with Hurst and Cotton?"

"He could be," Carmela said. "But the big trouble is, the cops are blind to all these other suspects. Quigg just looks so doggone guilty because of that fight he had with Lash."

Ava smirked. "I bet Quigg is thrilled to suddenly be your center of attention. You're running all over town, trying to be cagey and figure things out. Quigg must really love that."

Carmela gave a reluctant nod. "I guess."

"Does Babcock have any idea of what you're up to?"

"Let's put it this way," Carmela said. "Babcock's on a need-to-know basis."

"I think that's always the smartest philosophy when it comes to dealing with boyfriends."

"Especially *your* boyfriends," Carmela said. "They especially don't need to know about the other guys waiting in the wings."

"I told Roman Numeral that he was my first." Ava cackled wildly. "I meant that week."

"Ava!"

SOME TWENTY MINUTES LATER, ANNIE PLACED the black leather check case on the table.

"Ladies," she said, "if you enjoyed your dinner please tell your friends about us." There was a pleading note in her voice. "Because we sure could use the business."

Ava, happy from her wine, said, "The food was really good. I bet things will turn around for this place. Just give it a little time."

But Annie just looked morose. "I don't know. I have a horrible feeling we might be closed within the week. Maybe nothing can save this place. Why, Mr. Hurst even tried having a booth at the Winter Market last weekend."

Carmela was suddenly all ears. "Excuse me. *What* did you just say?"

Annie frowned. "You mean about his booth at the Winter Market?"

"He was there?" Ava screeched.

Annie nodded sadly. "He went there as a kind of last-ditch effort to drum up business. His booth was serving spaghetti and meatballs for, like, cost. And he was handing out two-for-one coupons. But it still turned out terrible. Most of the people at the Winter Market were only interested in chugalug drinking. And then some poor guy got himself killed! Stabbed to death. Right there in the middle of all the festivities."

"Amazing," Ava said, but she was looking directly at Carmela.

"That pretty much ruined it for Mr. Hurst," Annie said. She blinked back tears and pointed to the check. "Take your time. It's not like I'm busy or anything." Then, with a sniffle, she whisked their empty plates away.

"Yowsa, Carmela. Did you hear what she just said?" Ava was wide-eyed with excitement.

"I can't quite believe it," Carmela said. "Allan Hurst was actually at the scene of the crime."

"Maybe it's no longer a three-way tie," Ava said. "Maybe now you've got yourself a front-runner."

Chapter 15

CARMELA steamed through the front door of Memory Mine holding a cardboard tray aloft.

Gabby looked up from a page of stickers and said, "Be still my heart. Is that what I think it is?" Her eyes were shining like it was Christmas morning and there were diamond earrings to be found in her stocking.

"A quick stop at Café du Monde could only mean one thing, right?" Carmela produced two cups of coffee and dangled a grease-stained white bakery bag in front of Gabby's nose.

"Chicory coffee and beignets," Gabby said with great satisfaction.

"Abso-sugary-lutely."

Gabby grabbed the bag and tore it open. "Even though I swore off these things, one can't possibly hurt, can it?"

"The sugar is probably good for you. Revs up your metabolism."

Gabby's eyes fluttered as she bit into one of the beignets, sending a miniature avalanche of powdered sugar down the front of her navy blue sweater. "So good," she gasped. Then she noticed the powdered sugar. "Uh-oh." She brushed at her sweater, then snapped the lid off her coffee and took a sip. "What did I do to deserve such a great boss?"

"Only about a million things," Carmela told her. "Least of which is the fantastic job you did reorganizing our front window. I mean, who could walk by and *not* be lured in?"

Gabby nodded appreciatively as she chewed. "Before I forget, Baby called bright and early. She's bringing her daughter-in-law along to our handmade book class this afternoon. I told her it would be fine, that we always have room for one more."

"We do," Carmela said. "Oh, and one thing we have to remember is to put out those miniature brass keys I picked up at the tag sale in Natchitoches. I'm positive we can do something fabulous with them. Maybe combine them with a few Czech crystal beads."

"Strung on silk cord or gossamer ribbon," Gabby said. "To use as book binding."

Carmela carried her beignet and latte into her office, spread a napkin on the desk, and settled into her chair. She took another bite of beignet and munched thoughtfully. Although she knew she should be focused on work, on going through catalogs and ordering a treasure trove of new crafting supplies, her mind felt nervous and jumbled. Clearly, she was still preoccupied with Martin Lash's murder.

She sat back in her chair and thought about Lash. First Quigg had complained bitterly about Lash's review of Mumbo Gumbo. And then, last night, she'd seen with her own eyes how deserted and desolate Fat Lorenzo's was. Probably as the result of Lash's brutal review.

Martin Lash. The gift that keeps on giving.

But as the caffeine kicked in and the sugar churned its way into her bloodstream, Carmela was blessed with a brainstorm. She set down her coffee and did a quick search for the Glutton for Punishment website. When it came up almost immediately on her screen, Carmela was impressed by the format. The colorful splash page was a montage of landmark New Orleans restaurant signs skillfully morphed with images of oyster platters, bowls of gumbo, and elegant entrées of trout amandine. And the site was well organized, too. You could click on Type of Food, Neighborhood, Price, and New in Town. Plus there were lots of feature stories and ads for restaurants and bars.

As Carmela clicked around, going from page to page, she saw that Babcock had been right. He'd told her there wasn't a single sentence left on the website that had been written by Martin Lash. And, sure enough, Lash's restaurant reviews and columns seemed to have been completely expunged from the site. It was as if he had never existed.

In Carmela's mind, one of the places Babcock had made a wrong turn was in assuming Quigg was responsible for having all of Lash's columns removed. She knew that Quigg was way too self-absorbed to care about bad reviews on restaurants other than his own.

So . . . if he'd had the poisonous review of Mumbo Gumbo taken down, then who had removed the rest of Lash's reviews and columns? And why?

Carmela scoured the website, but still found no mention of Martin Lash. She couldn't find so much as an obituary or a "farewell to our colleague" notice.

Okay, so where does that leave me?

Maybe the better question was, where did that take her? Looking at the website's contact page, she saw that the Glutton for Punishment office was located on Frenchmen Street. That was just a few blocks away in the neighboring Faubourg Marigny. Carmela decided there was no time like the present for an informative little field trip.

"Gabby, I'm running out for a little bit. Can you hold down the fort?"

"No problem," Gabby said. She was helping a customer select handmade paper embedded with flower petals. "As long as you're back in time for our bookmaking class." Then her face clouded and she stepped closer to Carmela and whispered, "Carmela, are you . . . investigating?"

"Um, maybe," Carmela hedged.

"What do I do if Babcock drops in unannounced?"

"Well, for one thing, don't tell him I'm out there investigating."

Gabby looked nervous. "You want me to lie to him?"

"Technically, no. I just want you to take evasive action. Besides, Babcock's not going to ask you anything outright. He's too clever for that. He'll just casually fish around a little."

"Oh dear."

"Just put your head down and act busy," Carmela said. "Be busy."

"Okay, but be you careful, Carmela."

"No need to worry," Carmela said, smiling. "I'm just going to take a short walk through the prettiest, most elegant city in the world."

CARMELA STRODE ALONG THE SIDEWALK, ENJOYing the thin sunlight that streamed down, feeling the pulse of the French Quarter all around her. Tourists were shopping and snapping pictures, consulting maps and clamoring over strings of purple and green beads. A large group of folks wandered past her, all wearing bright green *MANNION FAMILY REUNION* T-shirts. They carried cameras and were arguing about where to go for lunch. Johnny's Po-Boys, Felix's, K-Paul's, or Napoleon House. Carmela could have told them that any one of those restaurants was an excellent choice.

It was never too early for music in the Quarter and some of the bars were cranked up, too. Carmela dodged around two women, geaux cups in hand, who were dancing on the sidewalk to hundred-year-old ragtime piano music that poured out of a corner honky-tonk.

When Carmela turned down Royal Street, she laughed out loud as she watched an antique-shop owner struggle to hang a wooden sign above his establishment. The words on the blue and gold sign said *ANTIQUES MADE TO ORDER*.

There's so much history here, Carmela thought as she strolled past the two-hundred-year-old Gallier House museum and the Old U.S. Mint. Then, skipping across Kerlerec Street, she wandered into what was the Faubourg Marigny. This neighborhood was ever expanding as a fun, funky area adjacent to the French Quarter. She turned onto Frenchmen Street, where the Creole cottages and three-story town houses had nearly all been turned into boutiques, galleries, restaurants, and bars. Word was even spreading that the music on Frenchmen Street was beginning to rival Bourbon Street.

The website's offices were located in a rehabbed yellow brick warehouse known as the Madeleine Building. The Bluebird Boutique was on the first floor and Glutton for Punishment had the second floor. They occupied a wide-open loft-type space complete with ancient hardwood floors and exposed brick walls. Gray contemporary furniture and a few pieces of artwork (mostly bright slashes of color) delineated the reception area from the actual workspace. People scurried to and fro while a bevy of writers (or maybe ad sales guys?) typed frantically on laptops at sleek gray desks without benefit of cubicle dividers. Everyone looked busy and productive although they could have been surfing the web, posting selfies, or checking out Tinder, for all she knew.

Carmela approached the young man who sat at the reception desk.

"Excuse me, I'd like to have a word with whoever's in charge."

He barely looked up. "That would be our editor in chief."

"Fine. Is he available?"

This time the young man did look up. "He's a she. Helen McBride. But Ms. McBride is in a terrible mood right now. Maybe you'd like to come back later?"

"Not really." Carmela cleared her throat. "Actually, I'm here about Martin Lash."

That got the man's attention. "I'm sorry, but that job has already been filled."

Carmela smiled. "I'm not interested in writing restaurant reviews. I want to talk to someone who can give me information about some of Lash's old columns."

Now he grimaced. "If you're looking for a rave review on one of your favorite restaurants, you're probably out of luck. Mr. Lash didn't do raves. It wasn't his thing."

"Perhaps I'd better speak with your editor in chief."

"Okay, but if she rips your head off, don't say I didn't warn you."

HELEN MCBRIDE SAT IN A SMOKE-FILLED OFFICE amidst a stack of papers, magazines, a set of ten-pound hand weights, an overflowing ashtray, and a tangle of purple elastic workout bands. Barefoot and dressed in black yoga pants and a black T-shirt, Helen looked like she could bench-press two hundred pounds without breaking a sweat or busting a bra strap.

"Okay, sweetheart," Helen said without looking up. "You've got thirty seconds. What's your problem?"

Carmela had a feeling this woman was one tough cookie. Still, she'd come this far.

"I have a few questions about Martin Lash."

Helen McBride looked up. "Lash? What do you want to know about him? Besides the fact that I hated the little twerp?"

"Obviously, you weren't the only one," Carmela said. "Since he went and got himself murdered." She sat down in a chair across from Helen and smiled sweetly.

"Who are you? What exactly is your interest in this?"

"My name is Carmela Bertrand and I had the misfortune to be there when Lash was murdered. And also when my friend Quigg Brevard was unjustly accused by the police."

"Quigg, yeah," Helen said. "I'm well acquainted with that rogue." She leaned on one elbow and yawned. "I hear the police grilled him pretty hard."

"I'm curious. If you disliked Martin Lash so much—and it sounds like you did—then why was he working here?"

"Because Lash was force-fed to me when I took this lousy job." Helen's eyes bored into Carmela. "What is it you want again?"

"Just some basic information about Lash. The kind of stuff you're giving me right now."

Helen blew out a plume of smoke and chuckled. "So I am."

"Let me get this straight," Carmela said. "Lash was on staff here when you took this job . . ."

"Three months ago," Helen said. "Yeah, the powers that be wanted me to keep him on. Heck, Lash wanted me to keep him on. He loved eating in fancy restaurants for free and then writing nasty, snide reviews. He used to argue that his reviews were the heart and soul of Glutton for Punishment." She shook her head. "That was so not true. In fact, he cost us money every time his greasy little fingers hit the keyboard." Helen set her cigarette in the lip of a black triangle-shaped ashtray that sat at her elbow.

"How is that possible?" Carmela asked.

"If you've ever read his reviews . . . well, of course you have or you wouldn't be here. His reviews were so poisonous, some so close to libelous, that we were turning off our advertisers. You realize, advertisers are our bread and butter. They're how we make money here, not by posting reviews. You understand revenue producing?" Helen blew out another plume of smoke. "Revenue equals money and money is what fuels the engine."

"Okay, I get that," Carmela said. "So why didn't you just dump Lash if he was causing you so much trouble? I mean, he was basically a freelancer, right? He was running his little environmental nonprofit group while he was writing reviews on the side. Couldn't you just work with some other restaurant critic who had a gentler touch?"

Helen sighed and lit a second cigarette. Now she had two cigarettes burning in her ashtray but didn't seem to notice. Or care.

"The thing is, our owners, Corvallis Media, operate a number of foodie websites in different markets and *they* decided to keep Lash on. The powers that be thought he added a certain degree of spice. 'Cachet,' as they used to call it back in the good old days when we actually had *printed* magazines. Me, I saw what Lash's toxic reviews were doing to us, so I wanted to lop his fool head off."

Carmela was temped to ask, "Did you?" But decided against it. Getting more information was her primary goal here. Instead she said, "Do you know if Martin Lash had enemies?"

Helen offered a thin, lizard smile. "That's what the police asked me, too."

"What did you tell them?"

"That Lash was an insubordinate pig who didn't get along with anyone. And that, yes, pretty much everyone hated him."

"Especially you?" Carmela asked

Helen exhaled a huge glut of smoke. "Honey, I detested the guy. I can count a dozen times that Martin Lash put my head on the chopping block and almost cost me my job." She venomously stubbed out a cigarette, spilling ashes all over the papers on her desk, then looked up at Carmela with a sly smile. "So you're investigating, huh? You like to nose around and ask questions."

"I told you, I'm helping Quigg."

"Yeah, well, it's too bad Lash got skewered the way he did—it must have been a hard way to go. But I'm not one bit sorry he's gone."

"And his columns?" Carmela asked. "What happened to them?"

Helen lit another cigarette. "I took great joy in personally deleting every single one of them from our server." She grinned and her smile took on a dark, malevolent look. "Now it's as if Martin Lash never existed!"

Chapter 16

CARMELA arrived back at Memory Mine in plenty of time for their handmade book class. As usual, Gabby had arranged a fabulous array of craft materials on the back table.

"I put out an assortment of cardstock and decorative papers," Gabby said. "Along with some of the twines and ribbons that work best for lacing pages together."

She'd also put out scissors, tape, glue guns, and an assortment of paints, rubber stamps, and charms.

"How did your investigation go?" Gabby asked, trying to look offhanded, but clearly dying of curiosity.

"I had an impromptu meeting with Helen McBride, the editor in chief at Glutton for Punishment," Carmela said.

"The website Martin Lash wrote for." Gabby noodled

this information around for a few moments. "Okay. So what did you find out? Anything?"

"Basically, that everyone pretty much despised Martin Lash. Especially his editor."

"But you don't think she killed him." It was said as a statement.

"I don't know that at all," Carmela said. "Helen McBride spewed out a ton of vitriol about Lash. I mean, she really hated the man. Plus, she looks strong and athletic enough to have shish-kebabed Lash with one hand tied behind her back."

"You see what I was talking about before?" Gabby asked. "This is veering into crazy-weird territory. I think you'd be better off sharing this kind of information with Babcock. Let him either discount her opinion as the snarkiness of a disgruntled boss, or follow up with hard questions if he deems this Helen person a legitimate suspect."

"You want me to *share* my information?" Carmela's brows rose in twin arcs. "With a man who's tried to remain totally mum with me?"

"Yes, I do."

"I'll think about your suggestion, okay?"

But this time Gabby was standing her ground. "Think hard, Carmela. For everyone's sake."

BABY FONTAINE SAILED INTO MEMORY MINE looking like she'd just stepped out of the pages of *Town & Country* magazine. Black-and-white tweed jacket, trim black slacks, supple black ankle boots. Her daughter-in-law, Priscilla, wearing a navy jacket, was almost Baby in miniature.

"Carmela!" Baby cried. "Gabby!" She rushed up to both ladies and distributed copious air kisses as if she hadn't seen them in weeks. "You remember Priscilla, don't you? Percy, we call her for short."

"Of course," Carmela said warmly, while Gabby just beamed.

Baby glanced around the shop. "Where's Tandy? She was supposed to be here, too. Especially after she made such a big stink about *me* being late."

The front door whapped open and they all four turned to look, but it was three more women rushing in for the class.

"Maybe she got held up?" Gabby said.

Five minutes later, with still no Tandy in sight, Carmela started the class.

"HANDMADE BOOKS," CARMELA SAID, STANDING at the head of the craft table, "are one of the hottest crafts today. Think about it—who wouldn't love to have their very own one-of-a-kind journal, photo book, or notebook? And when you give one as a gift to someone, it tells them they're special. That you took time out of your busy day to create a gorgeous, personal gift."

Carmela reached for a small book that sat in front of her and held it up.

"This is just one example of a handmade book. The cover is cardstock, the inside pages are a crinkle paper that we carry right here in our shop, and the binding is hand sewn—really just eight running stitches—using white silk cord."

"It's so gorgeous," one of the women exclaimed. "Look at the cover, all that gold and glam. How on earth did you do that?"

"I began making the cover by gluing some marbleized paper onto a piece of cardstock," Carmela explained. "Then I dabbed a little gold paint over the marbleized paper and, using bronze ink, stamped on an image of a Renaissance lady." She held up the actual rubber stamp. "From there I glued on some silk flower petals, a tiny gold bee charm, and a strip of gold gossamer ribbon. The inside pages are crinkle paper, about ten sheets. To finish everything off I made punches on the left side of the paper and cover, and bound it all together with the silk cord."

"It's absolutely gorgeous," Percy said.

"The thing about a craft project—any craft project—is that the more layers you build up the better it becomes," Carmela explained. "You start with a nice paper, add a few more paper bits or photos, sponge on some paint, and add a few stamped images or text. It's like making a good gumbo, the richer the ingredients the better the flavor."

"And you also threaded on a little gold tassel," Baby said.

Carmela smiled down at her book. "Yes, I did. But I'm quite positive all of you will come up with designs that are even better than this one."

"I'm not so sure about that," one of the women said.

"Just think about what kind of book you'd like to create," Carmela said.

The woman squinted. "Maybe a book I could write poetry in?"

"Perfect," Carmela said. She grabbed a sheet of pink vellum. "What if you used this as your album cover, then added some nature or floral images? You could enhance those with a rubber stamp of a sun image and maybe even add a dragonfly charm."

"I'm loving this," the woman said. She shrugged out of her jacket and rubbed her hands together. "Time to get started."

Everyone seemed to have an idea then and wandered through the scrapbook shop picking out various papers, ribbons, rubber stamps, and even small bags of ephemera.

When her crafters had finally settled down to some serious work, Carmela slipped into her office.

She had to make a call she really didn't want to make. A call to Babcock telling him about Allan Hurst of Fat Lorenzo's fame and how Hurst had actually been a vendor at the Winter Market a few nights ago. She figured it was hard evidence that could point his investigation in a totally different direction.

Carmela stared at the phone for a few moments, let out a long, slow sigh, and hit the speed dial for Babcock's number. She half hoped she'd get his voice mail, but no such luck. He picked up on the second ring, sounding very distracted.

"Carmela?"

"If this is a bad time . . ." Carmela was hoping for a way out.

"No, no, it's okay. If I sound abrupt it's because I'm up to my eyeballs in work. My caseload right now is a nightmare." He paused. "What can I do for you?"

"I've got some information I need to pass along to you."

"And that would be . . . ?"

"Here's the thing," Carmela said. "I found out that Martin Lash wrote a scathing review of Fat Lorenzo's, this restaurant over on Magazine Street."

"Yes?" Babcock's voice was just this side of chilly.

"And then I found out that Allan Hurst, the owner of Fat Lorenzo's, was pretty much gobsmacked by Martin Lash's review. I mean, people have been staying away from his restaurant in droves. His business is in a shambles."

"Uh-huh." Now Babcock's voice had dropped below the freezing point.

Carmela gritted her teeth and pressed forward. "And then I found out that Allan Hurst had a food booth at the Winter Market. He was *right there*, for gosh sakes, the night Lash was murdered. So you see . . ." Her voice trailed away.

A long silence spun out. Then Babcock finally said, "You've been investigating. When I specifically asked you not to."

Carmela tried her best to whitewash her information, to cover her trail. "I heard about the bad review in passing. And then Ava and I just happened to have dinner at Fat Lorenzo's last night. There was a talky waitress and . . . well, big deal. There's no law against what I did."

"Au contraire, Carmela. You've been doing more than just twirling forkfuls of fusilli pasta and munching focaccia bread. You've been meddling and poking your nose in where you shouldn't."

"Okay, yes, I'm guilty of asking a few questions. Maybe more than just a few, because you know I'm a naturally curious person. But please tell me if you knew that Allan Hurst had a food booth at the Winter Market?"

"Of course I knew that. I *am* a homicide detective and investigating is my job. The first thing we did was take a look at the roster of food vendors."

"Because of the nature of the murder weapon?"

Babcock was losing patience. "Obviously the fork was one of the key factors, yes. As you know, we also discovered rather quickly that Martin Lash wrote restaurant reviews as a sideline. Again, we are the NOPD."

Carmela was well acquainted with that tone of voice. Babcock was reminding her, yet again, that she'd crossed the line.

"Now that we're actually sharing information," Carmela said. "Please tell me you checked to see exactly what type of meat forks are used in Allan Hurst's kitchen."

"We did check. And you know who else we looked at? Your slippery-when-dry friend Quigg Brevard. As it turns out, Mumbo Gumbo's kitchen staff use the exact same kind of meat fork that our killer planted in Martin Lash's throat."

Carmela was quick to defend Quigg. "Same type of fork?

That's all you have? Babcock, quit fooling around. You
know Quigg didn't kill Lash. You're just making him your
personal patsy. When you get tired of jerking him around
you'll just kick him to the curb. Besides, there must be
hundreds of those forks around. New Orleans is a restaurant
town. Where there are restaurants, there are meat forks."

Babcock let out a half chuckle. "You sound so earnest.
Like you're really into this."

"Because I am."

"Don't be. I'm handling things, okay?"

Carmela sighed. "Okay." She wasn't about to capitulate
but she did know when to back off. "So . . . is the mayor
still on your back?"

"Lord, Carmela, everybody from the dog catcher on up is
on my back. Everyone wants this crime solved posthaste.
They're still worried it's going to impact tourism."

"Do you have any room in your schedule for dinner tonight? My place, my treat?"

"Listen, sweetheart, you're the reason I have to work such
long hours. The quicker I close this case, the sooner I can
stop worrying about you throwing yourself in harm's way,
trying to make an end run and catch this killer."

"Tomorrow, then?" Carmela asked.

"We'll see."

Carmela had barely hung up the phone before it rang
again. She snatched it back up and said, "Did you change
your mind?"

"I hope you haven't," Ava drawled. "Because it's party
time tonight, baby girl."

"What? What's going on tonight?" *Certainly not a hot date
with Babcock—sob.*

"It's the Holiday Art and Wine Stroll. The entire French
Quarter will be jumping with Christmas cheer. *Cher*, please

don't tell me you forgot. The galleries are all having open houses and you know what that means. They'll be trying to liquor people up in hopes of selling them overpriced art and photography."

"Oh jeez."

"Don't back out now. You promised to go with me."

"Ava . . . we've been going out a lot lately. I'd seriously rather stay home tonight and kick back with a book."

"You can sit and veg when you're ancient. Which we are a long ways from. So tonight we party. Besides, have you forgotten that Harrison will have some of his photos on display?"

Carmela gave it one more try. "Do I have to go?"

"The short answer is yes. The long answer is, when you were married to Shamus you endlessly dragged me to see his out-of-focus photos of egrets and herons. Now you are in-debted to me. You have to come ooh and aah over Harrison's out-of-focus shots of turtles and alligators."

"Quid pro quo, huh?"

"You got it, babe. See ya tonight."

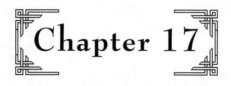

Chapter 17

THIS Wednesday evening the French Quarter smelled of roasted chestnuts, spun sugar, chicory coffee, and cigar smoke. A nice, sweet, familiar mélange that appealed to Carmela as she and Ava strolled down Royal Street. The French Quarter's most fabulous and hideously expensive antique shops and galleries were located here, of course, and they could barely go a few feet without being drawn in by some tasty bauble or piece of art.

"Look at this," Ava said. They stopped and gazed in the window of Madelaine's Sculpture Gallery. Colored lights circled the window, illuminating a large pewter statue of a nineteenth-century gentleman in top hat and tails, posturing with two dogs. At his feet, a lady in an enormous bell-shaped skirt sat and gazed adoringly at him. A bronze marker titled it *Enchanted*.

"I don't get it," Ava said. "Why is she sitting on the ground in what has to be the most uncomfortable dress imaginable?"

"This probably isn't feminist art," Carmela observed dryly.

"Better if it was. Better if that dude was gazing at *her* with stars in his eyes."

Carmela glanced at Ava, who had genuine diamond studs along with two pairs of gold hoops in her ears, wore a shiny red faux-leather micro jacket, and had shimmied (probably with the aid of a can of Crisco) into gold stretch pants. She looked, Carmela decided, like a mash-up of *Hillbillies for Hire* meets Tiffany jewelers. And because it was the Holiday Art and Wine Stroll, *wine* being the operative word, Ava clutched a geaux cup filled with sparkling rosé. Carmela, who had worn a black leather jacket and black slacks, decided she looked like a slightly hip undertaker.

"What's Babcock going to get you for Christmas?" Ava asked. She came to a stop in front of Trifles Estate Jewelry and pressed her nose up against the window. "Maybe a big honkin' engagement ring?"

Carmela gave a sarcastic chuckle. "The way things are going between us right now I'll be lucky to get a ring from a Cracker Jack box."

"It can't be that bad. You've been on the outs with Babcock before and he's always come around. Face it, the guy is nuts about you. Anyone can see that."

Ava slid along to the next window, marveling at every shiny piece that caught her eye, wishing she could find every last one of them nestled in her Christmas stocking.

"Ooh," Ava said. "You see that fancy diamond bracelet?"

"They're all fancy," Carmela said. She didn't quite share Ava's thirst for shiny stuff.

"The one in white gold with the panther clasp. I bet it's vintage Cartier." She grinned. "You know what they say . . ."

"No, Ava, what do they say?"

"The older the jewelry, the older the money." She bent suddenly and dug in her purse. "I almost forgot. I brought you something."

"What's that?" Carmela asked.

"The answer to all your trouble," Ava said. She pulled out a little white cotton voodoo doll and handed it to Carmela.

Carmela stared at it. The little guy looked like a puffy, naked gingerbread man with two black cross-stitched eyes. "What am I supposed to do with this?"

"Every time Babcock acts like an ass, I want you to stick one of those red pins into that doll."

"Ava, this is a cute little novelty, but you know I don't believe in voodoo."

Ava spun to face her. "Don't knock it until you've tried it. You'd be surprised at all the spells and charms that have worked for me."

"Okay, okay." Carmela dumped the doll into her purse and promptly forgot about it as they approached a cluster of street vendors. Some were selling holiday candles, two more had boards that displayed colorful bead necklaces. But when they hit the purse vendor, a guy in a long coat and tweed cap who was chomping on an unlit cigar, Ava really went nuts.

"Look at this bag," Ava screeched, pointing at his display. "It's gorgeous!"

Carmela stared at a brown oval-shaped bag that had so much fringe it looked like a lion's mane.

"That there is a genuine Carlos Femberly," the vendor said out of the corner of his mouth. He unhooked the bag and handed it to Ava

Ava clutched the bag tightly to her chest. "Did you hear that? It's a genuine Femberly!"

Carmela did not exactly share her enthusiasm. "I can't say I'm familiar with that particular designer."

"Trust me, lady, he's important," the vendor assured her.

Ava was over the moon with her discovery. "I'm positive Carlos Femberly is big-time European."

"You mean like it was jacked out of some warehouse in Bulgaria?" Carmela asked.

Ava slung the bag over her shoulder. "No, silly, like an anorexic supermodel lugged it down a Paris runway."

"Right before she fainted from hunger," Carmela said.

"I've gotta have it!" Ava cried. She held the bag up to the vendor. "Is this genuine leather?"

The vendor chomped down hard on his cigar. "I can see you have a very discerning eye. What you have here is genuine aminoplast stitched with cellulose."

"I just knew it was genuine," Ava said, digging out two twenties.

"Aren't you afraid it might melt in the first big down-pour?" Carmela asked as they walked down the street, Ava cuddling her new bag.

"Don't be silly," Ava said. "It's mega-gorgeous and totally me. What better to go perfectly with all my animal prints?"

Carmela couldn't argue with that.

THE VERY UPSCALE GALLERY NAPOLEON CAR-ried some of the finest paintings and sculptures on Royal Street. The brick interior walls were painted stark white, the gray industrial carpet lent a hushed atmosphere, and pin-prick spotlights illuminated the art to perfection.

Tonight the focus was on modern art. Which meant paint-ings with broad streaks of color, twisty metal sculptures, and black-and-white photography. The well-heeled, artsy crowd that had turned up for the gallery opening tended to favor all-black clothing, chic Oliver Peoples glasses, and hair that was either clipped extremely short or worn long and straight. And that held true for both sexes.

The gallery's proprietor, William Deveroux, had been known as Billy Donaldson in his former life. But that was back when he sold aluminum siding on the South Side of Chicago. Now that he'd moved to New Orleans, he'd upgraded his name and his merchandise.

"Carmela," Deveroux exclaimed, gliding over to greet her. "And Ava. Lovely to see you both."

"How-de-do," Ava said. Deveroux wore a blue-and-white-striped cravat tucked into the open neck of his crisp white shirt. A casual, but affected attitude.

"I am enchanted, just enchanted, that you two ladies have elected to grace my gallery," Deveroux said. "Could it be you're shopping for a special piece of art for that special someone?"

"Monsieur Deveroux, these charming ladies are my guests." Harrison Harper Wilkes III came up behind Deveroux and clapped him on the back.

"But of course," Deveroux said. Then, sensing the absence of a big-ticket sale in the making, he melted away to greet his other guests.

Harrison planted a smacker on Ava's right cheek. "Can you believe this!" he exclaimed. "Here I am in one of the most prestigious art galleries in the French Quarter and they've put three of my photos on display. Three of them!" He swallowed hard and caught his breath. "Come on, I'll show you."

He led them to a small display at the very back of the gallery where three completely out-of-focus eighteen-by-twenty-four-inch black-and-white photos hung on the wall next to a red fire extinguisher.

"Wow," Ava said. "This is very impressive." She squinted at one of the photos. "You captured quite a nice-looking log sunk into that mucky water."

"It's an alligator," Harrison pointed out. "Can't you see the row of teeth?"

She tilted her head. "Oh yeah?"

Harrison beamed. "You see how I managed to capture such a peaceful look on the gator's face?"

"He looks positively beatific," Carmela said. "He must have just eaten."

A skinny woman dressed completely in black, one of the gallery's young interns, touched Harrison on the arm. "Excuse me, but Mr. Deveroux would like to introduce you to one of his clients."

"Yes, of course." Harrison turned to Carmela and Ava and gave a delighted shrug. "Could be a sale. Talk to you later." He hurried after the woman.

Carmela rolled her eyes. "And I thought Shamus's photos were bad."

"Who cares about talent?" Ava said. "All the good stuff is airy-fairy and out of focus these days anyway. This gallery show is a huge step for Harrison. It could be the start of a real career."

"Versus him being an indolent trust-fund baby who whiles away most of his afternoons at a private men's club?"

"Yes, of course. If he keeps shooting photos it could mean he's got an actual future."

Carmela studied the photos more carefully. No matter which way she cocked her head or squinted, they were still wacky and out of focus. As for composition, Harrison displayed no real gift in that department, either. "A future, yes," she said. "Just probably not in photography."

"Come on, Carmela. Don't be so dang . . ." Ava suddenly realized she'd lost Carmela's attention. "What?" She turned and followed Carmela's gaze. Then she wrinkled her nose and said, "Holy Hannah, isn't that . . . ?" But the man Carmela was staring at was walking straight toward them.

"Josh Cotton," Carmela said, just as Cotton came to a stop in front of them. "From the Environmental Justice League."

"As I recall, you're . . . Carmela?" Cotton said.

"Yes, and this is Ava. We met at . . ."

"The visitation," Cotton said. "Yes, I remember." He smiled, revealing his enormous teeth. "And you two were at the funeral service as well."

"You delivered a very nice testimonial," Ava said.

Cotton pulled his lips into a sedate smile. "Thank you."

"So," Ava said, "you come here often?"

Cotton blinked. "To this gallery, you mean? No, I'm just out enjoying some of the art and wine. I was supposed to meet up with some friends here." He glanced around. "Don't see them yet."

Carmela decided to do a little probing. "How is your organization doing? I'm sure Martin Lash's death must have been a devastating loss to everyone involved."

"Absolutely it was," Cotton said. "But I'm hanging in there, trying to rally the troops as best I can. After all, we're committed to carry on our good work."

"And you're going to stay on?" Carmela asked. She recalled Martin Lash's notes, the ones they'd found at his cottage, that seemed to indicate Cotton might be on his way out.

"I'm probably going to become executive director," Cotton said. "That is, if the board will have me."

Carmela smiled. "Did I hear a rumor that you'd been

preemptively talking to some of the board members about changes in the leadership of the organization?"

Cotton's face flared pink, looking slightly flustered and guilty as charged. "Yes, well . . . the direction and methodology of the Environmental Justice League has always been important, always critical." After a couple of false starts he began to blather on about the importance of the group.

Carmela realized he hadn't answered her question at all. Rather, he had launched into a rambling monologue about maintaining the stability of the organization.

"And the grant from Crescent City Bank doesn't hurt, either," Carmela said, interrupting him.

Cotton's mouth snapped shut and he looked at her sharply. "How would you know about that?"

"Your benefactor, Shamus Meechum, is Carmela's ex," Ava explained sweetly. "Carmela's one of the ex-Meechums. Kicked out, ostracized, and once removed from the family."

"Which means I'm out of the money," Carmela said. "Though I doubt I was ever in the money in the first place."

"Still," Cotton said, "the Meechums are a wonderful family. So generous and civic-minded."

As Cotton prattled on, praising his benefactors, Carmela wondered if he was the one who'd tried to break into Martin Lash's house two nights ago—after they had already broken in. "I was wondering," she said, interrupting him again, "if you're familiar with the developer Trent Trueblood?"

"The man who's building the Parson's Point Townhomes," Cotton said immediately. "Of course I know *of* him, but I've never met the man personally."

"As far as you know, the town houses won't interfere with the ecology of the area?" Carmela asked.

Cotton seemed to weigh her question. "I'm sure they'll have some impact, but our organization isn't putting up any opposition to them. Not to my knowledge, anyway. It's only a few smaller homes surrounded by protected land." He cleared his throat and peered at her. "You ask a lot of questions, don't you?"

"I'm a curious sort of person," Carmela told him. She wondered if Cotton was relieved that the lawsuit Martin Lash had filed against Trueblood would now be dropped. And if he was relieved, why would that be?

But before she could ask another question, Cotton held up his wineglass and rocked it back and forth.

"Time for a refill," Cotton said. And walked away.

"He wasn't very friendly," Ava said.

"He doesn't like to answer questions," Carmela said.

But twenty minutes later, Carmela and Ava were also ready to walk away. Because, seriously, how long can you guzzle cheap white wine and pretend to be intrigued by so-so amateur photos and paintings?

But Ava being Ava, she didn't want to call it a night just yet. So Carmela suggested they stop at Mumbo Gumbo for a nightcap.

QUIGG BREVARD WAS STANDING NEAR THE BAR when Carmela and Ava walked in. His dark eyes lit up at the sight of Carmela.

"My evening has reached maximum perfection when two lovelies such as yourselves show up at my restaurant," Quigg said in his trademark big-cat growl.

"Oh, you are so full of it," Carmela said. But did she mean to put him down? Or was she a little bit flattered? She wasn't sure.

Wearing a perfectly tailored navy blue Armani suit that accentuated his broad shoulders, Quigg moved to greet them.

He gently took each of their hands and raised it to his lips. Then he pulled Carmela into a tight bear hug and startled her with a light but serious kiss on the lips.

Oh my!

Then Quigg steered Carmela and Ava to a giant black leather bumper car booth. "Just tuck in here," he told them, "while I see about some drinks and appetizers."

"Nice to have a man who takes charge," Ava said as she settled into the plush booth.

"But he's trying to take charge of my life," Carmela said.

Ava gave a conspiratorial wink. "Oh, come on, you like it a little, don't you?"

"Yeah, but . . ."

"Just relax and enjoy the attention. Think of Quigg as a little somethin' on the side."

"I think Quigg would prefer to be my main course." Carmela leaned back and looked around. Mumbo Gumbo was a hip restaurant with sun-washed brick walls, sleek eggplant-colored bar, giant potted palm trees, and wicker ceiling fans that spun lazily overhead. "Louisiana Christmas Day" played discreetly over the sound system.

Quigg was back a few minutes later with a platter of cranberry crab cakes and a bottle of Veuve Clicquot Yellow Label Brut.

"Say now," Ava said as Quigg poured champagne into crystal flutes. "This is pretty fancy."

"Only the best for you ladies," he said, but he was smiling at Carmela. "Now please enjoy." He squeezed into the booth and sat close to Carmela.

Carmela was ready to hit the panic button. Coming here had been a bad idea—why hadn't she seen that? Babcock could come storm-troopering in at any moment. Or he could have undercover officers watching the place. Then where would she be? Maybe . . . maybe the best thing to do would be to bring up Babcock and put Quigg on the defensive.

"Babcock's been doing a fair amount of investigating," Carmela said. "And he's discovered that the fork the killer stuck in Martin Lash's neck is the same type used in your kitchen."

Quigg leaned back and rested his right arm along the back edge of the booth, precariously close to Carmela's shoulders. "Pretty much every kitchen in Louisiana uses the same brand. It means nothing."

"Actually, it does mean something," Carmela said. "It means you're still a suspect." She wondered why Quigg was suddenly so casual about this.

Quigg waved off her suggestion. "Me and who else?"

"You really want to know?" Carmela held up an index finger. "First we have Allan Hurst, owner of Fat Lorenzo's."

"Lash's horrible review must have cost Hurst a fortune," Quigg said.

"Hurst also had a booth at the Winter Market, not that far from yours." Carmela held up another finger. "Then there's Josh Cotton." At Quigg's questioning look, she explained. "He's one of the officers in Martin Lash's environmental group. And let me tell you, they did not get along."

"We just left him at the Napoleon Gallery," Ava said, munching a crab cake. "Cotton acted all nicey nice about Lash, but I'm not buying it."

"You've actually done some serious investigating," Quigg said. "I'm impressed."

"And do you know Trent Trueblood?" Carmela asked.

"I've heard the name," Quigg said. "He's some sort of real estate developer?"

"Exactly," Carmela said. "Against whom Martin Lash personally filed a lawsuit. Except now Lash is dead so the lawsuit goes away."

"Poof," Ava said.

A slow smile spread across Quigg's face. "Carmela, you are amazing—all the information you've dug out, I'm impressed. You have to keep working on this. You're going to clear me yet."

"Only if Babcock doesn't kill me first," Carmela muttered.

"You?" Quigg said. "Noooo."

Carmela shook her head. "He's ready to hawk a rat at me."

"But I need you!" Quigg said, his self-preservation kicking in big-time. "Look how much you've figured out. You're a regular Agatha Christie." He picked up the bottle of champagne and refilled their glasses. "What I want to know . . ." His eyes flicked over toward the bar and he said, "Hold everything, I've got to run over and talk to those people."

Carmela followed his gaze. Harvey and Jenny Jewel were standing near the bar, looking around. "Those people?" she said. "The caviar people?"

"You know them?" Quigg asked.

"I was just introduced to them at the Reveillon dinner this past Saturday night," Carmela said.

"Harrison knows them real well," Ava said. She made goo-goo eyes at Quigg. "You remember my sweetie, don't you?"

"Sure," Quigg said. "The rich kid."

Ava grinned. "That's right."

"Well, the Jewels have a new company that's sourcing some wonderful caviar," Quigg said. "From Finland, I understand." He slid away from Carmela, ready to get up. "I'm about to order an entire case for the holidays."

"Go for it," Carmela said. She was happy to be rid of him.

Ava picked up the bottle of Veuve and said, "Ready for another glass, *cher*?"

Chapter 18

"YOU'RE here nice and early," Gabby said as she let herself into Memory Mine and turned on the lights in the front window.

Carmela was bent over the craft table in back, working on a half dozen paper luminaries. Rulers, scissors, X-acto knives, and tape were spread out all around her. A hot glue gun, looking like a high-tech hair dryer, stood at the ready.

"Tell me about it," Carmela said. "I know it's weird that I'm here. Thursday's usually my late day when I swing by Century Printing and pick up orders for our customers. But I promised Toby Brewer a set of luminaries, so here I am. I've just got to get these done." Toby Brewer was the manager of Glissande's Courtyard Restaurant, located directly across the street from Memory Mine. Toby had seen the Halloween luminaries Carmela had created (bats with grinning faces) and fallen in love with them. Now, much to her distraction, he'd ordered a set of Christmas-themed luminaries for the restaurant.

"You're a regular little workaholic," Gabby said.

Carmela shook her head. "Not really. Truth is, I've been putting this project off for weeks. And now . . . well, I'm behind the eight ball."

Gabby smiled. "But I bet you still went to the Art and Wine Stroll last night."

Carmela ducked her head. Caught like a rat in a trap. "Well . . . yeah. But only because Ava coerced me."

"And only because you wanted to poke around and investigate some more."

Carmela put up a hand to smooth her hair, which she worried needed a trim. "Funny you should mention that."

Gabby slipped her tweed coat off and laid it on the counter. "What?"

"We ran into Josh Cotton, the second-in-command at the Environmental Justice League."

Gabby made a rolling motion with her hands. "And . . . ?"

"And I still think he's a viable suspect."

"You think everybody's a suspect. How many people are on your list so far?"

"Four?" Carmela said in a small voice.

"There you go."

CUSTOMERS DROPPED IN, A LARGE ORDER OF scrapbook paper was delivered, and still Carmela continued to work. Luckily, Gabby handled everything with ease and a deft touch as Carmela painstakingly cut shooting stars into her twelve-by-eighteen-inch sheets of specially ordered red cardstock. When the stars were finally done, she perforated each sheet along the top and bottom. When assembled, those perfs would emit tiny pinpricks of light.

The hard part, the cutting part, finally done, Carmela folded each sheet into a five-sided lantern and carefully glued it at the seam. A handle went on the top of the luminary, then a strand of silver silk ribbon, accented with silk leaves and a sprig of artificial holly, was tied around the middle of the luminary.

Between customers, Gabby had been over to check on Carmela's progress. When she saw the luminaries were all but finished, she said, "Those look fantastic. Now all you need to do is put a candle inside."

"To test one," Carmela said. "And hope that the design is perfect."

"Then let's do it."

"You mean light a candle and turn off the lights? But we've got customers."

Gabby turned to face the four customers who were browsing racks of paper. "Ladies," she said sweetly, "do you mind if I turn out the lights for two seconds? We're testing a paper luminary."

Nobody minded. In fact, everyone crowded around to see. So Carmela lit a candle inside one of the luminaries and Gabby doused the lights.

Perfection. The red lantern emitted a warm glow, the stars twinkled, and the tiny perfs cast just the right amount of light.

"That's just fantastic," one of the customers marveled. "Could you show me how to make a couple of those?"

"Of course," Carmela said.

Another woman squinted at the luminary. "Looks hard."

"Not really," Carmela said. "All you have to do is follow my pattern."

*   *   *

CARMELA WAS HALFWAY THROUGH HER COBB
salad from Pirate's Alley Deli when she looked at Gabby and
said, "Why don't we close up shop and have you join me this
afternoon?"

"What?" Gabby said, blotting her mouth. "At the tea party?"

"Sure. You're kind of a fancy-pants society-type gal."

"Oh no, I'm not."

"Well, you at least went to a private school. And you
know all about tea drinking."

"So do you, Carmela. What do you think you've been
ordering from the Indigo Tea Shop in Charleston these past
couple of years? Sawdust?"

"That's completely different. It's one thing to pick up the
phone, order Assam or Darjeeling tea that comes in colorful
tins, and charge it to your Visa card. It's another matter entirely to get all gussied up in a ladylike suit and pearls and
attend a formal tea party."

Gabby was bemused that Carmela seemed so nervous.
"Oh please, you must have been to tea before."

"Maybe once at Baby's house. But that was just tea and
cookies between friends. And Sampson, her pet snapping
turtle."

"Didn't two of Shamus's aunts hold an engagement tea
for you?"

"Yes, they did. Aunt Eulalie and Aunt Philomena from
over near Slidell. Two little ladies who smelled like moth-
balls and, according to family legend, may or may not have
accidently smothered their younger brother to death sometime back in the late '50s. But I was so nervous I hid in the
butler's pantry the whole afternoon and nipped at the sherry.
Please, won't you come with me?"

"You want to just close up shop right during our busy time? Our peak season?"

Gabby made a good point. "I guess not," Carmela said.

"I've got an idea. Why don't you take Ava along? If you've got her as your wingman, nobody will give you a second look."

Carmela considered this. First it sounded preposterous. Then it sounded absurd. Then, the more she thought about it, the whole idea sounded downright doable. "That's actually a very clever idea," she said slowly.

Gabby looked amused. "I thought you might like it."

"I'm going to call Ava right now and tell her to get changed."

"Changed? Oh no," Gabby said. "If Ava's going to function as your smoke screen, then you want her to show up in her full-blown leopard-and-leather glory."

"Looking like a streetwalker."

"If the stiletto fits, yes."

WHEN CARMELA FIGURED THE LUNCHEON CROWD (usually high-test brokers and bankers keeping watch over family fortunes) had finally departed Glissande's, she put her six luminaries in a cardboard box and carried them across the street.

"Knock, knock," she said as she stood in the entryway. Nobody was in sight. The hostess stand was abandoned and she couldn't see a single soul left eating in the elegant dining room. She stepped into the bar. Nobody there, either. No broker or banker knocking back a final finger of bourbon. But she could hear faint voices coming from the back of the restaurant.

Carmela threaded her way through the dining room, which was old-world glamour personified. Decorated in a French palette of pale blue, eggshell white, and yellow, the room was both posh and plush. White linens graced the tables, diners sat on richly upholstered high-backed chairs. Windows were swagged with linen draperies, and bunches of dried lavender and white roses were arranged in enormous French crocks.

Toby Brewer's office was down a long hallway, just past two private dining rooms. The carpet was whisper soft and she could hear voices talking a little louder now.

"Mr. Brewer," Carmela called out. "Toby?"

Just then, Cortina Clark, the restaurant's catering manager, stepped out of her office. Cortina was a petite African American woman with sepia-colored hair and wide-set oval brown eyes. Today she was dressed in an elegant paprika-colored skirt suit. When she recognized Carmela she broke into a welcoming smile. "Carmela. What are you doing here?"

Carmela offered her box of luminaries for inspection. "Delivering Toby's luminaries, I hope."

"I'm pretty sure he's in his office," Cortina said, turning to lead the way. She pushed open Toby's door and said, "Toby, Carmela's here to see you."

"Send her in," came Toby's muffled voice.

"Go on in," Cortina said. And with a whisper of Dior perfume she was gone.

Toby met Carmela at the door. "My topiaries," he said when he looked in the box.

"Luminaries," Carmela said.

"Ah, right. Well, come on in and set them down." Toby backed up and began clearing a space on top of his messy desk.

As Carmela entered his office, she saw that he wasn't alone. A distinguished-looking man in a pinstriped suit lounged in the club chair that faced Toby's desk.

"Excuse me," Carmela said. "I didn't realize you had a visitor."

"Not a problem," Toby said. "We were just finishing up." He smiled at Carmela and said, "Do you know Harvey Jewel?"

Jewel popped to his feet and stuck out his hand. "We meet again," he said. When Carmela hesitated, wondering if Quigg had mentioned her last night, he said, "The Reveillon dinner? My company furnished the caviar?"

"Of course," Carmela said, clasping his hand. "It's lovely to see you again. And I have to tell you, that was delicious caviar, a treat one is not soon to forget."

Jewel fairly beamed. "Glad to hear it," he said, rocking back on his heels, obviously pleased.

"It really is fantastic caviar," Toby chimed in. "Fact is, our head chef just placed an order for several cases. We were just going over delivery dates."

"I imagine importing caviar can be somewhat dicey," Carmela said. "Fish being what they are."

"Ha ha," Jewel chuckled.

"Although, as I recall from the other night, you mentioned that you had a fairly reliable vendor?" Carmela asked.

"A wonderful wholesaler in Finland," Jewel said. "Jakobstad Farms."

"Our chef was so taken with the quality of the caviar, he's already planning a special dish," Toby said. "Tagliarini pasta topped with poached salmon, crème fraîche, and a generous dollop of caviar."

"Wow," Carmela said, suitably impressed. "That sounds a whole lot better than plain old mac and cheese."

Harvey Jewel reached into his briefcase and dug out a small jar of caviar. He bounced it in his hand and then handed it to Carmela. "For you, dear lady."

Carmela was stunned. "For me? Oh my goodness. Thank you so much!"

"My pleasure," Jewel said. "Please enjoy it with the very best champagne you can possibly afford."

"I absolutely will," Carmela said. In her head she was already planning a special New Year's Eve treat for Babcock. If he didn't have to work, that is. Otherwise she would gladly go facedown in the tasty little eggs all by herself.

"Of course," Jewel said, "the very best caviar you can buy would be beluga from the Caspian Sea, but that's almost all fished out. Very difficult to obtain unless you're on a first-name basis with someone in the Russian politburo." He continued, "The next-best caviars are sterlet, ossetra, and sevruga. Then there are all sorts of fish roe that are commercially produced, some good, some just plain awful. But our caviar, Jewel Caviar, is comparable to very fine ossetra."

"It most certainly is," Toby said. "I've tasted your caviar and it's got that Caspian pop—a nice firm snap in your mouth as you bite into an egg. Absolutely first-class."

"I couldn't agree more," Carmela said. She held up the tiny jar and studied the blue and white image that was printed on the shiny label—a grinning fish happily blowing bubbles that, she supposed, were supposed to be caviar eggs. Delicious caviar eggs filled with tiny bursts of flavor. Yum yum.

Chapter 19

"THIS Gingerbread Tea Party is going to be a blast," Ava chortled to Carmela as they climbed the wide marble steps of the Evangeline Women's Club. "I've always wanted to see how Garden District ladies fritter away their afternoons while the rest of us poor peons are working our fingers to the bone." Ava made a quick check of her hands, just to make sure her jet-black nails still had rhinestones glued to each tip.

True to form, Ava had dressed in her chicest biker babe outfit. Tight black pants with silver studs running down the length of them, black lace-up suede vest without a blouse underneath, and studded stiletto heels. She was a vision in what she liked to call Goth couture. Carmela, on the other hand, looked so sedate in her beige knit suit she could probably be mistaken for either a missionary or a Republican. Which might not be a bad thing, considering this crowd.

Carmela rang the bell and held her breath. Two seconds later, a doorman opened the door and was practically rocked back on his heels by Ava and her understated getup. "Uh . . . welcome. Ladies?" he said, as if that particular moniker was severely in question.

"Thank you," Ava said as she sashayed past him, her confidence burbling over.

Estelle Slawson, grande dame of the Ladies Charity League and the chair of the board of directors of the New Orleans Art Museum, made it her business to stand in the foyer and welcome every guest. So when Ava came bouncing in, the large pink flying saucer of a hat that was perched on Estelle's sensibly coiffed head began to vibrate like it was ready to take off.

"Excuse me, miss," Estelle said in a frosty tone. "I do believe you're in the wrong place. This happens to be a private affair."

"I think all affairs should remain private," Ava replied. "Unless you're definitely hot to marry the dude. Then it's okay to tell your gal pals."

Estelle's eyes bugged out, her lips puckered, and she made an ugly sputtering sound. Then she spotted Carmela one step behind Ava and said, "Heavens to Betsy! This is *your* guest?"

"That's right," Carmela said. She recalled that Estelle was a good friend of Shamus's sister, Glory. And that Estelle was severely allergic to peanuts. Carmela made a mental note to see if there were any peanuts to be found on the premises.

Jade Germaine, proud proprietor of Tea Party in a Box, was standing just inside the dining room, conferring with the catering manager. When she saw Carmela and Ava, she rushed over to give them both a big hug.

"Thanks for coming," Jade said. She was over the moon with excitement. "Will you look at this high-class crowd? I sure hope my sweets and savories meet with their approval."

"They're going to love everything," Carmela assured her.

"I owe this all to you," Jade said. "Because you created such a fabulous scrapbook for me. That's what got me this job."

"Your own talent and personality won you this job," Carmela said. "You're the one with the smarts to match the right tea with the right pastry and tea sandwich. You're the one who knows how to pretty up a tea table with gorgeous linens and china. Remember, I only showed you how to showcase your work."

"And, from the looks of things, it's terrific work," Ava said, gazing at the half dozen or so tables that were already set up.

Each tea table was covered with a white linen tablecloth, trimmed with Venetian lace. Matching napkins were folded into elaborate bishop's hats. The tables were set with Royal Albert Lady Carlyle china and Wallace Rose Point flatware. Flower arrangements of pink and white tea roses graced each table along with tiny tea lights in glass holders.

"Your arrangements look like something out of a magazine," Carmela said.

"Ooh, thank you," Jade said. She gave each of them a quick air kiss and said, "Wish me luck. I'm off to check on my scones."

"Luck," Ava said as Jade dashed off. Then, "Maybe we should mingle?"

"Maybe," Carmela said. She noticed a pod of women staring curiously at Ava. "Or maybe not." *Maybe I shouldn't have brought Ava along after all. Maybe I did her a terrible disservice.*

"Oh, those ladies don't bother me," Ava said, practically reading Carmela's mind. She dropped her voice. "You see that woman in the red suit? She looks like the serious decorator type who probably buys artisanal toilet paper."

Carmela almost choked with laughter.

"And the one lady who's wearing the gray sweater that

looks like it's made from mouse fur? She's got what you'd call a bitchy resting face."

"You sure know how to call them," Carmela said, still chuckling. Then (thank goodness!) she recognized a familiar face and a skinny body. "Why, it's Jenny Jewel."

Jenny Jewel strolled over to greet them. She was gussied up in a white wool skirt suit with a jeweled pink flamingo pin on the lapel of her jacket.

"I thought I recognized a couple of familiar faces," Jenny said. She pointed at Ava. "Ava. From the Reveillon dinner, right?"

Ava nodded. "And last night, too. Carmela and I were sitting in a booth in Mumbo Gumbo when you walked in with your husband."

"Oh, for goodness' sake," Jenny said. "Of course. You should have come over and said hello." She smiled at Carmela. "You, too."

"You looked like you were right in the middle of doing business," Ava said.

"We were," Jenny said. "Harvey and I had our work caps on. We were popping into all sorts of restaurants, really talking up our caviar, inviting the owners and managers to the big wine and caviar tasting Saturday night." She rolled her eyes. "It's our new product launch, don't you know?"

"I just ran into your husband at Glissande's Courtyard Restaurant," Carmela said.

"They're one of our newest accounts," Jenny exclaimed. "We just adore Toby, their GM. He's been awfully gracious and given us some very nice referrals." She touched a hand to Carmela's arm. "Tell me what table you two are sitting at, so I can join you."

"I think the one with the pink teapot," Carmela said.

"Perfect," Jenny said. "You know, I was afraid this tea party would be all stuffy and staid. But with you two girls here I know it'll be lively." She glanced around. "But first I have to go make nice with Estelle Slawson. Gag."

AND THERE WAS YET ANOTHER SURPRISE GUEST. Helen McBride from Glutton for Punishment, looking casually ragged in a gray knit skirt and pink hoodie topper.

"Oh my goodness," Carmela said to Helen. "What are *you* doing here?"

"Social climbing?" Helen said, then laughed heartily until her laugh turned into a hacking smoker's cough. She fished a hankie from her pocket and held it to her mouth for a few seconds.

Carmela hurriedly introduced Helen to Ava, who, strangely enough, now seemed much more appropriately dressed.

"So," Carmela said, her curiosity burning. "You just popped in for tea?"

"Honey," Helen said, "I get invited to a ton of these things—charity dinners, tea parties, restaurant openings, wine tastings. If it's a happening thing involving food, I get an invitation. It seems that everybody has high hopes of being written up by Glutton for Punishment."

"Except if it's a bad review," Carmela said.

Helen frowned. "Ah, like I told you before, we're trying to steer clear of those for now. Just too much controversy."

"You're talking about the nasty reviews Martin Lash wrote?" Ava asked. "Those must have stirred up some major trouble."

"And it all landed—*kersplat*—on me," Helen said. She made a big point of dusting her hands together. "But not anymore."

Carmela decided to dig a little deeper. "So bygones are . . ."

"Never bygones," Helen said. "Martin Lash may be dead and buried—at least I hope he is—but he's still a toad, in my opinion."

Carmela found Helen's vitriol slightly alarming. "But what a strange death. To be stabbed with a meat fork . . ." She tried to look appropriately outraged. "I don't suppose you were there that night? I mean, at the Winter Market?"

Helen gave her a strange look. "No, I was at home popping Pepcid AC. I'd been to so many fancy dinners and restaurant openings that past week my stomach needed a night off."

The merry tinkle of a bell punctuated their conversation and alerted them to take their seats.

"Your friend Helen is a strange duck," Ava said as they sat down at their table.

"But is she a murderous one?" Carmela wondered.

Then, like butterflies in a garden, four women in pastel suits converged upon their table. Including Jenny Jewel, who took a seat on the other side of Carmela. Waiters arrived suddenly, pouring tea and delivering gingerbread scones with Devonshire cream.

Carmela turned to Jenny Jewel. "With Mumbo Gumbo, Glissande's, and your other new clients, I'm guessing the Jewel Caviar Company has gotten off to a rousing start."

"Actually," Jenny confided, "it's been fantastic. We've written so many orders we're kind of amazed. We thought caviar might be a difficult sell to restaurateurs but it hasn't been at all."

Ava leaned forward. "And you're manufacturing your caviar right here?"

"We're not manufacturing at all," Jenny said. "We import in bulk from Finland and package the caviar in our plant just across the river in Gretna."

"You know," Carmela said, "you have a great opportunity to get a write-up on the Glutton for Punishment website. Helen McBride, the editor, is sitting just a couple of tables away. I could introduce you if you'd like."

Jenny smiled. "Yes, I know Helen. You could call us nodding

acquaintances." Then she dropped her voice. "Wasn't it a terrible thing about that Martin Lash business?"

"You're referring to his murder?" Carmela wanted to be perfectly clear.

"The rumor I heard was that Lash was killed over one of his freelance reviews," Jenny said. "Which is just incredibly shocking to me." She looked thoughtful for a few moments as plates were whisked away and a three-tiered tea tray placed in the center of their table. Then she said, "You probably don't know this, but I'm on the board of directors for the Environmental Justice League."

"Are you serious?" Carmela had been reaching for a tiny chicken salad sandwich and almost fumbled it. "So you must have known Martin Lash quite well."

"I knew him slightly. Since I'm relatively new to the board and had only attended three meetings. Though I have to say, I understand some of his tactics were a bit rough, that he tended to strong-arm people. And I heard that he was forever threatening lawsuits or holding demonstrations."

"He must have been a passionate man," Carmela said.

"Yes," Jenny said. "If Martin Lash thought you were causing damage to the environment, he was not above bringing a mob to picket your business for all the world to see."

"So now that Lash is gone, there'll no doubt be some major changes."

Jenny sighed. "I hope so anyway. For the better."

"Josh Cotton seems to be the heir apparent," Carmela said. "Do you have faith in him as an executive director?"

"I think so. Josh seems like far more of a consensus-builder. He doesn't have that do-it-my-way attitude. He'd rather use a carrot than a stick."

Carmela was fascinated with Jenny Jewel's connection to Lash and wanted to find out more.

"I understand that before Lash, um, died, Josh Cotton was talking to some of the board members about changing the direction of the group."

"That's true," Jenny said. "But in a good way. A thoughtful way. Josh wanted the group to become a real part of the community. He felt it had been perceived as too much of an outside agitator and wanted to soften the image." She hesitated. "It sounds like you've done some investigation into Martin Lash's murder."

"It's just that I'm . . . interested," Carmela said. She didn't feel the need to tell Jenny Jewel that she'd seen Martin Lash breathe his last.

Jenny fingered her teacup. "Uh-huh."

The waiter returned and was hovering at their table with a blue and white Chinese teapot. "For this course we're serving a Chinese black tea with apple cinnamon spice," he told them.

"No apple tea toddy?" Ava asked, while all around her the ladies tittered politely.

"I'm afraid not," the waiter said as his face reddened slightly.

Carmela wasn't sure if he was embarrassed over Ava's "tea toddy" remark or because he'd been looking down her cleavage.

"You know," Jenny said, "I wouldn't mind a toddy myself."

Which broke the ice and made everyone laugh in a nice, friendly way.

WHEN CARMELA FINALLY RETURNED TO MEMory Mine late in the day, Gabby was all over her.

"How did it go? Who all was there?" Gabby asked. She'd just been helping a customer select a number of rubber stamps with holiday themes.

"It couldn't have gone better," Carmela said. "During the

final course Ava started talking about a new leather bar that had just opened in the Bywater District and she had everyone pretty much shocked and eating out of the palm of her hand. I could have danced around the room in my birthday suit and nobody would have noticed. It was great."

"Glad to hear it. Was Glory Meechum there?"

"Thank goodness, no. Maybe she went off her meds again and is hiding under the bedcovers." She glanced around. "Anything happening here?"

"We were just busy, busy, busy," Gabby said. "Everyone's gearing up for the holidays. Oh, and a few customers wanted to know about upcoming classes, so you might want to work on that sooner than later."

"I hear you," Carmela said. She shuffled off to her office and flopped down in her chair. She spun the chair from side to side, looking at the sketches and ideas she had tacked to her walls. She'd gazed at them the other day, but hadn't really translated anything into an actual class. But now that the pressure was on . . .

Her eyes lit on some old sheet music. Maybe she could do a collage class right after the holidays? Yes, that might fit well between New Year's and Mardi Gras.

And then there was the cigar box class she wanted to teach. Decorating or decoupaging wooden cigar boxes to use as purses or trinket boxes. And paper sachets. And masks with mojo. She really had to start working on all those classes as well.

Carmela was staring at her desk calendar, trying to come up with a reasonable schedule for the new classes when her phone rang. She checked the caller ID.

Babcock? No, the number wasn't familiar.

"Hello?" Carmela said. "This is Carmela Bertrand. How can I help you?"

"Perhaps it's I who can help you," came a familiar voice.

"Who's I?"

"This is Trent Trueblood." He paused. "Is this Carmela?"

"Oh, hi," she said.

Trueblood jumped right into his sales pitch. "You seemed so interested in the Parson's Point development that I wondered if you might like to take a look at it? Well, not at the actual townhomes per se, because we haven't quite broken ground yet. But we have a lovely sales office with a rather extensive model. And I have some very detailed blueprints and artist's renderings on our walls. You could get a good idea of what the development will eventually look like."

Carmela thought about this for all of two seconds. "I'd love to see it. When would be a good time for you?"

Anticipation colored Trueblood's voice. He had a potential buyer on the hook. "I'm going to be down there tonight. Would that work for you?"

"I'll make it work."

"Excellent. Our sales office is just two miles south of Boothville. Turn on Ridgemount Road, hang a right on Briarwood, then left on McClean."

"Got it," Carmela said. "I'll see you around seven."

CARMELA PUNCHED SPEED DIAL AND, WHEN AVA answered, said, "Adventure calls, my little tea diva. Are you ready for another trip down south to bayou country?"

"Ordinarily I would be your girl," Ava said. "Especially if you promised a stop at Sparky's Tap again. But Harrison and I are going to see a play tonight. A revival of *Dracula*."

"They revived him? Again?"

"I think it's an updated hipster version where he ditches his cape for duds from Hollister. But, *cher*, where exactly are you going?"

"I've got a meeting with Trent Trueblood."

"About those Parsnip Point Townhomes?"

"Parson's Point."

"Whatever. The thing is, I don't like the idea of you going down there all by your lonesome. If this guy is high on your suspect list—and I'm guessing he still is—then you could be putting yourself in danger. I mean, what if this guy Trueblood is the killer?"

"Don't worry, I'll be fine."

"It sounds like you're whistling in the dark. Like you really are worried."

"Tell you what," Carmela said. "I'll take the dogs. They can stand guard over me."

"That's just peachy," Ava said. "Since Boo is a crackerjack shot with a Ruger and Poobah's got his black belt in karate."

"I'll be fine. Really."

"I hope so, sweetie." But Ava didn't sound one bit hopeful.

Chapter 20

I T was full-on dark when Carmela pulled up in front of the Parson's Point sales office just south of Boothville. Trent Trueblood had given her fairly detailed directions, but she'd still made a couple of wrong turns. Now, as she stared at the small white building with its windows still dark, it looked as if she was the first one to arrive. There were no other cars in the small parking lot and no other buildings around that she could see. Just a dark expanse of pine trees looming up on either side of her, a sparkle of water far off to her right.

"What do you think, guys?" Carmela asked Boo and Poobah, who were hunkered in the backseat of her car. It had been a long, boring ride for them and now they were panting like a couple of steam engines, fogging up the windows, whining, begging to escape.

Carmela, on the other hand, was suddenly feeling a touch

uneasy. Had she gotten the time wrong? Had Trueblood canceled on her at the last minute? Maybe something had come up. A real estate emergency, if there even was such a thing.

She checked her phone and found nothing from him. No text messages, no missed calls.

Okay. Whatever.

Easing herself out of the car, Carmela stretched languidly. She glanced around and again felt unsettled by how quiet everything was. There were no cars on what looked like an almost deserted stretch of road. No lights glimmering off in the distance. Just a faint sliver of moon scudding along on gray, low-hanging clouds. And a barely audible *chr-chr-chr* coming from deep in the woods.

What was that sound, anyway? Crickets? An owl? Hopefully not a band of marauding alligators with toothy grins that were slithering silently in her direction.

As the wind came up and riffled her hair, a chill seeped deeper into Carmela's heart. Dang. What if Ava had been right? What if Trueblood really was the killer? What if he'd neatly set her up?

No. I can't think that way, she told herself. *I'm here because I'm onto something. This is the part of Louisiana that had an almost magnetic attraction for Martin Lash. This is where the answers are going to be.*

Squaring her shoulders, making up her mind to remain calm, to maintain an open, inquiring mind, Carmela headed for the sales office. Maybe it was open, after all. Maybe Trueblood's car was parked in back and he was sitting in an office with the door closed, earbuds stuck in his ears listening to the Rolling Stones. Or Beethoven.

It was worth a shot anyway.

Carmela climbed two low steps and stood in front of the door. To the right was a sign that said *SALES OFFICE,*

PARSON'S POINT TOWNHOMES. She leaned to the left and tried to peer in a window, but it was no good. Just too dark. Nervously, her fingertips touched the doorknob. Maybe if she jiggled the handle . . . if Trueblood was inside, he'd hear her and turn on the lights. Greet her with a smile, eager to show off his models and his plans.

It didn't work that way. It never does.

Instead, the door to the sales office swung open with a low moan.

Carmela's heart caught in her throat.

"Hello?" she called out, fighting to keep her voice from quavering. "Mr. Trueblood? Anybody home?"

There was no answer.

Carmela felt a sudden flash of anger. "Well, somebody must have been here," she called out. "Because the door wasn't locked."

She took a step inside and stood there listening. Waiting for . . . what? Finally, her heart starting to flutter in her chest, she stuck her right hand out and batted around, trying to locate a light switch.

Success.

She flipped the switch and the flood of bright light practically blinded her. Her eyes flashed on white walls hung with floor plans, giant posters of postcard-perfect bayou vistas, and artist's renderings of sleek, modern-looking townhomes.

She took a step inside, starting to feel a wash of relief.

And that's when she saw him. Trent Trueblood lying on the floor, arms flopped out to his sides. He was faceup, just a few feet in front of her.

Her mind reeled sickeningly. *Is he dead?* She blinked and looked away. And then had to look back. Yes, of course he was dead. His eyes were open wide, as if he'd just encountered a big fat surprise, and an enormous butcher knife was sticking straight out of his chest. All around him, the beige industrial carpet was soaked through with blood. Lots of bright red blood.

The first thing Carmela thought was, *That stain's not coming out.*

The second thing she thought was, *I've got to get the hell out of here.*

Carmela spun wildly, slammed her right shoulder against the doorjamb, and sprinted for her car. She pawed frantically at the car door handle and flung herself inside. Click-click went the door locks as she turned frantically in her seat, looking out the car windows, searching for the raging maniac who must surely be charging after her, a fresh knife in hand, this very minute.

Instead, she saw Boo and Poobah staring at her, mild curiosity lighting their limpid brown eyes.

Fumbling for her phone, Carmela punched 911. When an operator answered, Carmela started babbling so rapidly, the woman had to beg her to slow down.

SLOW. THAT SEEMED TO BE THE OPERATIVE WORD. The call center sent an officer out, all right. But he turned out to be Deputy Bill Klunder, a good old boy–type sheriff's deputy who looked like he had hung on about ten years beyond retirement. Thinning gray hair, potbelly, bowlegs, flat feet, the works.

When Deputy Klunder knocked on her car window, Carmela screamed so loud the dogs joined in with a bloodcurdling cacophony. Then she climbed out and practically fell into the deputy's arms.

"Trent Trueblood," Carmela told him. "The real estate

developer." She fanned her arms wildly and pointed repeat-
edly in the direction of the sales office. "I found him dead
inside. Well, he's *still* dead inside."

"Dead, you say?" Deputy Klunder sounded like he didn't
quite believe her.

So Carmela grabbed him by the arm and pulled him
across the gravel parking lot to the sales center, where the
lights still blazed. Trent Trueblood was still there, of course.
Splayed out on the floor, looking waxy and pale and a little
less surprised. As if he had finally, reluctantly, come to terms
with his own untimely death. The puddle of blood had seeped
a little closer to the front door.

"He was dead when I got here," Carmela said. "The door
was unlocked. You see . . . I was supposed to meet him here . . .
concerning his town house development."

The deputy cocked an eye at her. "You a buyer?"

"No," Carmela said. "Well . . . yes. Maybe."

"I think it's best we go back outside and have ourselves a
talk."

Carmela's words continued to pour out in a disjointed
tumble, but Deputy Klunder's questions were slow and
methodical. Five minutes into their conversation, Carmela
was beginning to feel a hard ball of frustration deep within
her gut. Precious minutes were being wasted. Deputy Klunder hadn't yet called in the murder or sounded the alarm.
No other deputies were blazing down the road, setting up
roadblocks, hot on the trail of Trueblood's killer.

When Carmela answered the same question for the third
time, she did what she knew she had to do. She pulled out
her phone and called Detective Edgar Babcock.

Of course, once Carmela poured her situation out to Babcock, the cat was out of the bag. She was forced to explain a

few pesky details to him. Like why she'd driven down here to Boothville all by her lonesome. And how she'd come to stumble on a dead body, no less.

When Carmela finished her story, Babcock wasn't just angry, he was infuriated. But thank heavens and God bless his raving, ranting heart, he was coming to her rescue.

FORTY-FIVE MINUTES LATER, WHEN BABCOCK finally arrived at the murder scene, the place was buzzing. The sheriff and two more deputies had arrived, along with an ambulance and two EMTs.

Babcock confabbed with the local sheriff and inspected the body while the EMTs lounged against the back of their ambulance, talking and smoking, assuming a casual wait-and-see attitude. Just two guys out on a typical evening run.

Then Babcock corralled Carmela.

"How much have you told them?" Babcock asked her, hooking a thumb at the cadre of sheriff's deputies. He was trying to contain his anger but was both irritated and frantic over her safety.

"Everything," Carmela said.

"You've been absolutely straight with them?"

"Yes. Cross my heart."

"Because you haven't been with me."

"Edgar, I . . ." But he was already walking away from her.

Babcock was drawn into yet another conference with the sheriff and his deputies. As Carmela watched, she knew he was getting more and more annoyed by the slowness of local law enforcement. Finally, after what evolved into a fairly heated argument, Babcock got on his cell phone and called the Louisiana State Police, who also promised to send out their Criminal Investigations Division.

Once this higher level of law enforcement came swarming in, jurisdiction was reluctantly handed over by the locals. The murder scene would be analyzed, processed, recorded, and photographed by serious, hard-core professionals.

At which point, Babcock relinquished any authority he might have had and pulled Carmela aside once more.

"Before we start I'd like to let the dogs out of the car," she said.

Babcock waved an arm. "Forget about the dogs. This is about you right now."

Carmela knew she was in for what would probably be a difficult and highly contentious conversation.

"I want you to start from the very beginning," Babcock said. "Why on earth are you even here?"

Carmela winced at his hard-bitten tone of voice. "I told you on the phone. I found out that Martin Lash had filed a lawsuit against Trueblood, so I thought maybe . . ."

But he didn't bother to let her finish.

"Do you realize what kind of risk you took by coming down here? You don't even *know* anyone down here."

"No, but I . . ."

"You had no business driving down here in the dead of night and meeting with some random real estate person who may or may not have been involved with Martin Lash. It was a foolish mistake on your part. For all you know, Trueblood could have knocked you on the head and dumped your dead body in a bayou."

"But he didn't." Still, she was horrified by the idea of snapping turtles and alligators darting in to munch her fingers and toes.

"No," Babcock said, gripping her arm. "Because somebody killed him first." He glowered at her. "Are you getting this?"

"Yes. Of course I am."

"*Think* for a moment, Carmela! What you did is incredibly foolhardy. Stupid, even."

"I'm sorry," Carmela said. "I'm sorry to pull you into this mess, I'm sorry I've upset you."

"This *is* a mess."

"But really . . . don't you see this as kind of a clue as well? Like a piece of the puzzle dropping into place?"

Babcock put both hands on his head as if he feared his brains might explode and come shooting out his ears. "What are you talking about?"

"The murder weapon," Carmela said with urgency. "The butcher knife. Don't you think it points to someone familiar with the restaurant industry?"

Babcock's mouth worked silently for a few moments. Then he said, "I think it points to a psychopath."

"And the fact that someone wanted Trueblood dead. You have to ask yourself why! What was the reason? Was Trueblood about to reveal something important?"

Babcock placed his hands together and then pulled them apart. "Carmela . . . I have no words."

THANK GOODNESS BABCOCK GAVE CARMELA A slight break. He allowed her to clip leashes on Boo and Poobah and take them for a short walk. She walked them down the shoulder of the road for about a hundred yards, then turned around and came back. When they returned, she saw that another car had pulled into the parking lot. It was a state patrol car, with light bars pulsing red and blue and an enormous flop-eared, sloe-eyed bloodhound sitting in the backseat, staring silently out the window.

Suddenly, Boo was doing her best prance dance, her triangle ears pricked forward and her muzzle quivering with interest. When they walked past the bloodhound, Boo gazed up at the bloodhound with an expression that was almost akin to love.

"I'm glad somebody still thinks romance is alive," Carmela murmured. She gazed across the parking lot at Babcock. "Because I have a terrible feeling that mine might have fizzled."

But no. Babcock was holding up a hand, signaling to her. She put the dogs back in her car and walked over to him.

"Everything okay?" she asked.

"Hardly," Babcock said. "Come. Sit with me in my car."

They climbed into his BMW and she turned sideways to face him. "You're angry. I feel like this is going to be an inquisition."

"You should be so lucky." Her rubbed the palm of his hand over his chin and said, "So you've been investigating. Tell me. Give me the whole enchilada. And don't sugarcoat it."

"There's no sugar on enchiladas."

"Carmela. Just tell me. And don't leave anything out."

So Carmela laid out the whole story for him. About finding out about all the lawsuits. About meeting Josh Cotton at Martin Lash's viewing and then talking to Allan Hurst. She detailed all the things that had made her suspicious of Cotton and Hurst. And, more recently, how she'd had an impromptu meeting with Helen McBride, who professed to despise Lash and practically chortled over his death. What she left out was the break-in that she and Ava staged at Martin Lash's cottage. That would have really tipped Babcock over the edge.

When she'd finished, Babcock said, "What you've done is absolutely preposterous. Ridiculous."

"I was trying to weed out suspects."

"So I'm guessing you're no longer suspicious of Trent Trueblood?"

Carmela's brows pinched together. "Well . . . no. Obviously he's not a legitimate suspect. Now that he's been taken out of the equation."

Babcock put an arm on the back of Carmela's seat and leaned toward her. "What am I going to do with you?"

"Help me follow up on those other possible suspects?"

He pinched his thumb and forefinger together. "Carmela, I'm this close to putting you under house arrest."

Carmela tilted her head at him. "Whose house? Mine or yours?"

Babcock glared at her, but pain flickered in his eyes, too. "You tell me. Maybe it should be Quigg Brevard's house."

"That's so unfair!" she cried.

"Is it, Carmela? Is it really?"

"You know there's nothing between Quigg and me."

He reached over and pulled her close. "Except for the fact that you're trying very hard to pull his fat out of the fryer."

"I love *you*," she said.

Babcock sighed. "I wish I could believe that."

Carmela threw herself into his arms and buried her head against his chest. "I do." Hot tears streamed down her cheeks and burned into his shirt. "I love you."

Babcock circled her with his arms. This time he spoke a little more gently to her. "And I love you, my crazy Carmela."

Chapter 21

CARMELA'S ears were still stinging from the tongue-lashing Babcock had given her last night. Her tummy was in turmoil. Not even a new shipment of handmade paper or the promise of new wax seals could lift her out of her nervous funk.

Gabby was concerned. "You're like a zombie this morning, Carmela. What's wrong? Are you feeling poorly? Maybe you should go home and rest."

"Aw," Carmela said. "I'm just really screwed up."

"Tell me. Maybe I can help."

So Carmela told Gabby about her trip down to Boothville the previous night, about finding Trueblood's dead body and then calling Babcock to come down and straighten things out.

Gabby listened breathlessly, making little eeks and squeaks

in all the appropriate places. Then she said, "I don't think I can help you. That's some serious doo-doo you stepped in, Miss Carmela."

"And don't think I didn't get seriously chewed out," Carmela said. "I know I've pushed Babcock's buttons before, but this time I might have gone too far. I'm not sure our relationship—the tattered remnants of it, anyway—is going to survive this."

Gabby shook her head vigorously. "Please don't say that, Carmela. Don't you dare put that negative thought out there in the ozone where it can buzz around and gather steam. You and Babcock are *crazy* about each other. Anyone can see that you're both deeply in love."

"Babcock was positively apoplectic about my being down there. He basically wants me in a no-fly zone."

"Carmela, think about it. You can't blame Babcock for being upset. He's worried about you. I mean . . ." Gabby knew she was treading on eggshells here. "You *are* a little headstrong. And you *might* have gotten a little too involved in this Martin Lash business."

"I didn't mean to." Carmela's voice was as gloomy as the sky on a foggy day. "I was just trying to help Quigg."

"You were trying to help Babcock's rival."

Carmela waved a hand dismissively. "They're not rivals."

Gabby held up an index finger. "In Babcock's mind they are. Men are like that, they're territorial beings. And they like to fight over territory."

"Me being the territory?"

"Yes. Absolutely. You're like the Falklands or something. Small, but worth going to war over."

"Then how do I make Babcock stop obsessing over this . . . this silly turf war?" Carmela asked. She reached under the counter and grabbed her handbag. She pulled out the little cotton voodoo doll Ava had given her two nights ago. Frowning at it, she took one of the bright red pins and stuck it deep into the doll's shoulder. *There, maybe that will put a stop to it. Or at least give Babcock something to think about.*

But Gabby was talking quietly, trying to impart her gentle guidance. "You just have to put aside your investigation and start to rebuild some trust."

Carmela glanced up. "Huh?"

Gabby put her hands on her hips. "You know what? Enough with my advice. Because I can see it's going in one ear and out the other."

"Sorry."

"You're incorrigible, Carmela. Better you should help me with a project." Gabby pointed to a cardboard box that contained six white pumpkins. "I don't know if you remember this or not, but we promised to decorate those pumpkins for Betty Ritter's holiday table."

Carmela shook her head, unenthused. "I really don't remember."

"Do you have any idea how great a white pumpkin can look once it's been decoupaged with gold foil and Uzumaki lace paper?"

"No," Carmela said, a smile finally playing at the corner of her lips. "But I bet we're going to find out?"

"We're going to wave our magic wands and transform these pumpkins into gorgeous centerpieces." Gabby paused. "Picture, if you will, a lovely bed of green moss set against a white linen tablecloth. Then add our elegantly decoupaged white pumpkins along with stalks of dried red bittersweet and a handful of ripe red apples."

"It does sound rather beautiful."

"I see it as a cornucopia of creativity," Gabby said. "So. Do you want to work on a pumpkin?"

"You've more than convinced me," Carmela said. "But

first . . . I think I have to call Babcock and eat a little more crow."

"Poor baby," Gabby said. "Crow is never very tasty."

SITTING AT HER DESK, STILL FEELING A LITTLE glum, Carmela reached for the phone. When her fingers were mere inches away, it shrilled loudly. Oh my, was mental telepathy at work? Was Babcock calling to tell her that all was forgiven? She could only hope.

But, no, when she answered the phone, she found that it was just stupid old Shamus.

"Hey, babe," Shamus said. "I'm calling to remind you it's my weekend to have the dogs."

This was not what Carmela was expecting and it rubbed her the wrong way. "Honestly, Shamus, this really isn't the best time . . ."

"C'mon," Shamus wheedled. "You know darn well that it's my turn. I've been looking forward to having the dogs all week long. I even bought a new Kewpie doll for Boo. Pink velour, just what she likes."

"Shamus, I need to keep the dogs with me this weekend. How about we work out a swap? You can take them next weekend." Carmela was feeling needy and wanted the dogs to stand guard in her apartment. Of course, cuddling was good, too.

But Shamus was a stickler. "No way. It has to be *this* weekend. Next weekend is all booked up. Hey," he said, sounding petulant, "we made a deal, remember?"

"We made lots of deals, most of which you didn't bother to keep. Remember our marriage vows?"

"Don't start with me. Just tell me what time can I pick them up."

"There's no wiggle room here?" Carmela asked.

"None."

Typical Shamus. What a jerk.

"Tell you what," Carmela said. "I'm supposed to attend a concert at St. Louis Cathedral tonight, so maybe you could swing by there and pick them up. That will at least give me a chance to walk Boo and Poobah and spend some quality time with them."

Shamus sighed heavily to convey his disapproval. "I suppose. What time and where?"

"How about seven-thirty in Jackson Square?" Carmela asked.

"No. No way," Shamus said. "I detest having to dodge all the street musicians, palm readers, and crazies that populate that place. To say nothing of a few panhandlers. No. You'll have to make it someplace quieter, someplace where the dogs won't get upset. They're very sensitive creatures, in case you hadn't noticed."

Exasperated, Carmela tossed out the first place that came to mind. "Okay then, how about that little park right behind the cathedral? You know, the Place de Henriette Delille down Pirate's Alley?"

"Just be there," Shamus snarled.

CARMELA SAT THERE WITH THE PHONE IN HER hand. Talking to Shamus, aka The Rat, was always a drain. But now . . . now she had to call Babcock and do some penance. She steeled herself and hit speed dial.

"Carmela," Babcock said when he picked up his phone. His voice carried a faint whiff of *Why are you bothering me now?*

Carmela decided to dive right in with her apology. "Listen, I know you're still upset with me about last night . . ."

"Yes?"

Carmela wondered if that meant *Yes, what else do you want?* Or *Yes, I'm still upset.* Too soon to tell. She stumbled on.

"I honestly didn't think I'd be in any danger," Carmela explained for about the forty-seventh time. "My plan was to meet up with Trueblood, ask a few pertinent questions, and then head right back home."

"By 'pertinent questions,' you mean 'investigate,'" Babcock said. "Haven't we been over this enough? Or should we beat it to death a few more times?"

Carmela took a deep breath. "How many ways can I say I'm sorry?" She crossed her fingers, hoping for forgiveness. Was that too much to ask? Apparently so.

"Carmela, you have to stop getting involved in every crazy murder that comes down the pike."

His demeanor was so cool and distant, she was almost grateful that he wasn't screaming at her. Hadn't she had enough of that last night? Oh yes, she had. But wait, Babcock sounded like he was just warming up, working himself into a nice angry tirade.

"Now a second person is dead and there's a shitstorm brewing over here at City Hall!"

"I'm sorry," Carmela cooed, trying to sound as meek as possible.

"Yeah, sure you are."

Carmela hesitated. "Edgar. Are you feeling okay?" Did she detect something else in his voice besides anger?

"As a matter of fact, I'm not. I'm getting tons of flak from the mayor's office as well as from the police chief. And now some flunky councilman down in Plaquemines Parish has jumped on my case, too. To top it all off, my left shoulder is killing me. I don't know what happened, maybe I slept on it wrong." He snorted. "Thanks to you, it's a wonder I slept at all."

"If there's any way I can make this up to you . . ."

"Aw . . ." Babcock seemed to regroup and shake off some of his anger then. "I'm just frustrated because nothing seems to make sense. Lash filed suit against Trueblood but now Lash and Trueblood have *both* been murdered. It's a barrelful of crazy."

"You're right," Carmela said. "Nothing adds up. There's got to be another factor at work here. An x factor. Something—or someone—we don't know about. It feels almost like a Machiavellian plot."

"I might have to agree with that. But, Carmela, I can't solve the Martin Lash case if I have to spend all my time worrying about you. Nothing related to the Lash murder has fallen into place. I'm almost considering going back to square one."

"Square one?"

"Bobby Gallant thinks it's possible that Martin Lash *was* killed over a nasty review that drove some restaurant out of business." Bobby Gallant was another detective who worked closely with Babcock. "So I'm going to have my team try to look at *that* angle."

Carmela flinched. That path could boomerang right back to Quigg Brevard. And she didn't want that to happen.

"There were that many nasty reviews?" she asked. "Are you telling me that Lash actually had the power to drive several restaurants out of business?"

"We're checking that information right now. So far we've come up with four possibilities, but I'm going to meet with that editor, Helen McBride, and try to hash out some more stuff."

"I thought all Lash's reviews were permanently deleted."

"We have cyber experts. They'll try to recover them from the magazine's servers."

"But if you look at restaurateurs now, how do you explain Trueblood?" Carmela asked. "I figured there had to be a Martin Lash connection, considering the lawsuit and all."

"I don't know. There's always the possibility that Trueblood's murder wasn't related to any of this. That he had some kind of nasty dispute with one of his contractors. It wouldn't be the first time. Apparently he's been in knock-down, drag-out fights before. Put a guy in the hospital over a project near Baton Rouge."

"Was Trueblood charged with assault?"

"No," Babcock said. "The guy he beat up dropped the charges. Said it was just a business misunderstanding."

"I had no idea housing was such a rough-and-tumble industry."

"These days, I guess any business can be dangerous. People are angry over the economy and just more hostile in general."

"Well . . . maybe you'll get lucky," Carmela said.

Babcock sighed. "It's not exactly smart police work when you have to count on being lucky."

"Can I change the subject?" Carmela asked.

"I sincerely wish you would."

"Did you remember that we have a date tonight?"

It took Babcock a while to answer. "We do?"

"The cathedral concert. Over at St. Louis Cathedral. I bought tickets, like, a month ago."

"I did promise to go with you, didn't I?"

"Don't sound so enthusiastic."

"Do I have to dress up?" Babcock asked.

"Formal attire is not required, but your presence is." *Hopefully*, Carmela thought to herself.

"What time does the concert start?"

"I think eight o'clock."

"I'm really under the gun here. Is it okay if I work late and meet you there?"

"Does that mean you're coming? For sure?"

"Ah . . . yes," Babcock said.

"In that case I'm happy to meet you there," Carmela said. "I'll be the one hanging around the front door waving an extra ticket. Probably trying to scalp it if you're a no-show."

"Okay then."

"Can I ask you a question?"

"Is this about the murder?" Babcock asked. "Murders?" He sounded wary.

"Yes."

"Then just one question, Carmela. And only one."

"Are the carving fork and the butcher knife from the same manufacturer?"

A long silence spun out and Carmela was afraid that Babcock might have hung up on her. Then he finally said, "Yes. Both utensils were manufactured by a German company named Bocker."

Chapter 22

"NO more moping," Gabby ordered. She was standing at the craft table, where the white pumpkins and stacks of colorful paper awaited them. "From this moment forth I declare Memory Mine to be a mope-free zone. A murder-free zone, too."

Carmela touched a hand to the side of her head, saluting Gabby. "I read you loud and clear."

"And just look at how perfect these pumpkins are." Gabby tossed Carmela a soft cloth and they each rubbed a pumpkin to a dry sheen. "This is gonna be great."

"I think you're right."

"So how do you want to start? Go for the gold foil or do you have another idea?"

Carmela studied her pumpkin for a few moments. "I'm thinking we should decoupage some Christmas sheet music on."

Gabby grinned. "See? I knew you'd come up with a great idea. You want me to start on that? What sheet music should I use?"

Carmela grabbed a stack of vintage sheet music from one of her flat files and handed it to Gabby. "How about 'O Holy Night'? Just cut it into strips and don't worry if the lyrics and stanzas don't match up. We just want to convey a fun, musical concept."

Gabby quickly painted her pumpkin with a thick layer of Mod Podge, then began placing strips of sheet music up and down the pumpkin. Carmela, meanwhile, had dug out some artisan tissue paper that featured a cheetah print against a bronzy gold background.

"You're going to do an animal-print pumpkin?" Gabby cried. "I love it!"

Carmela's pumpkin was easier to decorate just because the tissue paper was more pliable and easy to work with. Like Gabby, she painted on a layer of Mod Podge and then pressed her cheetah-print tissue paper all over the pumpkin. When she gave it a good squeeze, the cheetah print crinkled a bit but then it conformed directly to the pumpkin as the glue took hold. And as Carmela continued to smooth and fine-tune her pumpkin, it began to look rather gilded and spectacular, while still retaining its pumpkin essence.

"For some reason, I thought we'd be slaving over these silly things all day," Gabby said. "But this is really quite easy."

Once the paper completely covered their pumpkins—except for the stems, of course—topcoats of Mod Podge were painted on and they set their projects aside to dry.

"What's next?" Gabby asked.

"What if we just spray-painted one of these pumpkins gold?" Carmela said.

"And then left it plain?"

But Carmela was already digging into her ephemera file. "I was thinking we'd decoupage some antique Christmas decals onto the gold pumpkin." She held up a handful of paper. "We've got decals of woodblock Santas, antique sleighs, old-time carolers . . ."

"Perfect," Gabby breathed.

Carmela grabbed a spool of gold cord and cut off a few two-foot lengths. Then she wound it around her cheetah-print pumpkin, pulling it tight at the seams and tying the cord at the top. The pumpkin was now sectioned off and looking even prettier.

"I think I'm going to tie a sprig of holly at the stem," Carmela said. "Not real holly, the silk stuff that we have."

She was pulling a sprig of holly from a plastic pack when she heard her ringtone. She slid the cell phone from her pocket and saw the name *QUIGG*.

Uh-oh.

She passed the cell phone over to Gabby and shook her head vehemently.

Gabby clicked on the phone. "Memory Mine, this is Gabby. How can I help you?" She gazed at Carmela and grimaced. "Yes, you did call her cell phone, but Carmela is teaching a class right now and really can't be disturbed. Can I give her a message? No, I . . . yes, I do realize how busy you are and I promise to let her know you called. Okay, thank you, Mr. Brevard. Okay. Thank you, Quigg."

Gabby hung up and handed the phone back to Carmela. "He's a persistent fellow, isn't he?"

"Yes, he is. And thank you for fending him off like that. With Babcock so crazed about Quigg . . . after everything that's happened . . ."

"Carmela, you have to settle down and let Babcock do his

job. Then he'll start to relax, too, and everything will get back to normal."

"You think?"

"No," Gabby said. "I hope."

CARMELA WAITED ON A COUPLE OF CUSTOMERS, finding some sheets of Nepalese handmade lokta paper for one lady, a black antique-looking photo album for another, while Gabby worked on the last three pumpkins. Once Gabby was finished, Carmela was able to duck into her office. There were a couple of hot potatoes she needed to take care of.

First, she grabbed the little voodoo doll and pulled out the pin. Had her stabbing the pin into the doll caused Babcock's shoulder to hurt? She didn't think so, but she wasn't taking any chances. This was New Orleans, after all. A city that celebrated their above-ground cemeteries, set up vampire cams at Halloween, had actual voodoo high priestesses, and featured a number of haunted houses.

Then Carmela leaned back in her chair and thought about Martin Lash. Closing her eyes, she could still picture the man staggering toward her, making hideous gagging sounds as the serving fork quivered in his throat. As that image slowly faded, it was replaced by one of Trent Trueblood lying on the floor with a butcher knife stuck in his belly. Both the fork and knife seemed like terrifying murder weapons. Like something Alfred Hitchcock would have dreamed up. Ordinary utensils used to commit horrifying crimes.

And Babcock had told her that both utensils were from the same manufacturer. Bocker.

What were the odds of that? Practically nil, she decided.

Her curiosity whirring at a frantic pace, Carmela began

tapping the keyboard of her computer. When the search engine spat out the results for "restaurant supplies" she was surprised at how many suppliers there were in New Orleans. Of course, it was a restaurant town. A foodie town, though she had come to loathe the term.

But it's strange that I've never noticed any of these places. Never walked by one on the street.

She scrolled down through the list and realized she had probably walked by quite a few restaurant supply houses. In fact, the nearest shop, Hawking's Restaurant Supply, was only a few blocks away on Esplanade Avenue.

Impulsively, Carmela shut down the computer and pulled on her leather jacket.

"Gabby, I'm going to skip out early today."

"Hmm?" Gabby looked up from the stack of Asian-inspired papers she was flipping through. "You're leaving? I hope you're not going to get in any more trouble."

"I'll try not to. I just have to, um, run a couple of errands and then get ready for the cathedral concert tonight."

"Lucky you. I wish I was going to that concert. But Stuart's mother is hosting a command performance dinner tonight for the entire family. I'd like to blow her off, but Stuart will never knowingly disappoint his *maman.*" Gabby cocked her head. "I assume the illustrious Detective Babcock will be your escort?"

"He'll be running late but he promised to be there."

"It sounds like things between you two aren't nearly as bad as you think."

Carmela fervently hoped Gabby was right.

IT WAS A COOL, CLOUDLESS DAY AND ROYAL Street was vibrating with just as much excitement as it had during the Art and Wine Stroll. She breezed past Temperley's Antiques and the Rosebud Gallery and, in less than the distance from the fifty-yard line to the goal post in the Superdome, was suddenly standing in front of a window filled with everything from pie plates to chef's toques. The name *Hawking's Restaurant Supply* was painted across the window in a scroll of yellow letters nearly a foot high. Carmela chuckled to herself. She'd hurried down this block a thousand times and never noticed this shop. Well . . . duh for her.

Pushing open the door was like entering a veritable chef's paradise. Floor-to-ceiling stainless steel racks were stacked with fry pans and stockpots, many of them large enough to cook Christmas dinner for a small army. Carmela also saw pans for baking sheet cakes, drawer warmers, proofing ovens, and banquet carts, as well as tables stacked high with round, square, and oblong-shaped plates and bowls. Restaurant dinnerware, she supposed.

As Carmela wandered through the shop, she spotted an intriguing display of kitchen hand tools—ladles, graters, wire whips, scoops, and wooden spoons. She picked up a long-handled whip and was beating eggs for an imaginary soufflé when a voice behind her said, "That one's a beauty. At twenty-four inches, the nylon handle is long and lean. And you'll notice that the bulbous cage has plenty of spokes to whip any food you want into a delicious frenzy."

The salesclerk, a middle-aged man with a gray goatee, was wearing a full-length white chef's apron with the name *Ned* embroidered over a top pocket.

"We also have it in sixteen- and eighteen-inch handles if that one is a might long for you," Ned said. "Depends on how deep your mixing bowls are, of course." He stopped his pitch and cocked an appraising eye at her. "You using another kind of whisk or just learning how?"

"I can handle a whisk," Carmela said. "But I think maybe the sixteen-inch would be better." She put the longer one back as the clerk reached under the table and pulled out a box.

"Here you go. A sixteen-inch Jacob's Pride by Vollrath. Guaranteed for a lifetime."

"I'm familiar with the brand. Do you carry their cookware, too?"

"Sure do," Ned said. "You want to take a look?"

"Not today, I'm afraid. What I am interested in are kitchen knives and serving forks."

"You want a complete set?"

"Maybe."

"Well, you've come to the right place. We have the largest selection of cutlery in Louisiana." Ned crooked a finger. "Come along with me." He led her to a large display case near the rear of the store and made a sweeping gesture.

Carmela stepped forward and eyed the gleaming cutlery. The first thing that struck her was how long and dangerous-looking the forks were. She'd never thought of a carving fork as being deadly before, but now, after seeing Martin Lash impaled, that notion seemed to be firmly implanted in her brain.

"These are all carving forks?" she asked.

"Carving forks, cook's forks, and what we call pot forks," Ned said.

Carmela pointed to a dangerous-looking fork with long, curved tines. "What kind is that?"

"That's made by Victorinox," Ned said. "Extremely popular. We also carry lines from Mercer and Dexter-Russell."

"I was wondering . . . do you carry the Bocker brand?"

The clerk moved a few feet down the display case and Carmela followed.

"Right here." He waved his hand over a set that included

a carving fork as well as a large knife. "These are stainless steel with rosewood handles. Very durable. Very reliable."

Carmela reached a hand toward the carving fork. "May I?"

Ned handed the fork to her.

Carmela gripped the fork's handle and balanced it in her hand. It had a serious weight and heft to it, almost like a good dueling sword or rapier.

Ned gave an approving smile. "Feels comfortable, huh?"

"Very nice." Carmela thought the gleaming tines looked razor-sharp. As if they could pierce a piece of flesh with ease. She handed the fork back to him. "Do you sell a lot of these? Forks, I mean."

"They're some of our best sellers. With more than fourteen hundred restaurants in New Orleans, we help outfit a lot of chefs."

"And many of them prefer the Bocker brand?" Carmela asked.

"Yeah, even the sous chefs seem to like them." Ned smiled. "We get a lot of younger guys and gals who are apprenticing or working as sous chefs, dreaming of the day when they can open their own restaurant. So they're hot to get their own tools."

"I can just imagine," Carmela said. But her mind was elsewhere. Back to a dark night with a stumbling man . . .

"You know, you're the second person in here this week to ask about these forks."

Carmela was instantly jerked back to the here and now. "Who else asked?"

Ned scrunched up his face. "A police detective by the name of Gallant. He was quite interested because . . ." Looking uncomfortable now, he let his voice trail off. "Well, because . . ."

"Because of the murder," Carmela said. "At the Winter Market."

"You know about that?" Ned shook his head. "Hell of a strange thing."

"Tell me about it," Carmela said. "I was there."

JUST AS CARMELA APPROACHED THE FRONT door of her apartment, she did a quick about-face. She crossed the courtyard and slipped in the back door of Juju Voodoo. She hadn't talked to Ava all day, so her friend had no idea of the horrible murder that had taken place in Boothville the previous night. Time to clue her in.

Ava was standing behind the counter, busily arranging red and blue moon goddess pendants and earrings. She looked vaguely Christmasy in her bright red plastic bustier paired with a dark green leather skirt. Her four-inch stiletto sandals had white furry pom-poms on the toes.

"Are those pom-poms on your toes or did you just mug a bunny rabbit?" Carmela asked.

Ava looked up and dimpled prettily. "Be careful. You might just find a pair of these tucked under your Christmas tree."

"Be still my heart."

"Speaking of which, what's the latest on your love life? Still two-timing Messieurs Babcock and Brevard?" Ava fluttered a hand to her chest. "And I say that with the utmost respect, no judgment intended."

"Things have taken a slightly wacky turn," Carmela said.

Ava's eyes twinkled. "What? In your life? Nooo."

Carmela drew a deep breath and proceeded to give Ava a blow-by-blow description of what took place the previous night. The dead guy, the blood and gore, the slow-talking cop, and, finally, Babcock swooping in for the coup de grâce rescue with a modicum of screaming and scolding on the side. When she'd finally finished her tale of woe, Ava's eyes were bugged out and her mouth hung open.

"Wha . . . so somebody whacked your real estate guy?" Ava squeaked. "Seriously?"

"Either that or it was a very elaborate hoax and the joke's on me."

Ava sped around the counter, swept Carmela into her arms, and gave her a big, squeezy hug. "Doggone it, I knew I shouldn't have let you go down there all by yourself!"

"I wasn't exactly alone. A crazed killer put in an appearance just before I got there."

Ava gave a final squeeze and then gawked at her. "So who do you think did it? I mean, why was this Trueblood guy stabbed?"

"I don't know. There must be some connection to Martin Lash that we don't know about . . ."

"Besides the defunct lawsuit," Ava said.

"Besides that. Or maybe Babcock's theory is correct after all. He thinks Trueblood might have been embroiled in a horrible dispute with one of his contractors and things turned ugly."

Ava put up a hand and twirled a twisty gold earring. "It all sounds very weird."

"Tell me about it."

"And Babcock was furious with you for going down there? He completely exploded?"

"About a seven-point-nine on the Richter scale."

"So what's *your* theory about this second murder?" Ava asked. "You're the one who's a regular little Nancy Drew."

Carmela held up both hands, then dropped them to her sides. "I don't know. I've turned it over in my head a million times and I still can't figure it."

"The connection I see is that Martin Lash lived down near the bayou and Trueblood was building townhomes there."

"Isn't that what a clever lawyer would call *circumstantial evidence*?" Carmela asked.

Ava shrugged. "I don't know. I'm not very legal. Legal-minded, anyway."

Carmela held up an index finger. "There is one other thing that links them."

"What's that?"

"They were both murdered with Bocker cutlery."

Ava eyed Carmela carefully. "So you're saying maybe a chef did it? You think it was that Fat Lorenzo's guy? What was his name again?"

"Allan Hurst."

"Or what about that woman at the tea party who dresses like a cover girl for *Muscle Magazine*? The one who's connected to the food website?"

"Helen McBride."

"Could the killer have been either one of those two characters?" Ava asked.

Carmela shrugged. "I don't know. Both of them hated Lash with a vengeance, but I can't imagine that either of them was remotely acquainted with Trueblood. So your guess is as good as mine."

Ava frowned. "I don't have a guess."

"Well, there you go. It looks like we're still up a creek without a paddle."

Chapter 23

CARMELA walked back across the flagstone courtyard toward the appealing solitude of her apartment. She figured she had just enough time to flake out and take a nap before she had to get dressed up and walk the dogs down to Jackson Square. After she handed them off to Shamus she'd hopefully meet up with Babcock and they'd . . .

She stopped short when the leaves on her banana palm began to tremble and shake.

"Who's there?" Carmela called out. What she was really thinking was, *What now?*

The palm shook again as Quigg Brevard stepped out of the lengthening shadows.

"This is getting to be a bad habit of yours," Carmela said. She decided she was also honor bound to discourage it.

Quigg grabbed her by both arms. "I had to see you, Carmela. I know you've been avoiding me and, believe me, it's been torture. May I come in?" He threw a hopeful glance at her front door. "Just for a few minutes so we can talk? We need to catch up."

Visions of Babcock danced in Carmela's head. He definitely wouldn't approve of her spending any time with Quigg, much less any time alone with him in her apartment. Still, Quigg had materialized of his own accord and they did have a few things to talk about. Trent Trueblood being one.

"Well?" Quigg said.

Carmela made a hasty decision. She knew that Babcock was busy at work, defending the city from evildoers, so he probably wouldn't show up unexpectedly. Thus, she was safe. For now.

"Okay," she said, unlocking the door. "But just for a couple of minutes. I have to deliver my dogs to my ex and then I've got a date."

"My, my, such a full social schedule," Quigg said.

Carmela turned around and said, "Be nice." Then she pushed open the door. As she knew they would, Boo and Poobah flung themselves at her, kissing, licking, dancing, and whining. When they suddenly noticed Quigg standing behind her, they stopped and gave him a chilly look. A look that clearly said, *Who dat?*

"It's okay, babies," Carmela said. "He's just a friend."

"*Just* a friend?" Quigg said as he walked into her apartment and looked around. "Mmn." He spun in a half circle. "Nice. Cozy."

Carmela gestured toward the dining room and pointed at a cane-backed chair. "Why don't you have a seat over there while I take care of these two rascals."

Quigg ignored her direction and plopped himself down on

the leather sofa in the living room, acting as if he owned the place. "You've fixed the place up since I was here last," he said. "Upgraded the furniture and bought some nice artwork."

"Hard to resist with all the galleries around here," Carmela said. "And the settlement from the divorce helped, too." She poured food into the dogs' bowls and gave them pans of fresh water.

"Where do you keep your wine? Oh, never mind, I see the wine rack." Quigg stood up, stretched languidly, and moved into the dining room. His fingers moved across the wine rack, almost judgmentally, until he finally found a bottle he approved of. "This looks like a decent rosé." He walked into the kitchen. "Have you ever tried Domaine Chandon Étoile Rosé? It's California grown, but it could easily pass for Italian. Corkscrew?"

Carmela pulled open a drawer and passed him a corkscrew. She flattened herself against the refrigerator, feeling stressed. Feeling uncomfortable that the two of them were smooshed so close together in her tiny kitchen.

"Why don't you take the wine into the dining room?" Carmela said. "I'll bring in the glasses." She ushered Quigg out of the kitchen and grabbed a silver tray. She placed coasters, cocktail napkins, and two wineglasses on the tray and carried it into the living room.

Quigg had put the opened bottle of wine on the coffee table and was once again sprawled on the sofa, legs crossed and an arm stretched across the sofa back as if waiting for Carmela to snuggle in.

Carmela placed the tray on the coffee table and sat down primly in a small leather club chair that was conveniently out of Quigg's reach.

Quigg picked up the bottle and poured them each a glass of wine. As he passed one of the glasses to Carmela he said, "I called you earlier today. Not only did you avoid taking my call, you didn't bother calling me back."

Carmela wasn't about to take criticism, not after all she'd been through on his behalf. "Quigg, did it ever occur to you that I have a personal life as well as a business to run? I can't always be at your beck and call."

"You don't want to be my beck-and-call girl?"

"Quigg!"

"Sorry, sorry." He held up a hand, chuckling. "Bad joke. You know that I appreciate everything you've done for me."

Carmela continued to glower at him.

"I do, I really do."

"Glad to hear it," Carmela said. "And please chew on this. In case you haven't already heard, last night I went down to Boothville to meet with Trent Trueblood."

"The real estate guy, yeah. You said you were gonna check him out."

"That's right. Only when I got there, Trueblood was dead. Somebody had stuck him with a butcher knife and he bled out on the floor of his shiny new sales office."

Stunned by her words, Quigg rose up from his seat and leaned toward Carmela, but she put up a hand to ward him off.

"No, Quigg, sit down and let me finish."

Carmela filled him in about calling the local sheriff, then making the decision that she pretty much had to call Babcock. Quigg whistled and rolled his eyes at that part.

"As you might have guessed," Carmela said, "Babcock's coming down there precipitated a horrible fight between the two of us. Which ended with him telling me to unconditionally back off on any kind of investigation."

Quigg moved his wineglass around, making little wet circles on her coffee table. "I suppose you can't blame him for being worried. I mean . . . a second murder?" Her words finally seemed to be sinking in. "My Lord, Carmela, *you* could have been the one who was killed!"

"I know that."

They sat in silence for a while, sipping their wine.

Finally, when Quigg thought an appropriate amount of time had passed, he gave her a puppy dog look. "Carmela, what about me?"

She shot him a hard look. "What about you?"

"You've been an incredible help so far in clearing my name and narrowing down some potential suspects. Why, if it wasn't for you, I'd probably be sitting in jail by now."

"Don't flatter yourself, Quigg. They're not nearly ready to drag you to the slammer."

"No, I'm serious!"

"Quigg, are you listening to me? I don't see what more I can do . . ."

"You can keep on digging, that's what you can do," Quigg urged. "You must be incredibly close to finding the murderer." He was getting agitated now. "I mean . . . you scheduled a meeting with Trueblood and then . . . wham! Somebody goes and kills him. That's just amazing—you have to be on the right track!"

"More like being on the right track to becoming the next victim!" Carmela yelped. She said it so loudly that both dogs bounded over to make sure she was okay. "Would that suit you, Quigg? If they found the killer standing over my body and a meat fork dripping with blood, would you finally feel exonerated?"

Boo and Poobah cast stern doggy looks at Quigg.

"Carmela, you know I didn't mean to imply anything of the sort. Heck, your safety is *everything* to me," Quigg said hastily. "It would shatter me if something happened to you."

Now the dogs glanced back at Carmela as if the ball was in her court.

"Oh jeez," Carmela said. Where *was* this conversation going?

Quigg leaned forward and said, in a hushed whisper, "And what about our personal relationship? Did our kiss the other night mean nothing to you? Carmela, I have feelings for you. Genuine feelings."

This was the moment Carmela had been dreading, the moment she hoped would never come. But here it was, sitting in front of her like a giant meatball plopped on top of a plate of spaghetti.

"Quigg," she said, picking her words carefully, "you are a dear friend. I will always hold you special in my heart, but I am truly in love with Babcock."

Quigg waved a hand as if completely dismissing her words along with her feelings for Babcock. "Carmela, I know you believe you and Babcock are meant for each other, but I know that isn't true. You won't be with him forever. So until then, my dear, I'm prepared to wait." He flashed her a triumphant look. "For as long as it takes. Because I know my day will come."

Carmela reached over and patted his hand. "I don't think so."

Quigg smiled confidently. "Oh, but I do. Which is why I know you're going to keep helping me."

"Quigg, I don't dare."

"I know you're not going to abandon me. Even if your investigation has to be incredibly covert." Quigg picked up his wine, drained his glass, and stood up. "So thank you, my dear. Thank you for still believing in me. For still going out of your way to help me."

"Don't thank me, Quigg. It's not like that." Carmela stood up.

Quigg took two steps toward her. "How would you like to be thanked, Carmela? Do you want me to kiss you again?"

"No!"

Watching them eagerly now, Boo and Poobah both wagged their tails.

"Stop that!" Carmela told the dogs. "Don't you dare give him an ounce of encouragement."

"Smart dogs," Quigg grinned. And with that he strode out of her apartment.

Chapter 24

IT was seven fifteen at night and dark as the inside of a tomb. As the days got shorter and shorter, Carmela felt like her life was getting more and more complicated. She pondered this as she walked Boo and Poobah through her courtyard and out onto the sidewalk. Actually, she decided, it was more of an HR issue, a personnel problem. The personnel consisting of two dead guys, Detective Babcock, and the I-won't-take-no-for-an-answer Quigg Brevard.

Well, the dead guys hadn't come back to haunt her dreams, but Quigg certainly had. And every time she had a conversation with Babcock, straight up, romantic or contentious, Quigg's specter lurked in the background like Casper the Friendly Ghost. And after tonight, his presence would probably lurk in her apartment.

How to exorcise Quigg's presence? Holy water? Prayers? Garlic and a silver bullet?

Gabby would advise her to politely turn her back on Quigg. Ava would tell her to have fun, kick back, live life to the absolute max, and string both men along.

So what was the answer? Where was the balance?

Well, Carmela *had* made a promise to Quigg early on and she didn't like to renege on a promise. It was one of the things she held true to. And she was definitely in love with Babcock, even though he'd been acting like Mr. Grumpy Pants for the last couple of days. Still, there was no way she was going to two-time him. That simply wasn't in her nature, either.

No, she was just going to have to see this thing through to the bitter end. Whatever that entailed.

Carmela had been walking at a fairly good clip, pulled along by the dogs. But now they stopped to carefully sniff and inspect a candy wrapper that lay curled in the gutter. Which made her glance around and realize how quiet the neighborhood was at this hour.

In this slightly more residential part of the French Quarter, there weren't a lot of bars and restaurants. Which was wonderful if you wanted a quaint neighborhood that wouldn't be disturbed by late-night bar-goers and partiers, but bad if you were the nervous type out for a walk. There were lots of pickpockets and thugs hanging out in New Orleans. Lots of crime. Of course, she had the dogs along. And once Shamus met her and picked them up, she'd be with Babcock. Which was always a comforting thought.

Carmela's nervousness waned as soon as they reached the edge of Jackson Square. She knew she'd be perfectly safe mingling with the crowds in such a lively place. As far back as the founding of New Orleans, this block, once known as the Place

d'Armes, had been the city's public square. After the famous
Battle of New Orleans, it had been renamed Jackson Square
in honor of General Andrew Jackson. Of course, a statue of
the heroic general, sitting tall on his horse and waving his hat
in greeting, stood at the very center of it all.

And Shamus had been right about one thing: Jackson
Square was filled with people. Tourists posing for selfies
with the general, jugglers in colorful costumes, palm readers trying to make a buck, artists showcasing their drawings, and dozens of lively street musicians. In stark contrast
was St. Louis Cathedral, an imposing edifice with three
towering spires just across Chartres Street. People would be
gathering here soon in anticipation of the concert. She would
be meeting Babcock here, providing he showed up.

Boo tugged at her leash, sniffing at the empty saxophone
case of one of the street musicians.

"Boo, come on, baby," Carmela said. They quickly crossed
Chartres, skirted left, and headed down Pirate's Alley. The
music and craziness faded immediately as they turned into
the Place de Henriette Delille, the small, secluded garden
that was tucked behind the cathedral.

The hedges surrounding the garden were tall and bushy
and seemed to close in on her right away. And while the foliage made for a lovely contemplative garden, the place suddenly felt dark and cut off from the rest of the world. Boo
and Poobah didn't seem to mind. They strained and danced
on their leashes, anxious to explore the overgrowth of bushes
and shrubs.

Okay, a few sniffs and that's it.

Carmela led the dogs over to a small stone bench and sat
down. Looked around and shivered. It felt a little too dark and
lonely here. She probably should have been more insistent

about meeting Shamus in the safer, more populated Jackson Square.

Oh well, he'll pop in here any minute now.

Boo looked up at Carmela and put her chubby muzzle in Carmela's lap. Poobah shook his head and gave a lopsided grin. One of his eyes caught a shaft of light and gleamed eerily.

"Daddy's going to be here real soon," Carmela told them. "And I want you both to be on your best behavior this weekend." Boo wagged her tail. "But if Daddy has any strange young women staying at his condo, it's more than okay to gnaw on their shoes. Or whatever else they leave lying around. Daddy may get cranky, but I'll give you extra treats."

Poobah's ears perked up at the word *treats* and Carmela said, "Good boy. You know what I'm talking about, don't you?" She dug in her purse and pulled out a small liver treat for each of them.

As the dogs chewed happily, Carmela glanced at her phone. Seven forty.

Really, Shamus, this is getting ridiculous.

Here she was, sitting all by her lonesome in a deserted garden. If it weren't for the dogs she would feel . . .

There was a rustle up near the gate.

"Shamus," Carmela called out. "Is that you?" She knew her voice sounded a little shaky.

Nobody answered.

Feeling spooked, Carmela stood up and gathered the leashes tighter. If something went really wrong and she had to run, she wanted the dogs running with her.

There was another sound, this one more muffled. Like leaves rustling, somebody pushing through the hedge?

Oh crap. This feels so bad.

"Shamus?" she called again.

Carmela was just about ready to get the hell out of there when Shamus suddenly lurched from the shadows. His hair stuck up crazily and his tie was askew. A sprig of evergreen was stuck to the lapel of his navy blue jacket.

Carmela turned on him with a vengeance. "You scared the crap out of me, Shamus Meechum! Where have you been? I've been sitting here in the dark, waiting forever!"

Shamus held up a hand as if to fend her off. "Chill, babe. I'm here now."

She peered at him carefully. "You look a little dopey. Did you get mugged or something? Wait a minute, have you been *drinking?*"

"What if I have?" Shamus managed a crooked grin and stood up a little straighter.

"Then I'd have to say you're an unfit pet parent. That you shouldn't be trusted with Boo and Poobah." She looked at the dogs. "Right?" Boo wagged her tail as if in agreement.

"Come on, Carmela, you know better than that. I had one lousy drink. An after-work cocktail. That's it."

"Just one?"

"Just one."

"Then please promise me that you'll take the dogs right home? That you won't stop at some stupid club or cocktail lounge and make them wait in the car?"

"I wouldn't do that," Shamus said. "It breaks my heart to think of their little noses pressed against the car window, waiting for me."

"Then promise me, okay?"

"Cross my heart, I'll take them right home."

Shamus held out his hand for the leashes and Carmela reluctantly handed them over. She bent down and gave both dogs a kiss on the nose before she watched Shamus lead them away.

* * *

STILL FEELING JITTERY, CARMELA WALKED BACK down Pirate's Alley, turned left, and took up a spot in front of the cathedral. She stood just to the left of the massive front door, waiting for Babcock. It was getting close to the start of the concert now and people were chattering excitedly as they hurried inside.

Glancing into the crowd, Carmela was surprised to see Allan Hurst, the owner of Fat Lorenzo's, go by. And then, strangely enough, she spotted Josh Cotton. He was in the middle of a group of people that passed by almost on the heels of Allan Hurst.

Talk about a weird coincidence. Or was it some kind of omen?

Both men had looked so carefree that it made her wonder if either of them could have been down in Boothville last night, taking care of some nasty business.

Josh Cotton certainly had a strong connection to Trueblood, because the developer had been planning to build homes near one of the bayous. But she couldn't imagine how Hurst would be connected to Trueblood. Although, if you looked at the killings of Lash and Trueblood as murder mysteries—and they certainly were—a possible connection might just be another aspect.

As the crowd of concertgoers slowed from a flood to a trickle, there was still no sign of Babcock. Finally, Carmela was standing all alone on the cathedral steps as the ushers leaned out to close the stately, wooden doors.

What to do?

At the last possible moment, Carmela slipped inside. She stood in back in the semidarkness, next to a white marble statue of a winged angel, and put in yet another call to Babcock's cell phone. Of course, he didn't pick up.

Luckily, the concert was open seating and there were several vacant seats left at the rear of the church. Feeling scattered and alone, Carmela took a seat in the very last pew.

Babcock, Babcock, where are you?

Carmela was worried, but tried hard to ease her mind by taking in the magnificent surroundings. The soaring Gothic arches seemed to extend all the way to heaven, while flickering candles cast shadows on the benevolent faces of saint statues that graced every alcove. On the altar, dozens of tall, white candles were set amongst giant baskets overflowing with red roses. The cathedral looked elegant, moody, and contemplative.

Minutes later, the altar lights came up and a chorale group, all wearing white cassocks over their red robes, came marching down the center aisle. They climbed the altar steps and arranged themselves in three rows. In the audience, throats cleared, pews creaked, and programs rustled. Then the chorale director, a tall man in an all-red robe, walked out and raised his baton.

Voices suddenly soared like angels as they broke into a rousing rendition of "The Holly and the Ivy."

Carmela listened, enjoying the lively tune, then slipped her phone out of her purse and checked the time. Five minutes after eight. And there were still no texts or messages.

She half listened to the choir but was becoming more and more concerned about Babcock. It wasn't like him to leave her in the lurch, even if he was still annoyed by her behavior.

When the chorale group moved on to "Afternoon on a Hill," a song based on a poem by Edna St. Vincent Millay, Carmela was in a complete tizzy. Where could he be? More important, why didn't he answer his phone? Impulsively, she got up and stepped to the back of the church. Should she try calling him again? No, it wouldn't be right. Not with the choir singing their hearts out and the audience listening with rapt attention.

She hurried out a side door and huddled against the building in the rapidly chilling air. She dialed Babcock again but there was still no answer. That earned him a clipped voice mail: "I'm at the cathedral concert. Did you forget about me?" She clutched the phone for a couple of minutes, waiting, and hoping that Babcock would receive her message and call right back. But no such luck.

Either Babcock wasn't getting her messages or, worse, he was ignoring them. It was easier to believe that his phone was dead or that maybe he'd left it in his car. Carmela slid the phone back into her purse and glanced across the street, hoping to see him, bent over, long legs pumping, hurrying toward her. But nobody was in sight and the street was deadly quiet. Even the musicians and performers way over in Jackson Square seemed to be on break.

Now doubt crept into her mind. Had she given Babcock the correct time and place? Was it possible that, in all the excitement, she might have screwed up and told Babcock to meet her in the back garden where she'd arranged to meet Shamus? Could she have gotten her locations mixed up? Oh dear, it was definitely possible.

Carmela decided she'd better run back there and check. It would be awful if Babcock was standing in the dark in the Place de Henriette Delille waiting for her!

She scooted down Pirate's Alley once again and slipped into the small garden. The place seemed even darker than it had before, mournful and completely lost in shadows. And it was certainly lonelier without the company of her two dogs.

"Babcock?" Carmela called out. "Edgar? Are you here?"

The wind had picked up and was hissing through the trees as the white statue of Christ glowed eerily in the dark.

Carmela crept back toward the stone bench where she'd been sitting earlier and sat down to wait. Now she could just barely hear the faint tones of the choir. They had switched to something madrigal, but their voices sounded far away.

She fidgeted, crossing her arms and then uncrossing them. Doing the same with her legs. Her nervousness continued to build. Leaves swirled, tree branches rattled like dry bones, and then the wind slowly died down.

The silence was suddenly broken by what sounded like a footfall shuffling over cement. Was someone walking across one of the graves out in back? She looked around nervously. Why couldn't she see anyone? Carmela shivered and pulled her shawl tightly around her shoulders.

"Babcock," she called out again, trying to sound confident.

There was dead silence.

Now the wind came up again, gusting and practically drowning out the chorale group. Beneath it all, Carmela could swear footsteps were drawing ever closer to her, snapping twigs, scraping hard against cement.

Carmela stood up just as the tiny hairs on the back of her neck rose, too.

What am I doing here? This is crazy.

Her heart fluttered; a bad premonition began jackhammering at her brain. What if Josh Cotton or Allan Hurst had followed her out the side door? What if one of them was the killer and knew full well that she was investigating? What if one of them was lurking here in the garden with her right now? If they'd killed twice, they wouldn't hesitate to kill a third time!

I've got to get out of here!

Carmela took off as if a starter's gun had just been fired. She dashed through the little garden, spun through the narrow gate, and hit Pirate's Alley at a dead run. Clattering along the cobblestones, running as fast as her silver high heels could carry her, she was positive she could hear footsteps coming after her!

Should she stop? Should she look back? No. If it was Babcock who was behind her, he would have called out to her by now.

She pounded down Pirate's Alley in a full-out, gasping-for-her-next-breath sprint, trying to get away from whatever madman was chasing her.

Carmela spun around the corner of the cathedral, trying to hold a tight line and suddenly ran—wham!—right into someone's arms. She shrieked, backpedaled like mad, and tried to push the man away.

But the man had wrapped his arms around her and was holding her tight.

"Please!" she struggled, pleading with him. "Let me go!"

"Carmela, honey," came a calming voice. "It's me."

"What?" She forced herself to focus, to stop shaking her head and actually *look* at the man. Holy Hannah, it was Babcock! "It's you!" she cried out, close to tears now.

Babcock pulled her closer. "Carmela, calm down. What happened? What were you doing back there? Why were you running down the alley like that?"

Carmela nestled against him, still shaking and barely able to force out a whisper. "I went back there looking for you. And then someone . . . somebody came after me. They were chasing me."

Babcock drew back, alarmed. "Chasing you just now?"

Carmela bobbed her head.

"Wait here!" Babcock practically lifted her out of the way and stuck her in the doorway of the church. Then he pulled out his Glock and, with barely a hint of hesitation, sprinted down the alley.

As she waited, Carmela was not the least bit comforted by the voices of the chorale group that filtered out of the cathedral. All she wanted to hear was Babcock cornering someone in the garden, yelling at them to kneel down and put their hands on their head, and then calling for backup.

No such thing happened.

A few minutes later, he came walking around the corner and emerged into the faint yellow glow of a streetlamp. "There wasn't anybody there," he told her. He looked a little puzzled.

"Are you positive?"

"I did a sweep of the park, checked the perimeter."

Her was giving her cop lingo now, but Carmela wanted more. She wanted answers.

"I wouldn't have even been back there if you'd met me like you promised," she said in an accusing tone. She felt scared and heartsick. She feared he didn't believe her. Or maybe that he didn't want to be with her anymore.

"The deputy chief called an emergency meeting just as I was about to leave," Babcock explained. He gazed at her in what appeared to be complete earnestness. "I could hardly say no."

"You could have at least texted me."

"You're right. I should have done that and I didn't." He lifted his hands and then dropped them. "I'm very sorry. I screwed up."

Carmela gazed at Babcock. He really did look sorry.

"The meeting was about the Martin Lash case?" she asked.

"Yes. Of course."

"Anything new?"

"Short of holding a séance, I don't know how we're going to figure this out." Babcock stepped closer to her and gave her a gentle squeeze. "Do you want to go inside and catch the rest of the concert?" His lips nuzzled the top of her head.

Carmela shook her head. "No. I've kind of lost my taste for it. Please, could you just take me home?"

"You're still mad."

"No, I'm not." Yes, she was. She was mad at herself for being so twitchy, mad at him for being late.

Babcock walked her to his car, held the door open, and waited until she was settled. Their drive home was very quiet until they pulled up outside her apartment.

She felt his gaze in the dark.

"May I come in?"

Carmela wanted him to, she really did. But something inside her prompted her to say, "Probably not tonight."

"If that's how you feel, okay. And please believe me, I really am sorry."

"I know that." Carmela reached into her purse to grab her keys and caught sight of the little voodoo doll she'd stuffed down inside. The one she'd pulled the pin out of. She looked at him and said, "How's your shoulder?"

"Funny thing about that," Babcock said. "The pain went away."

Chapter 25

WHEN Carmela answered her doorbell the next morning, she found Ava standing there hugging a bulging red tote bag that was decorated with rhinestone skulls.

"Not to worry, *cher*," Ava sang out. "I brought all the supplies we need." She pawed around inside her tote and pulled out a chilled bottle of Bollinger Brut. "When you called to invite me to your impromptu little brunch, I dug around in my fridge and it was either this or a two-week-old head of iceberg lettuce."

"The champagne should do the trick," Carmela said. "Get in here, you."

Ava scooted inside and, with one swift kick with her leather bootie, shut the door behind her. "I figured we could add a dash of orange juice and a smash of Grand Marnier and—boom—we've got ourselves the perfect Grand Mimosa."

"Sounds like a plan," Carmela called from the kitchen, where she'd gone back to her chopping and stirring.

Ava peeled off her tiger-striped sweater coat and used both hands to straighten her leopard-print bustier. Then she smoothed her painted-on denim jeggings and looked around. "Seems strange not having Boo and Poobah around. They add so much . . . um . . ."

"Frenzy?"

"Well, they are active little buggers, that's for sure. So Shamus has them for the whole weekend?" Ava sauntered over to watch Carmela in the kitchen.

Carmela nodded. "The one thing, the only thing, I regret about my divorce is that Shamus gets time with the fur babies. Oh well, too late to screw him over now. You want to fix the mimosas while I whip up some eggs française?"

"*Cher*, just hearing the words *eggs française* puts me into sheer ecstasy."

"You must be awfully hungry, because they're really only fancy French scrambled eggs."

Ava clutched her chest. "Ooh, don't burst my bubble."

Carmela grabbed two champagne flutes from the cupboard and handed them to Ava. "Drinks, please."

"Gotcha." Ava grasped the bottle of champagne and eased out the cork. It gave a nice satisfying pop. "You know I'm always ready to party, but I was plenty surprised when I got your call this morning. That you decided not to go in to work."

Carmela cracked eggs into a blue-and-white-speckled bowl. "It's Saturday and I just needed a day. Besides, when I phoned Gabby and told her I wouldn't be in, she said she could manage just fine. We didn't have any classes scheduled, so . . . I think she was happy to run solo."

"Well, two can play the hooky game." Ava pulled her cell

phone out of her bustier and tapped at the keyboard furiously. "*Hola*, Miguel. *Sí.* I'm fine, really. But I'm having breakfast over at Carmela's and then I've got a ton of pressing errands to run." She gave Carmela a slow wink. "So if you can manage Juju Voodoo on your own . . . oh, you can? It's not a problem? Well, okeydokey. Call me if something pressing comes up."

"So . . . you're cool?" Carmela asked.

Ava poured out a long draft of champagne. "We have a long day of freedom stretching ahead of us. And to help kick it off, a nice bottle of champagne."

"OJ's in the fridge," Carmela said.

"I'm getting to that." Ava poured champagne into the second glass, grabbed the orange juice, and added a couple of judicious splashes. Then she gave both drinks a quick stir and topped them both with Grand Marnier.

"Looking good," Carmela said. "And I could use a fortifying sip before I start the eggs."

"Then drink up." Ava handed her a Grand Mimosa.

Carmela sipped her drink. "Delicious."

"I give good mimosa." Ava took a long sip of her drink and said, rather cryptically, "I have something to tell you."

"Me, too," Carmela said. "But you go first."

Ava let out her words in one enormous whoosh: "Roman Numeral asked me to house-sit for his parents while they're away on vacation."

"Okay," Carmela said cautiously. "You're referring to their ginormous Garden District house?"

"Yup."

"And where, pray tell, will your dear Harrison be during this time? Cozying up alongside you in the ginormous Garden District house?"

Ava's brows pinched together. "I'm afraid he's got different plans. He's traveling with his parents to Majorca."

"What!" Carmela stared at Ava. "And he didn't ask you to go along?"

Ava shook her head. "Disappointing, no?"

"Disappointing, yes. So while you're blowing out the steam pipes and checking the furnace, Harrison will be having a grand old time . . . strolling the beaches of the Mediterranean, enjoying the local dives, the amusing house vino . . ."

"And the local women," Ava spat out.

"Hey, no relationship is perfect. Look at me and Babcock."

"Are you kidding? You two are crazy perfect."

"Oh, honey. Wait until you hear my story."

"Yeah?"

"Give me two minutes to whip up these eggs."

"Go for it," Ava said.

Carmela whipped her eggs with her new wire whisk, slid them into her fry pan along with fresh chopped chives and scallions, and pulled a pan of cranberry muffins out of the oven. A few more whisks of the eggs and, five minutes later, she and Ava were sitting at the table together.

They lifted their glasses and clinked them together.

"Here's to playing hooky," Ava said. "Now would you please tell me *why* we're playing hooky?"

"It's a long, complicated story."

"We've got all day."

"Some jackhole terrorized and chased me last night."

"What!"

So Carmela had to tell Ava all about handing over the dogs to Shamus, waiting for Babcock outside the cathedral, then going back to the Place de Henriette Delille because she thought maybe she'd given Babcock the wrong instructions. And then she told her all about getting chased.

"And you think you got chased by a real-life bogeyman?"

"I think so, yes."

"But you didn't see who it was?" Ava asked.

"I was too terrified to turn around. But I gotta tell you, I saw Allan Hurst, the Fat Lorenzo's guy, and Josh Cotton, from the Environmental Justice League, go into that cathedral right before the concert started. So I kind of think it might have been one of them."

Ava picked up the bottle of champagne and poured them each a straight shot. No OJ to dilute it this time. "Do you think one of them followed you out? I mean, when you left to call Babcock."

"I don't know. Neither of them seemed to notice me, but that could have been a charade. So, yeah, I guess either one could have followed me."

"Poor baby. And you didn't have any kind of weapon on you?"

"For some strange reason, I left my Uzi at home in my sock drawer. But you're right, I should have been carrying something. A can of mace, a hatpin even. I didn't even have a big clunky purse."

"With a hatpin," Ava said, "you have to stick it right square in the jerk's eye."

"I think I'd stick it somewhere else."

Ava let loose a high-pitched giggle and said, "These eggs are real good."

"Aren't they?"

"What's your secret?" Ava asked.

"Heavy cream, some butter, and lots of whisking."

"So lots of fat and a nimble wrist."

"You could say that, yes."

"Are there more of those muffins? To add to my muffin top?"

"Of course." Carmela grabbed two cranberry muffins from the kitchen and carried them to the table. "You know. Everybody that's a suspect—Josh Cotton, Allan Hurst, Helen McBride—they're all well aware that I've been investigating."

Ava finished buttering her muffin and looked up. "Okay."

"I know this is going to sound weird, but maybe Trueblood's murder was just collateral damage. Maybe somebody figured out that I was driving down to the Parson's Point sales office and Trueblood just happened to show up first. Maybe he came stumbling in, the place was dark, and they figured it was me."

Ava looked alarmed. "*Cher*, that's awful. To think that *you* were the intended victim?"

"I know it's awful."

"Do you think that possibility has crossed Babcock's mind?"

Carmela thought for a few moments. "No, I don't think so." She aimed her fork at Ava. "And don't you tell him."

"Even if it means saving your life?"

"Please don't put it that way."

Ava speared a bite of egg and said, "You know something."

"What do I know?" Carmela asked. "What are you talking about?"

"That's the thing. I don't know what you know. But *somebody* thinks you know more than you do. That's the reason somebody chased after you last night."

"I'm not sure I follow your logic," Carmela said.

"Because it isn't logical," Ava said.

"Wait a minute. Now I'm really getting confused."

Ava agreed. "It's a confusing issue."

Carmela thought for a few minutes. "All I really know is . . . there's something weird going on down in the bayous south of here. First Martin Lash is murdered—maybe because of his environmental organization, which was very involved in protecting that area. And then Trent Trueblood—who was trying to build townhomes in that exact same area—gets killed."

"So you think the two killings are related?" Ava asked.

"I don't know. I still don't see the how or the why. But I don't think either of those men was killed for the reason Babcock thinks they were."

"Explain, please," Ava said, looking intrigued.

"Babcock is becoming more and more convinced that Lash was murdered in retaliation for a poison-pen restaurant review that he wrote."

"But you don't think so."

"I *thought* that was the reason at first, but now it doesn't feel right to me," Carmela said. "And I don't believe True-blood was killed because he had some kind of falling-out with one of his contractors."

"Then what's really going on?"

"That's the mystery, I guess. I don't know how those two killings are linked, but it feels like they are." Carmela took a sip of champagne. "But I don't think we're going to find the answer sitting on our butts drinking champagne in the French Quarter."

Ava cocked an eye at her. "Yeah? Then where are we going to find it?"

"South of here in bayou country?"

"You don't sound all that convinced."

"Probably because I'm not." Carmela thought for a few moments. "What we need to do is to make contact with some-body down in that area who's really plugged in. Someone who's familiar with the people and who knows the lay of the land."

Ava shook her head. "I can't imagine who that would be."

But a germ of an idea was forming in Carmela's brain. And it was starting to feel pretty good. "Ava, do you re-member what you said to me yesterday afternoon?"

"I don't remember what I said five minutes ago. What did I say? Was I brilliant?"

"Kind of. You said we were up a creek without a paddle."

"Carmela, I was speaking metaphorically."

"And I'm thinking that we should go up a creek literally!"

"Wait a minute," Ava said, her eyes taking on an excited gleam. "Are you talking about . . . ?" She cocked an index finger at Carmela.

"That's right," Carmela said. "We need to get in touch with our old pals Moony and Squirrel."

Chapter 26

MOONY, really Eddy Moon, was a swamp rat that Carmela and Ava had run into a few years ago. He had helped them when the widow of a crooked tycoon had pulled them into a tangled web of lies and jewelry heists.

Moony lived down in Venice, Louisiana, close to his buddy Jake Ebson, also known as Squirrel, who was even more of a swamp rat. Squirrel, a sort of swamp hermit, lived in a tar paper shack where he poached alligators, trapped illegally, and probably cooked up vats of blow-your-brains moonshine whenever he felt like it.

Still, they were decent guys. Well, they were if you didn't put too much stock in them being upstanding, card-carrying, law-abiding citizens.

Carmela dialed Boomer's Boat and Bait, where Moony worked on a semi-regular basis. He answered on the second ring as "Hotel California" played in the background.

"Carmela, darlin', long time no hear."

"It has been too long and I apologize," Carmela said.

"We need to get ourselves to a *fais do do* one of these days and do some dancing." A *fais do do* was a Cajun party.

"That's what I'm thinking, too. But first I need your help."

"What trouble did you get yourself in now?" Moony asked.

Carmela quickly explained about the two murders. And how they might or might not be connected.

"Murder," Moony said slowly. "That's serious business. A person crosses that line, they end up with a life sentence. Not just a slap on the wrist for poaching. So why call me when your boyfriend is a hotshot police detective?" He pronounced it *po-lice*.

"I have kind of a strange request," Carmela said. "I need a guided tour through the swamp down in your parts. Just a little south of Boothville where that developer I told you about was going to build some townhomes, called Parson's Point."

Moony was instantly accommodating. "Why didn't you come right out and say that in the first place? Cruising around the swamp? That's what I do best. Better yet, I'll give Squirrel a holler and tell him to gas up his flatboat. Of course, if we happen to trap a couple of nutria or shoot us an alligator along the way, that would be what you'd call your lucky strike extra."

"Just as long as we don't get arrested."

"Say, is that hot chick girlfriend of yours coming along, too?"

"You mean Ava?" Carmela glanced at her friend, who'd just dumped her entire cosmetic bag on the table and was dabbing on eight coats of bulletproof mascara in preparation for a foray into the swamp.

"That's the one."

"She's coming."

There was pure delight in Moony's voice. "So what are

you waiting for? Get on down here—I'll close up the bait shop and see you gals in an hour or so."

FLYING DOWN LOUISIANA'S STATE ROAD 23, Carmela violated the speed limit about twenty-seven times before she skidded into the gravel parking lot at Boomer's Boat and Bait. Moony's place of employment, if you could call it that, was a rickety cabin built on stilts. It was located on the swampier side of Tide Basin Road right on the edge of Venice, deep in bayou country.

Carmela pulled in behind an ancient Silverado with a rusted-out truck bed and honked her horn.

Moony burst out the front door and flew down the half dozen steps, waving and hollering, "How do!" the whole time. He wore a plaid shirt, tied at the waist but hanging open, to reveal his suntanned chest. His cutoff jeans were slung low on narrow hips. A tangle of sun-bleached blond hair completed his bayou biker look.

"I forgot how cute Moony was," Ava purred as she watched him boogaloo across the parking lot. "Look at those high cheekbones, that cute nose."

"We're here on business," Carmela reminded her. "Keep your mind on Roman Numeral and off present company."

"But will Roman Numeral keep his mind on me?"

Then Moony was leaning into the car, smiling broadly, his green eyes flashing. "You two are looking finer than a Mardi Gras float on Fat Tuesday," he proclaimed.

"Hey there," Ava said, batting her eyelashes.

"Hello, beautiful," Moony said. Then he gestured to his truck. "We best use my vehicle if we're fixin' to get to Squirrel's place in one piece. I hear his road is pretty torn up."

They piled into Moony's truck and took off. Two minutes

later, they were bumping down a rutted road while the swamp closed in around them.

"Peaceful down here," Ava observed. "A person could get . . . lost."

They humped along, twisting and turning, following what was barely a trail as brackish water lapped up on both sides of the road. Clumps of tupelo trees, at least fifty feet high, stretched upward to block out the sun, their roots intertwined like ancient sculpture. In some spots, swamp water had seeped across the road, turning it to mud. Still they muscled on, past stands of bald cypress, once clattering across a narrow wooden bridge. Drifts of grayish-green Spanish moss hung down from the trees, swishing against the windshield, making it feel like they were clawing their way through some kind of strange, primordial world.

When they finally went from bumpy to rutted to no road at all, the trees parted and a clearing seemed to magically open up. They'd arrived at Squirrel's place.

"I see Squirrel is still using the same decorator," Carmela remarked.

Squirrel's house was a weathered silver-gray cabin with a corrugated metal roof that was tarnished and corroded in so many places, Carmela was sure it probably leaked like a sieve during even the lightest sprinkle. Animal hides and antique traps were tacked to the walls. Shoved up against one side of the building (helping to prop it up, perhaps?) an old truck rested on cinder blocks. Brown and white hound dogs barked and spun all over the place and two boats were anchored at a rickety dock that stuck out into a small lake.

Moony clambered out of the truck and waved a hand. "Howdy, Squirrel."

Squirrel waved back from where he was lounging in a torn canvas hammock. He was drinking an Abita Beer and eating crawfish that were liberally sprinkled with Pleasure & Pain Hot Sauce. When he saw the three of them ambling toward him, he hopped out of his hammock, pulled a baseball cap on his head, and grinned.

"Bless my soul," Squirrel said. "Moony brought me a gift from heaven. Two fine ladies." He gave a deep bow. "How you been. Anybody want some crawfish?"

Ava murmured "yum" and Carmela had the feeling it wasn't the crawfish she was eyeing. It was Squirrel in his cut-off jeans and tight T-shirt. At least three days' worth of stubble on his face gave him a bad boy action hero look.

Squirrel grabbed Ava in a giant hug and swung her around so hard her feet flew off the ground. "Girl," he said, "you are hot as fish grease."

"Aren't you the sweet talker," Ava giggled.

"Honey, that's why they call me the Cajun Casanova."

After grabbing a six-pack of Abita Beer—"For emergency purposes only," Squirrel said—he led them onto a shaky dock and they all gingerly stepped aboard an ugly green boat.

"What kind of boat is this?" Ava asked as she sat down.

"This is your basic sixteen-foot aluminum flatboat," Squirrel told her. "With a Mercury outboard engine."

"That's good, huh?" Ava asked as Carmela sat down next to her.

"The best," Squirrel said.

"Does that mean we . . ." Carmela began, just as a floppy-eared hound dog took a flying leap from the dock and landed in her lap. "Whoa. Nice doggy," she said as his pink tongue tried to wiggle across her face.

"That friendly guy is Cooter," Squirrel said. He cast off from the stern while Moony jumped into the bow of the boat. "He likes to ride along."

"What about his buddies over there?" Carmela asked.

Two other mangy dogs had padded out onto the dock and were gazing at them with crazy, rolling eyes.

"Lobo and Bufford," Squirrel called out to the dogs as he pulled the starter cord and the engine roared to life. "You guys stay home and take care of Dixie, Dolly, and Banjo."

"How many dogs do you have anyway?" Ava asked.

"Uh . . . six," Squirrel said.

"What about that spotted one lying under the porch?" Carmela asked.

"Seven," Squirrel said. "I forgot about Mateo. He isn't home all that much. He's what you'd call a part-timer. Likes to wander. Visit the lady coonhounds."

"I can identify," Moony said.

Squirrel guided the boat out into the middle of the lake, where a green flotilla of water lilies bobbed on the waves.

"Gorgeous out here," Carmela said.

"There's nothing like it," Moony agreed.

"So where we headed?" Squirrel asked.

Carmela turned around to face him. "I want to look around just a little south of here. Where a developer by the name of Trueblood was supposed to build a neighborhood called Parson's Point Townhomes."

Squirrel bobbed his head. "I know where that is. Too bad somebody's going to throw up a bunch of ticky-tacky houses and ruin all that natural beauty."

Ava rolled her eyes at Carmela. "*He's* worried about ticky-tacky houses?" she said under her breath.

Carmela shrugged. Then, "We're not sure he's going to build the town houses after all. But I still want to look around over there."

"Then hang on to your hats, folks." Squirrel goosed the engine, there was a deafening roar, and they were suddenly flying across the lake.

"This is terrifying," Ava shouted, trying to make herself heard above the thunder of the engine.

But Carmela, speed demon that she was, found the trip totally exhilarating. The wind whipped her hair, the prow of the boat practically lifted up and hydroplaned across the water, tiny beads of water spattered her face. She was having the time of her life even though . . . oh my . . . they did seem to be closing in on the shore at a most alarming rate.

"Are we going to hit the . . . ?" Ava cried.

At the very last moment, Squirrel throttled back. There was a high-pitched whine as he cranked the boat hard left into a dizzying one-eighty-degree turn and they suddenly found themselves spinning down a narrow creek.

"Wheee!" Moony called out. "I think I lost my sunglasses back there."

"I almost lost my lunch," Ava said.

But Squirrel was dialing back his speed even more, floating them gently down the narrow waterway as if they were on an adventure ride at Disneyland. Tupelo trees rose like silent sentinels while bald cypress poked bulky knee-like knots out of the water to capture oxygen for their underwater systems. A brown and black marsh hawk flew low over their heads, causing Cooter to look up and growl. The hawk circled their boat complaining, *"Pee-pee-peeeee."*

They cruised down one channel and then another, Squirrel seeming to have some kind of bayou GPS embedded in his head.

"This is very spooky," Ava said. She swatted at an insect. "And buggy."

But Carmela loved it. Being in the bayou reminded her of the times she used to spend with Shamus, back when they were first married and actually got along with each other. They'd paddle a pirogue out to his camp house in the Baritaria bayou and spend the weekend. Light a fire, cozy up in the loft, fish for redfish. But that was then and this was . . .

"We're getting close," Squirrel said. The narrow channels, the press of bright green flora and foliage, had caused everyone to reflect inward and speak a little more quietly.

"You sure you know where we're going?" Moony asked. "Because I would've thought we had to veer more to our left."

Squirrel nodded at something just ahead of them. "We gotta go past that capped energy pipe up there."

They were all silent as they glided past a white standpipe that rose out of the brackish water. A battered sign on it said, *WARNING DO NOT TOUCH.*

"What happens if you touch it?" Ava asked.

"I don't know," Squirrel said. "I guess there's a big explosion or something."

They motored on for another ten minutes and then Squirrel said, sounding pleased, "There you go. That's where your town houses were gonna be built."

Moony stood up in the front of the boat and pointed to an opening in the trees. "Doggone it, Squirrel, you brought us right in on the money."

"What a gorgeous area," Carmela said as Squirrel swung them in closer.

"But look," Moony said. "They cleared out most of the trees and vegetation."

As they pulled closer, Carmela could see that Moony was right. A large area had been clear-cut and a gravel road led out through the far stand of pine trees, presumably out to Highway 23 and civilization. All that occupied the clearing now was a large painted sign with an architect's rendering of a row of contemporary-looking townhomes and the words *PARSON'S POINT TOWNHOMES.*

Chapter 27

"NOTHING but a big sign," Carmela said, sounding disappointed.

"Not what you were hoping for?" Moony asked her.

Carmela shook her head. "I . . . I don't know." She hadn't expected to find an X-marks-the-spot type of clue, but she'd been hoping for *something*.

Squirrel sensed her dilemma. "Do you want to go a little deeper into the swamp?"

"I'd like to," Carmela said. "As long as we can find our way back out again."

Moony grinned. "That's no problem. Squirrel here can navigate by the sun."

"Can you really?" Ava asked.

Squirrel gazed up at the partly cloudy sky. "Sure. When the sun's out."

He putt-putted the boat out from shore, spun it around, and headed down a waterway that bent like an elbow. Tupelo stood like tiny islands, surrounded by stands of reeds and large ferns. Dwarf palmettos waved their fronds, green velvet moss crawled up the banks on either side of them. They twisted and turned in a dizzying tangle of ever-narrowing waterways.

"It's funny we haven't seen any alligators," Ava said.

"Oh, they're here," Squirrel said. "They just don't want you to see them. But they've seen us, I guarantee it."

"Now I don't feel so safe," she said.

Squirrel reached forward and patted her knee. "You're safe with me, darlin'."

Moony, who'd been crouched in the bow of the boat, suddenly stood up. "Look at that." He pointed ahead. "Another sign. Damnation. This bayou's filling up with billboards like it was a superhighway. Pretty soon there'll be a sign that says *McGATOR BURGERS, FIFTY GAZILLION SERVED.*"

Carmela squinted in the direction of the sign, curious. "What does the sign really say?"

"Not entirely sure," Moony said. "Better take us in closer, Squirrel." When they were ten feet from the sign, Moony read aloud, 'Recreational and Commercial Fishing Prohibited in These Waters.'"

"What?" Squirrel said.

"What's it say underneath?" Carmela asked. Now she was half standing, too. "There's more letters."

"It says 'By Order of the Environmental Justice League,'" Moony said. "Who dat to post a sign like this?"

"That's very weird," Carmela said. But she remembered Roman Numeral talking about being harassed by the vitriolic Martin Lash. Had Lash been posting signs all over the bayous? Had he really been—kapow—crazy?

Squirrel scrunched up his face in an approximation of deep thinking. "That doesn't sound right to me. My uncle Eustus and I used to fish here all the time. We never ran up against any kind of pro-hi-bitions."

"Maybe things have changed," Ava said. "There are lots more rules and regulations these days."

"Like from the IRS," Moony said. "The Infernal Revenuers."

"Like you pay actual taxes," Squirrel scoffed.

"But the Environmental Justice League doesn't have any real jurisdiction here," Carmela said. "To prohibit fishing in these waters, that order would have to come from the Louisiana State Fisheries, wouldn't it?"

"I guess," Squirrel said. "Sounds right to me."

Carmela furrowed her brow. This was awfully strange. If Lash were still alive she would have wanted to grill him hard about the sign. Demand what right he had to decide who could or couldn't fish here. But dead men tell no tales . . .

"Let's keep going," Carmela said. "As long as we're here."

"Makes no never mind to me," Squirrel said. He goosed the boat speed just a little and they continued up the channel. They stopped to explore a number of inlets and shallow areas, but didn't find anything unusual beyond a few nesting spots for egrets and herons.

"Not much here," Ava said.

"Except for nature's bounty," Carmela said.

Painted turtles dove off logs as they approached, a barred owl screeched from overhead.

"It's getting late," Ava said. She was more than ready to turn around.

"Time to head in?" Squirrel asked.

"I guess," Carmela said. The sun was low now and elusive through the dense foliage. Here and there she caught a few fleeting shafts of fading, dying rays. Carmela knew it was time to turn back. And realized that her journey down here—though it had proved to be an amusing diversion—was ultimately futile.

Squirrel turned the boat into an inlet and was about to nose it around when Carmela craned her neck and caught a flicker of something in the rapidly descending dusk. "Wait a minute." She held up a hand. "Keep going."

"You see something?" Ava asked. Her voice was filled with doubt.

"I'm not sure," Carmela said.

Squirrel cut back the motor until it was just putt-putting every few seconds and they were practically drifting up the small stream.

Carmela half stood in the boat and pointed. "There, up ahead. What is that?"

Everyone stretched to see.

"It looks like a hunk of fence," Moony said. "It's half submerged in the water, almost blocking the stream."

They pulled even closer and saw two feet of faded blue plastic fence sticking up out of the stream.

"Dang," Squirrel said. "It *is* blocking the stream."

"End of the line," Ava said.

"No, it isn't," Carmela said. "Keep going. Squirrel, see if you can pull up right next to it."

"Yes, ma'am." He maneuvered the boat even closer and then guided it around so they were parallel to the fence.

"What's a fence doing out here?" Ava asked. "I mean, what would it be keeping out?"

"I think," Carmela said, "that it might be keeping something in."

"What are you talking about?" Moony asked.

"Take a look over there," Carmela said.

They all looked over to where she was pointing.

Moony did a kind of herky-jerky double take. "The water's bubbling," he said, sounding surprised. "Almost like there's some kind of hot spring coming up from underneath."

"Is that normal?" Ava asked.

"I guess there could be natural springs out here," Moony said, though he didn't sound sure of himself.

Suddenly, the water on the opposite side of the fence from them began to bubble like mad. Then the dorsal fins of several large fish broke the surface.

"Those are fish!" Carmela cried as several more fish swam along the fence line. Cooter, squished in beside her, let out a series of high-pitched yips.

"This isn't right," Squirrel said. "There's something wrong here. This is supposed to be a free fishing area."

"What kind of fish are these?" Carmela asked suddenly.

Squirrel cut the motor, grabbed onto the fence, and hoisted himself up.

"Don't fall in," Moony warned. "There's probably snappers in that water. We don't want to haul you out with a few chunks missing."

Squirrel hung on tightly as he peered intently at the swirl of fish for a few moments. Then he eased himself back down, looking puzzled. "Those fish are what you'd call your Gulf sturgeon."

"Sturgeon," Carmela said.

Why was an idea suddenly pinging in her brain like crazy? Shaking her neurons and sending a tumble of messages to her prefrontal cortex. Maybe because she'd suddenly realized that sturgeon were a rich source of . . . caviar?

"Oh no!" Carmela cried. "Are these the kind of sturgeon that you can harvest for caviar?"

Squirrel looked thoughtful. "Well . . . yeah . . . I guess they could be. But, you see, these particular sturgeon are supposed to be protected. I mean, these fish, what you call your Gulf sturgeon, are pretty much untouchable. They're on the National Fish and Wildlife's endangered species list."

"Are you sure about that?" Carmela asked.

"Pretty sure." Squirrel took his cap off, smoothed his hair, and put his cap back on. "Whenever you go into a local bait shop or fishing supply place, they hand out these little cards from the Louisiana Department of Wildlife and Fisheries that tell you which fish are okay or not okay to hook or net."

"That's right," Moony said excitedly. "He's right."

"And these guys"—Squirrel hooked a thumb toward the roil of sturgeon in the enclosed area—"you're not supposed to touch a single whisker on their slimy little heads."

"I guess that's why they're in a pen," Ava said. "Because they're protected."

"I don't think so," Carmela said. "I think these poor creatures are being exploited."

"What?" Ava said.

"Pull the boat over to shore," Carmela said. "We need to take a closer look."

Chapter 28

COOTER hopped out of the boat first, happy to be back on dry land, delighted to be running around. Ava, unfortunately, didn't share Cooter's boundless enthusiasm. The heels of her rhinestone-studded slippers sunk into the mud the minute she stepped off the boat.

"Help!" Ava cried. "My feet are getting sucked down. I think I'm caught in quicksand or something."

Squirrel grabbed her under the arms, gave a quick tug, and hoisted her back up and out of harm's way. Both her legs were streaked with mud up to her knees and one dainty shoe was missing.

"My Capezio dance shoe," Ava cried. "It got sucked under."

"Oh dear," Carmela said. "You'll never dance *Swan Lake* again."

Squirrel stuck his hand down into the mud and poked

around for a few seconds. "I think I . . . got it." When the shoe popped out, the mud made an ugly sucking sound.

"My poor shoe is totaled," Ava mourned.

"Naw," Squirrel said as Moony tromped on ahead of them. "Just rinse it off and it'll be good as new."

"If it was good as new, I'd take it back to the store," Ava grumped. She shook the mud off her shoe, slipped it on, and turned toward Carmela. "Now what?"

"Let's just follow along after Squirrel," Carmela suggested. "He went ahead to . . ."

"Ah!" Ava screamed. She was suddenly batting her arms wildly, dancing a crazy jig, as if she were being attacked by a swarm of bees.

"What's wrong now?"

"Spiderweb," Ava said, sputtering. "I walked right into the dang thing." She shook her head. "I tell you, Carmela, I'm a city girl. I'm just not cut out for the wilds of Louisiana. It's . . . it's a jungle out here."

"Technically a bayou," Carmela said.

"Hey," Squirrel called as he came splashing back to them. "I found another one of those fish pens."

"Is it full of sturgeon?" Carmela asked.

Squirrel nodded. "Looks like."

"There's something really wrong here," Carmela said.

"Yeah," Ava said, curling a lip. "We should have never gotten out of the boat."

"No, I mean . . ."

A sudden crashing through the undergrowth had them all turning to stare. That's when Moony popped out, looking all red-faced and breathless.

"There's some kind of building back here that you-all should take a look at," Moony shouted.

Moony pivoted and headed back the way he'd come.

Carmela and Squirrel were right behind him with Ava stumping along as best she could.

A metal Quonset hut–type building was perched in the middle of nowhere. They approached it cautiously.

"This looks pretty new," Squirrel said. "Like it was just built." He thumped the back of his hand against the metal door. It sounded rock solid.

"I wonder how it got here," Moony said. He grabbed the door handle again and shook it hard, but the door didn't budge. "It's locked up tighter than a drum."

"I guess that's it." Ava shrugged. "No way in. Time to say adios to all the spiders, bugs, and squirmy things."

"Not so fast," Carmela said. "We have to somehow get inside there. I have an idea of what's going on, but I need actual . . . proof."

"Wait. What?" Ava said.

There was a loud grunt from behind them and they all turned to see Squirrel hoist a giant hunk of scrap metal onto his shoulder. He drew a quick breath and then ran full tilt at the door. "Waaaaatch out!" he bellowed at the top of his lungs.

"Holy cheese curds," Ava cried as Squirrel collided with the door in a cataclysmic crash. At which point the door bowed inward as if it had been struck by a moving freight train and was suddenly rent from top to bottom.

"You did it," Moony cried, jumping up and down. "Squirrel, you're a monster! You could star on *WrestleMania*!"

When Carmela saw that the shattered door was barely hanging from its damaged hinges, she said, "Come on, what are we waiting for?"

Moony shoved the door aside and they all tiptoed in. The place was dark, cavernous, and carried a distinctive fishy odor.

"Eew," Ava said.

"Fish," Moony said.

"And it ain't fresh," Squirrel added helpfully.

Taking a quick glance around, the first thing Carmela spotted was the generator. "There's a generator," Carmela said. Seeing it pretty much confirmed her worst suspicions.

"Why a generator way out here?" Ava wondered.

But Carmela was slowly working herself into an ice-cold rage. She was finally putting the pieces together. "Look at all the large metal tables. And the plastic coolers that are stacked up, waiting to go."

"I don't know," Moony said. "It looks to me like a place where's you'd clean fish."

"Not clean them," Carmela said. "This is a kind of processing plant where they extract the fish roe. You know, the caviar."

"Caviar?" Ava suddenly yelped. She was still confused. "Wait a minute. You mean like in the Jewel Caviar Company?" She stared at Carmela and wrinkled her nose. "I guess I still don't know what's going on."

"I'll tell you what I think is going on," Carmela said. "Harvey and Jenny Jewel are a couple of thieving snakes. They've been stealing caviar from protected Gulf sturgeon and passing it off as their fancy, imported brand. They've been making money off a bunch of innocent fish!"

"Holy mackerel," Ava said.

"No," Squirrel said. "That kind of fish would be legal."

Moony stood there with his hands on his hips. "This is a conspiracy," he said. "Just like Area 51 or Bigfoot."

"It's worse," Carmela said. "Because it's real."

Squirrel grabbed one of the coolers and tossed it aside with a clatter. "Outrageous," he snorted. "They keep this up, there won't be any Gulf sturgeon left alive."

"Just like overharvesting destroyed all the sturgeon in the Caspian Sea," Carmela said.

"So what are we gonna do to about it?" Moony asked.

Carmela thought for a few moments, staring at the metal tables that looked like autopsy tables to her now. Clenching her jaw so hard she just about popped a filling, she said, "For one thing, we have to put a stop to this. Like . . . now."

"We're with you on that," Squirrel said. "This is poaching of the worst kind. It's one thing to take a gator or two out of season. But this . . ." He looked around the building, at the metal tables, the generator. "This is poaching on an industrial scale."

"I'm afraid we actually have an even more pressing problem than just the illegal harvesting of fish," Carmela said.

They all stared at her.

"I believe that Harvey and Jenny Jewel probably committed murder to keep their little gold mine going," Carmela said.

Squirrel squinted at her. "No shit?"

"I'm betting that Martin Lash, the executive director of the Environmental Justice League, was in on this illegal operation, too," Carmela said. "But they probably killed him to get him out of the way."

"Whoa," Ava said. She clapped a hand to her chest and took a step backward.

Carmela continued. "And I wouldn't be surprised if the Jewels murdered Trent Trueblood as well. Just because he was going to build down here and had major plans to fund a research study in these very waters."

"Where do you think they take this caviar?" Moony asked.

Carmela thought for a minute. "I remember Jenny Jewel said something about an old shrimp processing plant over in Gretna."

Squirrel put one hand over the other and cracked his knuckles. "What are we waiting for?" he said. "Let's go close it down!"

*   *   *

THE RIDE BACK TO SQUIRREL'S CAMP SHACK WAS
a bit of a blur, but somehow they made it. Then, of course,
Squirrel and Moony wanted to come along to mix it up at
the caviar processing plant. So they all jammed into Carmela's small sports car (Cooter included—she never could
seem to ditch old Cooter) and headed back to New Orleans.

All the way back, Carmela struggled to keep the car on
the road as she fought to keep Cooter from slobbering on her
shirt while she tried to get hold of Babcock on her cell
phone. But no luck. For some reason he wasn't picking up.
So she found herself leaving about a million voice mails for
him, each one more frantic than the last one.

Just as they'd finally reached New Orleans and were hur-
tling across the Route 90 cantilevered bridge, closing in on
Gretna, Carmela called Babcock's office and his phone was
finally picked up.

"Yeah? What?" came a familiar voice. She recognized it
as Detective Bobby Gallant, Babcock's right-hand man. He
sounded like he was ready to call it a day and head home.

"Bobby, this is Carmela!"

"Hey, Carmela," Bobby said, his voice instantly warming.
"What's shaking?"

"I've been trying to get hold of Babcock," she said. "It's
kind of an emergency."

"What's wrong?" Gallant asked.

"Stop that!" Carmela cried. Cooter had his front paws on
the shift column and was trying to downshift from fourth
to second.

"Carmela, what's going on?" Gallant asked.

Cooter suddenly spun around, his tail whipping across

Carmela's face, nearly blinding her and sending her lurching into the next lane over.

"Cooter," Carmela screamed, "you've got stop this."

"Who's Cooter?" Gallant cried. "Carmela, don't tell me you've been kidnapped!"

"Please, Bobby . . . just tell Babcock to send a couple of cruisers, lights and sirens, to the Jewel Caviar Company in Gretna!"

"Carmela . . . what?" But she had already hung up.

"WE NEED A PLAN," MOONY SAID. "WE CAN'T JUST go cowboying into that plant and disrupt the whole shebang."

"Why not?" Squirrel demanded. They were in the parking lot outside the Jewel Caviar Company. The building was low and dark, hunkered on a flat piece of cracked concrete a block or so from the Mississippi. Tendrils of fog drifted in, the mournful hoot of a tugboat floated back to them. Night had stolen in to shroud what was a gloomy industrial area.

"Because . . ." Moony hesitated. He really didn't have a good, logical reason.

They debated what kind of approach to take and, after a few minutes of arguing, basically gave up and went storming into the Jewel Caviar Company, full steam ahead. The whole lot of them: Carmela, Ava, Squirrel, Moony, and Cooter.

Carmela had expected a well-lit plant bustling with busy workers and officious clipboard-wielding managers. Instead, all she saw were a handful of workers in white smocks and hairnets who barely even glanced up as their convoy came roaring in.

Still, the production line was humming away, with small glass jars bouncing down a rubber conveyor belt where they were being filled with drips and drops of precious caviar.

Thirty seconds later, an officious manager did turn up. A chubby, frowning, bespectacled man in a bad polyester suit that had the sickening green sheen of a barn fly.

"What's the meaning of this intrusion?" the manager demanded as he set his feet wide to block their advance.

"Who are you?" Carmela asked.

"I'm J. R. Teasdale, manager of this plant," the man said. "Who are *you*?"

"We're here to see Harvey Jewel," Carmela said. "We have important business with him."

"Important business," Squirrel reiterated. He was back to cracking his knuckles, trying to look intimidating.

Teasdale gave Squirrel one imperious glance down his knobby nose and said, "Get out of here, the lot of you, before I call the police."

"We're not leaving," Carmela said, "until we speak to Harvey Jewel."

Cooter gave an angry bark as if to underscore their words.

Startled, Teasdale glanced down and was met with Cooter's toothy grin. "You can't bring a dog in here," he thundered. "It violates all health regulations."

"Cooter's been cleared," Moony said. "He's working undercover."

"Are you people plum crazy?" Teasdale screamed. "Get out."

"Where's Jewel?" Carmela demanded. "Is he in his office?" She glanced around Teasdale toward the back of the plant.

"You're not setting foot back there!" Teasdale screamed.

"Watch me," Carmela said, darting forward, trying to push her way past him.

But Teasdale was ready for her, throwing a shoulder out, blocking her passage with his wide hips.

"Come on, Squirrel," Moony shouted. "Let's take this goober!"

That sent Teasdale backpedaling away from them, fists bunching as if ready to fight, his face as dark and threatening as a thundercloud. "I'm calling the police," he threatened. "Gonna have you people arrested!" He spun on his heels and waddled toward the back of the plant.

"Go ahead and do that," Ava said, darting in to add her two cents. "Call the police. We've been trying to get hold of them for the last hour!"

One of the workers, a skinny guy in a white apron and paper hat, who'd been watching the whole exchange, said, "Mr. Jewel isn't here."

"Do you know where he is?" Carmela asked.

The skinny worker shrugged. "I heard something about a fancy caviar tasting."

Carmela rocked back on her heels and clapped a hand to her forehead. "Oh my gosh. That's right! There's a wine and caviar tasting tonight—a black-tie event—over at the Hotel Vendue!"

Squirrel grabbed her by the elbow. "Come on, girl. What are we waiting for!"

THEY ALL SQUISHED INTO CARMELA'S CAR AGAIN and roared back across the bridge. This time Moony wanted to drive with Carmela riding shotgun. Ava got stuck in the backseat next to Squirrel with Cooter alternately licking her knees and trying to curl up in her lap.

"Hurry up," Ava cried. "I'm going crazy back here. It feels like I'm riding in some kind of clown car."

"That's because you are," Carmela said.

They zipped their way through the CBD, the Central Business District, Carmela waving her arms and shouting directions. At Canal Street, they almost collided with a streetcar, the driver wildly clanging his bell at them, chastising them. Finally, Moony brought them into the French Quarter.

"Lookie this!" Squirrel shouted as they turned down Bourbon Street. The colorful neon lights, the wall-to-wall bars and clubs, made it look like a fun house arcade for big kids. "They even got bars here with topless dancers. Ain't that something? Look at that one . . . Scarlett's Cabaret. Sounds classy. Think we got time to stop?"

"No, we don't have time to stop," Carmela yelped. "And get your mind out of the gutter." She glanced at Moony, who was driving but craning his head in a million different directions, clearly dazzled by the sights and *plinkety-plink* music that spilled out of the raucous clubs. "You, too, Moony. Stop looking around for loose women and keep an eye on the pedestrians and stoplights. This isn't some jerkwater town, you know, this is New Orleans."

"Yeah, yeah, I got it," Moony said. "Bright lights, big city. Where we headed again?"

"The Hotel Vendue."

"Is it fancy? Sounds fancy."

"More like ultraexclusive," Carmela said. "It's five star."

"Probably got free movies like the Super 8," Moony muttered.

"I wouldn't exactly say we're dressed for a black-tie event," Ava said. "I mean, my shoes are slathered in mud and I feel like I've got bugs crawling in my hair."

"Ava," Carmela said, "you can't take a shower just yet. So please try to deal with it, okay?"

Just as they were careening down Dauphine Street, Moony honking at a horse-drawn jitney, trying to get it to move out of the way, Carmela's phone rang. She grabbed it out of her bag and fumbled it, her phone immediately slipping to the floor. But when she scooped it back up, she could see from the caller ID that it was Babcock—*finally* returning her seventy zillion calls.

"Carmela, where are you?" Babcock cried as soon as she answered. He sounded anxious, bordering on upset. "What's going on? You left me something like fifty-seven voice mails. What's this about a Gulf surgeon?"

"Sturgeon," Carmela said. "Not surgeon."

"And sending squad cars, lights and sirens, to some former shrimp factory in Gretna?"

"Babcock, forget about that!" Carmela cried. "There's been a huge change of plans. Wait . . . hold on." She punched Moony hard on the shoulder. "Turn left here. Wait . . . watch out!" The Easy Slider food truck had veered in front of them, holding up progress. "Don't hit that truck!"

"Are you talking to me?" Babcock asked.

"No, I'm taking to Moony," Carmela said just as Cooter hung his head over the seat and started yapping loudly in her ear.

"Who the hell is Moony?" Babcock screamed. "And what's that dog I hear barking? Is that one of yours? I thought they were with Shamus this weekend."

"Never mind that," Carmela said. *Yip, yip, yap* . . . Cooter had spotted something that had set him off, probably a corner hot dog vendor. "The thing is . . . we need you to come to the Hotel Vendue! Like . . . immediately!" Carmela grabbed the dog's collar and twisted it, trying to get him to quit barking. "Shut up!"

"What!"

"Not you. Cooter."

"Who . . . why . . . ?" Babcock sputtered in sheer frustration. "What's going on?"

"Just meet me at the caviar and wine tasting in five minutes. I'll explain everything."

"Honey, I can't come to a caviar tasting. I'm not dressed for it. Besides, don't you know I'm working?"

"No, no, this *is* about the murders—and the Jewels. The murders were all about the caviar!"

"Caviar? Jewels? What are you talking about?" His voice rose to a squawk that became a tangle of static. "Carmela, you're not making any sense!"

Chapter 29

MOONY ran the car right up onto the sidewalk and lurched to a stop.

"Sir!" A valet stepped in front of the car, looking like a Napoleonic solider in his red uniform and gold braid. "You can't park here, sir. This is for drop-offs only. We have a red carpet event tonight, sir!"

"That's what I'm talkin' about," Ava cried as she pushed open the car door and stuck out a shapely mud-spattered leg. The rest of them spilled out, too. Moony and Squirrel, Carmela and Cooter.

The snippy society page reporter for the *New Orleans Star* rushed forward, eager to see who'd just arrived, pinching her photographer's arm to get his attention. But when she saw Carmela and Ava, all muddy and sunburned, and Moony and Squirrel, looking like flophouse refugees, she reared back, her prim and proper sensibilities utterly rocked to the core. Cooter saw the reporter staring openmouthed and immediately rushed over to jump up, christen her white dress with his muddy paws, and administer a big old doggy smackeroo. And just as the society reporter opened her mouth to howl in protest, a rival TV reporter aimed his camera at her.

Flashbulbs popped like cheap cheeseburgers, more cameras swung their way, and black-tie guests aimed stunned looks at Carmela's motley crew.

No matter. They all charged down the red carpet, heading for the Hotel Vendue. Into the lobby they went, following a gaggle of well-heeled people. A desk clerk caught sight of them and came rushing out, just about breaking his leg in an effort to stop them, but it was like trying to halt the Visigoths from raiding Saxony. No dice.

"Where's the wine and caviar tasting?" Carmela shouted.

The desk clerk looked to his left and then hesitated, deciding not to tell them.

"Never mind," Carmela said. "It's probably upstairs in the ballroom."

"You know where that is?" Squirrel asked.

"This way," Carmela said. She headed toward a wide flight of marble steps and everyone followed her. Up they ran, down the hallway and straight through the double doors of the Magnolia Ballroom. A well-dressed older couple saw them coming and flattened themselves against the wall, as if they were terrified of catching bubonic plague.

Carmela skidded to a halt just inside the entrance to catch her breath and look around. The ballroom couldn't have been more elegant. A string quartet played a sprightly tune. Guests were dressed to the nines in black tie and gowns. At least two dozen major wine vendors had makeshift bars set up, where they were pouring their finest vintages. And in the center of the room, an enormous ice sculpture of a leaping fish poked high above everyone's heads. Shimmering and spectacularly lit by colored lights, Carmela figured this had to be caviar central.

"You know," Ava said, "we do look a tad bedraggled. And the boys are wearing cutoffs." Of course, that didn't stop her from helping herself to a flute of champagne from the tray of a passing waiter.

"These folks are some heavy hitters," Moony said, awed by the crowd of two hundred or more.

Carmela had already spotted a deputy mayor conversing with a federal court judge. There were also pockets of Garden District socialites as well as local TV personalities, bankers, lawyers, and restaurateurs. She also noticed Helen McBride flirting outrageously with the wine vendor from Castle Cellars and Allan Hurst bending the ear of the man who she was pretty sure owned a chain called Captain Tommy's Seafood Restaurants.

But that was all irrelevant to her now. Driven by anger and a renewed sense of purpose, Carmela elbowed her way through the crowd, heading straight for Harvey and Jenny Jewel's caviar display.

And there was Harvey Jewel himself, resplendent in a Brioni tuxedo, white hair slicked back, looking like a foodie homecoming king. A smarmy grin lit his face as he glad-handed guests, accepted compliments, and urged everyone who hadn't already tried it to have a taste of his pride and joy Jewel Caviar. The ice sculpture fish stood on the table behind him, surrounded by enormous silver platters filled with smoked salmon and dozens of open jars of caviar.

Carmela flew through the crowd and accosted Harvey Jewel.

"You," she said, shaking a finger at him. "You're a thief and a murderer. I'm going to see to it you spend the rest of your living days behind bars." She was screaming and didn't care who heard her.

Harvey reared back as if slapped, then regained his balance and goggled crazily at her. "You're . . . you're insane!" he sputtered.

Carmela leaned in closer. "You want to tell me about the black market caviar?" she asked, fairly seething. "And explain why you murdered Martin Lash and Trent Trueblood!"

Harvey's head snapped back and forth like a trapped animal. "Where's hotel security?" he shouted. "This crazy woman needs to be removed at once!"

Ava moved in on Harvey now, Squirrel and Moony backing her up. "You're in big trouble," she said.

Harvey Jewel was waving frantically now. "Help, please! Have this rabble removed!"

Jenny Jewel came flying to her husband's side like the Wicked Witch of the West. "What's going on?" she shrilled. Anger and stress had pulled her face tighter than a death mask.

"We're taking you down," Carmela said. "Your days of thievery and murder are over."

Jenny bared her teeth and pinched her hands into claws. "Leave us alone," she shrieked. "Get out." She tilted her head back and yelled, "Securityyyyy!"

Five seconds later, a burly guy in a navy blue blazer was there. "What's going on?" he asked.

Jenny thrust out an arm and pointed to Carmela. "Evict this intruder!"

The security guy put a hand on Carmela's shoulder, hoping to steer her away with a minimum of fuss. But Moony and Squirrel jumped in to intervene.

"Take your hands off her, you varmint," Squirrel ordered.

"Call the police!" Jenny screamed.

"Yeah, call the police," Ava screamed back at her. "So we can get this out in the open."

By that time, a crowd of onlookers had formed around them. Everyone curious, fascinated, and maybe a little stunned by all the shoving and shouting.

"Don't you dare . . ." the security guard growled at Squirrel. Letting go of Carmela, he lunged for him.

Bad idea. Moony pulled his right arm back and clocked the security guard right in the jaw. And then Cooter, sensing his human might be in trouble, lunged for Jenny Jewel.

"Arghhh!" Jenny cried as Cooter's big paws began shredding the front of her silk dress. "I'm being attacked!"

But Cooter, suddenly spotting the trays filled with smoked salmon, bounced off Jenny and jumped onto the table.

"Crap on a cracker," Ava said. "Cooter, no!" She tried to grab his collar. "Bad dog!"

But Cooter was a dog on a mission. He lapped up hunks of smoked salmon faster than a Hoover vacuum could suck a rug clean. Bits of pink fish flew through the air, spattering everyone.

"Somebody help!" Harvey Jewel shouted as Jenny continued to freak out. Then another security guard rushed in and Moony and Squirrel started swinging at anyone in the near vicinity.

"Dear Lord," Jenny said, sinking against the table as if she was about to faint. Which is when the precariously balanced ice sculpture began to wobble like crazy.

"Watch out!" Ava shouted. "The ice sculpture!"

But everyone was too busy shoving and pushing to notice. And just as Harvey Jewel grabbed a silver fork and tried to jab Carmela, the fish tumbled forward and struck him directly on the head!

"Owww!" Harvey cried. His knees buckled like a cheap

card table as he went down. The fish followed him, shattering into thousands of bright little shards.

"Holy MacNamara," Ava shouted. Arms outstretched, she fought to maintain her balance as she—and everyone else—began stumbling on the ice shards underfoot.

Which was the perfect time for Babcock and a contingent of police officers to arrive. He gaped at the collapsed Harvey Jewel, shattered ice sculpture, and dog, Cooter, who was now lapping up spilled caviar with a vengeance.

"Carmela, oh my Lord! What happened?"

Carmela grabbed Babcock and pointed to Harvey Jewel, who was curled up on the floor moaning. "There's your killer." She waved at Jenny Jewel, who was spinning and hissing like an alley cat. "And I'll bet she's in on it, too."

"Murderer?" Babcock said. "These two?"

"It's all about hijacked caviar . . ." Carmela began, just as a metallic clatter sounded above the bickering and two EMTs rushed in pulling a gurney.

Babcock held up a hand to Carmela as if he were a traffic cop. "Hold, please." Then he watched for a few moments as the EMTs bent over the semiconscious Harvey Jewel. "Okay, go. Give me the whole thing."

As if she were on a game show and had only fifteen seconds to come up with the correct answer, Carmela quickly explained the matter of the illegally harvested fish, the caviar, and how she was fairly confident that the Jewels had murdered Martin Lash and Trent Trueblood.

Babcock blinked rapidly and his head seemed to bob back and forth on its own. He uttered only a few words during her entire garbled explanation. *Preposterous* and *unbelievable* were two of those words.

As Carmela's story wound up, Harvey Jewel began to

groan. Then he started muttering feverishly as the EMTs loaded him onto the gurney.

Carmela pointed at him. "You're going down."

But Harvey Jewel, playing possum now and figuring he might be in the clear, threw Carmela a smirking, triumphant smile as he was wheeled away.

"No," Babcock yelled. "Stop!" He gestured to one of his officers, who promptly whipped out a pair of handcuffs and cuffed Harvey Jewel to the side of the metal gurney.

"You're under arrest," Babcock said.

"I didn't do anything," Harvey Jewel screamed.

"You've been poaching Gulf sturgeon," Squirrel shouted. "We found the fish pens. We know you were harvesting fish illegally."

"I'm innocent," Harvey shouted back. "I swear I am. My caviar comes from Finland! I could show you actual invoices!"

"This fish story," Babcock said to Carmela. "It's really true?"

"I was just there," Carmela said. "We were all there. We saw the fish with our own eyes."

"Excuse me." Helen McBride had edged up next to them. "This sounds like the makings of a very tasty story."

"Stand in line," Babcock said.

"I'd portray law enforcement in a very favorable light," Helen said.

Allan Hurst elbowed his way in, too. "How about a new story on me?"

"Yeah, yeah," Helen said. "Okay." She glanced over her shoulder, frowned, and said, "Where do you think you're going?" Jenny Jewel had been surreptitiously trying to back away.

"Get over here," Babcock ordered. "I need to talk to you."

"Ask her about Martin Lash," Carmela said, practically baring her teeth at Jenny Jewel. "Tell him!"

"Yes, tell me how Martin Lash was involved," Babcock said.

"I-I-I . . ." Jenny chattered.

"Take your time," Babcock said.

"Bu-bu-bu . . ." she started again. Jenny had begun blub-bering like a baby, her mascara streaming down her face and pooling under her eyes, making her look like a sad raccoon.

Babcock was starting to lose his patience. "Come on, spit it out."

"I don't know anything," Jenny sputtered. "I'm innocent, I tell you." Her eyes were open wide, her chin was quivering. "I don't know a thing about this." She peered at Carmela. "Fish pens, you say?"

"She's in just as deep as Harvey is," Carmela told Babcock.

"I'm not, really," Jenny said. "I only handled a teeny-tiny part of the sales and marketing."

"Lies," Carmela said. "Which will all come out in deposi-tions from all their employees."

"You can't do that," Jenny squealed.

"I can and I will," Babcock said. "Unless you start talking."

Jenny Jewel snapped her mouth shut and shook her head.

"Then I have no other recourse but to take you down-town in the back of a squad car . . ."

"No!" she screeched.

"And have you booked, photographed, and strip-searched."

It was the strip search that did it, of course. Jenny Jewel began to weep copiously and moan like a banshee, but Bab-cock stood firm. Finally when she realized there was no way out, she said, "I want a deal."

"You want a deal," Babcock repeated. She'd finally stopped blubbering and managed to choke out four consecutive words.

"You see," Carmela said. "She's morally flexible.

Jenny Jewel stared at them with hate-filled eyes. "I can't go to jail, I'd never survive."

Babcock nodded. "Go ahead then."

Jenny Jewel took a deep breath and said, "Martin Lash was the one who discovered the Gulf sturgeon. You know, from all his forays into the bayous. Harvesting the fish for caviar was his idea. But Lash needed money to, you know, to set up the pens and handle the extraction."

"You mean destroy the fish," Carmela said.

Jenny pulled her mouth into a hard line. "Whatever."

"Keep talking," Babcock urged.

"Anyway," Jenny said, "Lash pulled Harvey and me into his scheme." She threw pleading eyes at Babcock. "But Harvey was just the money man, the investor. We didn't *do* anything."

Ava darted in and shook a finger at Jenny. "The money man is always the guilty one," she cried. "Just look at Bernie Madoff."

"Wait a minute," Carmela said. "So Lash wasn't really an environmentalist?"

"Oh, he was," Jenny said. "But he loved making money more than the bayou."

"So Martin Lash was your partner," Babcock said, "in the Jewel Caviar Company."

Jenny looked wary. "He was at first . . . yes."

Carmela swept in like an avenging angel. "But then you killed him," she cried. She felt vindicated, being able to hurl those accusing words at Jenny.

Jenny's face turned dark and her mouth pulled into a feral snarl. "You don't understand. We had to do *something.* Lash started making impossible demands!"

"I do understand," Babcock said. "He wanted a bigger piece of the pie. He wanted an additional cut of money."

"He . . . he wanted it *all*," Jenny hissed. "Martin Lash claimed that *he* was the mastermind, the brains behind the whole operation."

"What about Trent Trueblood?" Carmela asked. "How did he figure into all of this? Did you kill him, too?"

Jenny gave a furtive look and then sought out Babcock's eyes. "Will you give me the same kind of deal? I cooperate in exchange for my testimony?"

"I'll do my best," Babcock said.

"That whole incident was very unfortunate," Jenny said. "But Harvey convinced me that Trueblood had to go, too." She ducked her head nervously. "You see, Trueblood was building town houses down near the Gulf sturgeon pens and he was funding this huge water study. Somehow, he found out about the fish pens! He called Harvey and threatened to turn us in, to expose everything!"

"He threatened to turn you in? Just like that?"

Jenny's scrawny shoulders crept up to her ears. "Well, he wanted money." She spat the word out like she was talking about camel dung. "He wanted a cut. A *huge* cut." She shook her head. "I guess home sales haven't been so good lately."

"You killed two men for money," Carmela said.

"Well," Jenny said. "It was a *lot* of money."

A hand suddenly descended on Carmela's shoulder. She whirled around, only to find Quigg smiling at her, his warm hazel eyes dancing with excitement.

"You did it!" Quigg cried out joyously. "You solved Lash's murder!"

"How . . . how on earth did you find out?" Carmela stammered.

"Yeah," Babcock said, his jaw barely moving. "Who let you in?"

"I've been here all along," Quigg said. "Showcasing my wine."

"I ran over and grabbed him," Ava said, giving a mischievous smile. "I figured he deserved to share in the good news. He should know that his good name has been cleared."

"Is that true?" Quigg focused on Babcock. "Am I really cleared?"

Babcock stood there stolidly. Looking like he'd rather hawk a rat, rather have his fingernails pulled out one by one.

Carmela nudged Babcock. "Tell him," she said. "He deserves to know."

Babcock grimaced. "As much as it pains me to say this, Mr. Brevard, you are officially off the hook for the murder of Martin Lash."

"Thank you!" Quigg cried.

"The thanks should go to Carmela and her . . . ahem . . . rather unorthodox compadres here. They managed to locate the fish pens that were the source of all this mayhem."

"We exposed the entire operation," Ava said.

Babcock continued, "In the face of such overwhelming evidence, Mrs. Harvey Jewel has also given us what we believe is the beginning of a full confession. Of course, we need to take this to the district attorney and . . ."

But nobody was listening, they were cheering so loudly.

Quigg put his hands on Carmela's shoulders and gazed at her lovingly. "Babe . . . I could kiss you for this!"

Babcock hastily broke off his speech and said, "Oh no you don't, she's mine!"

Carmela gazed at him expectantly. "I am?"

"Was there ever a doubt?" he asked.

"Well . . . yeah."

"Not in my mind," Babcock said.

"Me neither," Ava added.

"A toast," Squirrel said. He grabbed a bottle of Perrier-Jouët champagne and began pouring flutes for everyone. "To true love."

Quigg stared at Squirrel. "Who are you guys again?"

Ava jumped in to explain. "Squirrel and Moony are the

guys who helped us find the fish ponds." She wrapped her arm around Squirrel and said, "This is Squirrel, and that handsome fella over there is Moony."

"Looks like I'm much obliged to you boys," Quigg said. "I owe you a ton of thanks."

Squirrel actually blushed through his sunburn, but it was hard to tell which embarrassed him more—Quigg's compliment or Ava's semi–choke hold. As if he wanted in on the good vibrations, too, Cooter sauntered over and plopped down at his master's feet.

"Hey, whose dog?" Quigg asked. He glanced at Babcock. "Police dog? Drug sniffer?"

"Oh, hell no," Babcock said.

"He's mine," Squirrel said. "One of my bayou pooches." He eyed Quigg carefully. "Say now, Ava tells me you own a restaurant right here in the French Quarter."

"That's right," Quigg said. "Mumbo Gumbo, one of the finest places you'd ever want to dine at. And if you ever want to enjoy dinner there, rest assured you'd be my special guests. Anything you want to eat, any wine you request."

"We was wondering," Moony said. "Do you know the fella who owns that place called Scarlett's Cabaret?"

"Well . . . sure," Quigg said. "That's Raymie Savoy's place. But that bar is kind of a . . ."

"Have you got any juice there?" Squirrel asked.

"I do," Quigg said. "But, you know, it's kind of a rough joint."

"No problem," Squirrel said, scratching his belly. "We'll fit right in."

"In that case, I'd be happy to arrange for you to sit in the VIP section," Quigg said. "Just let me know when you'd like to go."

"Now?" Moony said.

Quigg grinned. "Well, why not?" He chuckled. "You know, boys, I just might come along with you."

BABCOCK GRABBED CARMELA'S ELBOW AND steered her away from the crowd. "Carmela, we need to talk."

"I know," she said, a sinking feeling suddenly making her stomach ache. "We've had a pretty tough week, you and I."

"What I've been thinking is . . ."

Carmela held up a hand. "I know. You want to break up with me." Her voice was shaking now and she fought hard to control it. "I know I deserve this. I know I've been driving you crazy." She blinked away tears as she gazed up at him. He was so good-looking, so dear to her, and now she'd let him slip away. "But if sometime . . . you could find it in your heart . . ."

Babcock shook his head. "That's not what I was going to say."

"Oh." Carmela stared at him, befuddled. "Then what . . . ?" Did he want to yell at her some more? Tell her what a fool she'd been? Well, fine, she'd go ahead and let him have at it. She knew she probably deserved it.

"I was going to say that maybe we should get married."

Carmela's mouth literally dropped open. "What?" It came out more as a mouse squeak.

"What I was going to say was . . ."

Carmela waved a hand impatiently. "I got that already. Skip to the last part."

"Maybe we should get married?" Babcock said.

"Edgar, you're scaring me. This isn't some kind of joke, is it?"

"No joke. You want me to get down on bended knee?"

Carmela thought about it. "No. That would be too weird."

"What's weird is that we're arguing about this," Babcock said.

"Are we?"

"Of course. Then again, we argue about everything."

"So why would you want to marry me then?" Carmela asked.

Babcock squinted at her. "Because I love you?"

"I can't quite tell if that's a heartfelt declaration or a quasi-question."

"A little of both, I guess."

Carmela thought for a few moments. "If we did get married, nothing would change . . . right?"

"I never thought it would."

"I wouldn't have to . . . oh, I don't know . . ." Carmela tried to think of some odious task, something Shamus would have expected her to do. "Do wifely things like cook stewed okra or clean the lint trap in the clothes dryer, would I?"

"I'm sure I can handle those particular things myself."

"Then . . . okay. Yes, I will marry you." Carmela's heart was thump-thump-thumping out of her chest with joy as she held up a finger. "But not this very moment in time. I really, really love you, but you have to give me, like . . . oh my gosh . . . maybe six months. Okay?"

Babcock grinned from ear to ear. "That's great, Carmela! Fantastic!" Then he hesitated. "Wait a minute. What's going to happen in six months?"

Carmela reached up, twined a hand in his hair, and pulled his face down to meet hers. She kissed him lightly on the lips and then gazed at him, a crooked smile lighting her face. "You never know," she whispered. "You just never know."

Scrapbook, Stamping, and Craft Tips from Laura Childs

✂

Road Trip!

When creating a scrapbook page to showcase your most recent vacation, consider using a road map as your background. Tear a page from an old atlas or grab a car map and glue it on your page. Arrange your photos in a fun collage style and be sure to include ticket stubs, programs, hotel postcards, luggage tags, and other memorabilia you picked up on your trip.

Lollipop Flowers

Paper lollipop flowers are easy to make. Create a template for your flower petals and then cut out a dozen or so petals using tissue paper or crepe paper. Using a lollipop or Tootsie Pop as the center of your flower, tape the bottom of your petals to the lollipop stick and then pull the petals into shape, fashioning a lovely rose or daisy. The lollipop sticks can then be attached to a stiff pipe cleaner if you want a longer stem. These make great favors for kids!

Journal Your Page

A scrapbook page doesn't necessarily have to have photos. You can also journal your scrapbook page. With colored pens and a few freehand doodles, tell a story about a visit with a special friend, a trip to the museum, or a solitary walk through the woods. You can use free verse, rhymes, or even create a kind of rebus, where drawings illustrate some of your words. Whatever you do, tell your story straight from the heart.

Collage with Paper Napkins

These days paper napkins come in the most elegant designs and patterns, making them perfect for creating a collage. Napkin designs feature Renaissance angels, Parisian street scenes, autumn motifs, bridal-inspired designs, and so much more. Even background motifs like an elegant paisley or floral design will work well in a collage. And a pack of paper napkins is often more affordable than fancy paper.

Wrap the Map

For fun and inspired gift wrap, tear out pages from an old road atlas or use a map. Imagine an art history book wrapped in a map depicting the streets of Rome. Or a wedding gift wrapped in a map of Jamaica, the honeymooners' destination. Use the map as you would wrapping paper and then tie an elegant gossamer bow around it!

Punch It Up

Sharpen your favorite paper punches that have gone dull by punching them through a piece of tinfoil a few times. Your punch will soon be crisp and sharp again.

Wedding Scrapbook

For a perfect wedding scrapbook, start with a theme. Hearts and flowers, elegant lace, your wedding venue, etc. Organize your photo of the big event and add short stories as well as captions. A photo of you walking down the aisle (or watching your daughter walk down the aisle) will be more memorable if you share your inner feelings (yes, goose bumps, heart thumping, and all the good stuff!).

Favorite
New Orleans Recipes

✂

Mini Cranberry Crab Cakes

⅓ cup cream cheese, softened
¼ cup crabmeat, drained, flaked, cartilage removed
½ tsp. sugar
2 Tbsp. scallions, finely chopped
1 (1.9-oz.) pkg. frozen miniature phyllo tart shells
⅓ cup whole-berry cranberry sauce

Preheat oven to 375 degrees. In a small bowl, combine cream cheese, crab, sugar, and scallions until thoroughly blended. Place tart shells on an ungreased baking sheet. Fill each shell with 1 Tbsp. crab mixture. Top each crab mound with 1 tsp. cranberry sauce. Bake for 12 to 14 minutes or until heated through. Makes 15 mini crab cakes.

Cajun Pork Roast

2 lb. boneless pork loin roast
1 Tbsp. cooking oil
3 Tbsp. paprika
½ tsp. cayenne powder
2 tsp. oregano
2 tsp. salt
½ tsp. ground white pepper
¼ tsp. nutmeg

Preheat oven to 350 degrees. Rub pork loin with oil. Combine all seasonings in a small bowl and then rub onto meat. Place roast in shallow pan. Roast for approximately 1 hour, then let rest for 5 to 10 minutes before slicing. Serves 4.

Crock-Pot Lemon Chicken

4 chicken breasts, boned and skinned
¼ cup lemon juice
¼ cup brown sugar
¼ tsp. oregano
¼ tsp. paprika
1 (6-oz.) can mushrooms

Place chicken in Crock-Pot. Sprinkle with lemon juice, brown sugar, and seasonings. Then add mushrooms without draining them. Cook on high for approximately 2 hours. Serves 4.

Crock-Pot Cajun Pecans

1 lb. pecan halves
4 Tbsp. butter, melted
1 tsp. chili powder
1 tsp. salt
1 tsp. dried oregano
1 tsp. dried thyme
½ tsp. onion powder
¼ tsp. cayenne pepper

Combine all ingredients in your Crock-Pot and mix well. Cover and cook on high for 15 minutes. Remove cover, stir, and turn Crock-Pot to low setting. Cook for another 2 hours. Transfer pecans to a baking sheet and allow them to cool.

Big Easy Caramel Corn

2 cups brown sugar
1 cup granulated sugar
⅔ cup corn syrup
1 cup butter, melted
1 tsp. cream of tartar
2 to 3 gallons popped popcorn

In saucepan, bring first 5 ingredients to a boil, stirring constantly. Place popcorn in a large bowl and carefully pour caramel mixture over it. Stir immediately to evenly coat popcorn. Enjoy!

Boo and Poobah's Favorite Dog Cookies

2½ cups whole wheat flour
½ cup nonfat dry milk powder
1 egg
½ cup vegetable oil
1 beef bouillon cube dissolved in ½ cup hot water
1 Tbsp. brown sugar

Preheat oven to 300 degrees. Combine all ingredients in large mixing bowl. Stir until blended, then turn out onto a floured surface and knead gently for about 2 minutes. Using a floured rolling pin, roll dough out to about ¼-inch thickness. Use round cutter or bone-shaped cutter to cut out dog cookies. Place on ungreased baking sheet and bake for 30 minutes. Remove from pan and cool on wire rack. Makes about 40 cookies.

Apricot Barbecued Ribs

5 lbs. pork ribs or spare ribs
1 (16-oz.) can apricots, drained
¼ cup brown sugar, packed
1 tsp. chili powder
½ cup ketchup
½ cup white vinegar
2 tsp. Worcestershire sauce

Place ribs in a large pot and cover with water. Bring to a rapid boil, then cover, reduce heat, and simmer for 30 minutes. Drain ribs and arrange in a large, shallow baking dish. Combine apricots, brown sugar, chili powder, ketchup, white vinegar, and Worcestershire sauce. Blend until nice and smooth. Pour sauce over ribs, turning to coat. Cover and marinate in refrigerator 4 to 8 hours, turning occasionally. Preheat oven to 425 degrees. Remove ribs from marinade and place on a lightly greased rack in broiler pan, reserving marinade for basting. Bake for 40 minutes, basting twice. (Hint: these ribs can also be cooked on an outdoor grill.) Serves 4 to 6.

Cranberry Muffins

1 cup cranberries, fresh or frozen
½ cup sugar
2 cups flour
4 tsp. baking powder
¾ tsp. salt
1 egg
1 cup milk
4 Tbsp. melted butter

Preheat oven to 425 degrees. Chop cranberries and sprinkle with half the sugar. Sift flour, baking powder, salt, and remaining sugar together. Beat egg slightly, combine with milk and melted butter, and then add to dry ingredients. Stir only until blended. Fold in cranberries. Pour batter into a buttered muffin pan and bake for approximately 25 minutes. Yields 12 medium-sized muffins.

Baked Avocado Egg Rolls

2 large, ripe avocados, diced
juice of 1 lime
4 oz. (½ pkg.) cream cheese
2 Tbsp. sun-dried tomatoes in oil, drained and chopped
¼ cup onion, minced
2 Tbsp. cilantro, chopped (optional)
pinch of red pepper flakes
salt and pepper to taste
9 egg roll wrappers
vegetable oil

Preheat oven to 400 degrees. Place diced avocados in medium bowl and stir in lime juice. Stir in cream cheese, sun-dried tomatoes, onion, cilantro, red pepper flakes, and salt and pepper. Mix well. Lay out egg roll wrappers. Place 2 to 3 Tbsp. of avocado mixture down the middle of each wrapper. Fold one point of wrapper down over mixture, then fold in the two sides. Using a bit of water on remaining wrapper tip, fold that in and seal. Brush egg rolls lightly with vegetable oil. Place on lightly greased baking sheet and bake for 10 minutes. Turn rolls over and bake for another 10 minutes. Serve with your favorite dipping sauce.

Keep reading for an excerpt of
Laura Childs's next Cackleberry Club Mystery . . .

Egg Drop Dead

Coming December 2016 in hardcover
from Berkley Prime Crime!

IT was an autumn of particular intensity. Of riotous colors and delft blue skies, cool nights with smoke curling out of chimneys. Halloween was barely a week away and Suzanne Dietz was feeling mighty pleased with herself as she glanced at the puddle of black silk lying on the car seat next to her. She'd just picked up the wicked witch costume that her neighbor Laurel Kennedy had sewn for her. The woman was a creative genius when it came to three yards of fabric, six yards of black scalloped lace, and a Singer sewing machine. Suzanne, on the other hand, managed to impale her finger every time she picked up a needle to sew on a button or whip-stitch a hem. Which is why she was congratulating herself for outsourcing such an odious task and looking forward to her role as a well-stitched witch at the Cackleberry Club's upcoming Halloween celebration.

Changing lanes, Suzanne caught her own reflection in the rearview mirror and thought, *Correction, make that a modern-day witch.*

Just a hair past forty, Suzanne was lean, square-shouldered, and still golden brown from puttering around her herb garden in the summer sun. Her hair was a shoulder-length silvered blond, her eyes a deep cornflower blue. Today she wore a white blouse, nipped tightly at her waist by a silver concho belt, and a pair of slim-fitting jeans. She had on her favorite cowboy boots, the well-worn brown ones with turquoise leather steer heads inset at the ankles.

Suzanne was the self-appointed purveyor of foods and the driving force behind the Cackleberry Club, a cozy little farm-to-table café she ran with her two BFFs, Toni and Petra. She was also recently engaged to Dr. Sam Hazelet, who had to be the most handsome and skilled doctor in the small Midwestern town of Kindred.

Suzanne smiled to herself as she drove along, the noon sun lasering down upon the windshield of her Taurus. Sam was quite a catch, she mused. Four years younger than she was, great sense of humor, and, most important, in love with her. (Okay, truth be told, he might even be a little besotted with her.)

If she hadn't hit the boyfriend jackpot, she probably would have (horrors!) been forced to venture onto one of those Internet dating sites. Then her character sketch might have read something like, *Overworked café owner, dog mom, and curiosity seeker hopes to meet fun-loving guy for wine dinners, occasional trout fishing, and long-term mischief.* And after a few sketchy responses, someone like Sam would have popped up. Or not.

Suzanne drank in the scenery as the blacktopped country road dipped down and the woods closed in on either side of her. Late October meant the oaks and maples had erupted in a riot of crimson and orange, and every time a puff of wind came along, leaves fluttered down in perfect golden swirls. It made her think of bonfires and pumpkin spice muffins, and, of course, Halloween.

Coming up out of a valley onto a slight ridge, the road suddenly hooked right and ran alongside a rustic fence of silvered, weathered wood. That fence marked the property line for Mike Mullen's dairy farm. Mike was Suzanne's go-to guy for the homemade wheels of tasty cheddar and Swiss cheese that she served and sold at the Cackleberry Club. Tapping her brakes lightly, Suzanne coasted along until she spotted Mike's familiar tilting mailbox up ahead. This behemoth of dented metal was surrounded by a tangle of bright red bittersweet and sat beside a hand-painted sign that read *Cloverdale Farm—Farm Fresh Milk and Cheese.*

Suzanne turned into the driveway and crunched her way down a narrow gravel road. A quarter of a mile later, her car rolled to a stop in Mike's farmyard. The place was picture-perfect, an old-fashioned farm built in the early 1900s by hard-working German immigrants. Off to the right was a classic *American Gothic* farmhouse complete with finials, balustrades, and a rambling old front porch. Straight ahead was a faded red hip-roofed dairy barn. Several smaller buildings that housed bales of hay and farm tools were scattered off to the left, and a large, woodsy pasture butted up close to the house and barn.

Suzanne slid out of her car and scuffed the toe of her boot into the gravel.

"Hey, Mike," she called out. "It's Suzanne." She let out a breath. "From the Cackleberry Club."

The big sliding barn door stood wide open and she expected to see Mike's broad, grinning face appear at any moment.

When, after a minute or two, Mike didn't duck out and greet her, Suzanne decided he must be all the way back in the barn, tending his cows. Or maybe he was in the adjacent cheese workshop, a place with a pleasant, yeasty smell and gleaming stainless steel pipes, tanks, and tables. The place where all the cheese magic happened.

"No problem," Suzanne said, striking out for the barn. She'd talked to Mike a couple of days ago and told him she needed to replenish her larder with a few wheels of his delicious cheese. He'd told her to stop by anytime. Well, now was anytime.

Suzanne ducked inside the barn, going from dazzling sunlight to a dim interior. She blinked hard a couple of times, trying to adjust her eyes, keenly aware of the mingled sharp scents of cows and hay.

"Mike?" she called again.

This time Suzanne received an answer. But it wasn't from Mike. Instead, she was greeted by a cacophony of loud bellows.

"What?" she murmured.

A few steps down the center aisle and Suzanne was confronted by the urgent, upturned faces of four dozen cows bawling unhappily at her. Cows that clearly hadn't been milked yet.

Haven't been milked yet? But it's twenty after twelve. These poor things have been waiting all morning?

Where was Mike? Suzanne wondered as she tiptoed through the barn. On either side, cows continued to blat anxiously as they stretched their necks out to greet her. To plead for help. And the farther in she ventured, the more the cows' mooing turned to pitiful moans.

Where the stanchions ended there were two box stalls. Animals moved about restlessly in there, too. Horses that tossed their heads and banged their hooves hard against the wooden walls.

What was going on?

"Mike?" Suzanne called out, trying to keep a slight quaver out of her voice. "Are you back here?" She hesitated and peered into the dimness ahead of her where dust motes twirled lazily and worn leather halters and bridles hung on wooden pegs. Then she added, "Are you okay?"

Moving toward the wooden door that led into the cheese workshop, Suzanne felt a prickle of unease. The hairs on the back of her neck were starting to stand up straight. Really? Now, why was that? Then her heart did a little thump-bump inside her chest and her breathing became a little more rapid. Had something happened to Mike? Or was she simply over-reacting to the agitation of the cows?

Suzanne tamped down her fears and rapped her knuckles sharply against the white wooden door of the cheese workshop.

"Mike? Are you in there?"

No answer.

Gathering up her nerve, Suzanne put a hand flat against the door and gave it a shove. Instead of swinging open on its hinges, the door creaked open a couple of inches and stopped. Frowning, she pushed again, this time with a little more force.

No way. Something seemed to be blocking it.

Suzanne leaned forward and touched her cheek to the door, the smooth wood feeling cool against her skin. Then she poked her nose in, trying to peer around the edge of the door.

The first thing she saw was a green rubber boot turned sideways on the damp cement floor. That boot was clearly attached to a leg.

Mike? Something's happened to Mike?

Worry exploded in Suzanne's brain. She drew a quick breath, took a step back, and then flung her full body weight against the door. The door creaked open another foot. Suzanne eased herself into the room, where Mike Mullen sprawled awkwardly on the floor. His white hair was matted with bright red blood as if he'd sustained a dozen deep scalp lacerations, and his gnarled hands were crisscrossed with bloody defensive wounds. The blue-and-white-striped overalls he wore were completely slashed and tattered, as if he'd been existing as a castaway on some remote South Seas jungle island. The fabric was also completely saturated with blood.

Dead? Mike's dead?

Suzanne's mind spun like a runaway centrifuge. *Who? Why?* A hundred questions churned inside her head. She lunged forward, somehow thinking she'd check his pulse or hopefully clear an airway. But her foot slipped in the slick pool of blood and she fell forward. If she hadn't thrust her hands out to break her fall, she would have landed right square on top of his body. As it was, her ungainly fall put her on her hands and knees, looking directly into wide-open milky white eyes that stared sightlessly into a void.

"Mike?" Suzanne said again in a pleading, still-hopeful tone. Because she was still trying to make sense of how someone could cold-bloodedly murder this mild-mannered dairy farmer.

Writing as Laura Childs, this author has brought you the *New York Times* bestselling Tea Shop Mysteries, Scrapbooking Mysteries, and Cackleberry Club Mysteries. Now, writing under her own name of Gerry Schmitt, she has created an entirely new series of sharp-edged thrillers.

LITTLE GIRL GONE

AN AFTON TANGLER THRILLER

by Gerry Schmitt

On a frozen night in an affluent Minneapolis neighborhood, a baby is abducted from her home after her babysitter is violently assaulted. The parents are frantic, the police are baffled, and, with the perpetrator already in the wind, the trail is getting colder by the second.

As a family liaison officer with the Minneapolis Police Department, it's Afton Tangler's job to deal with the emotional aftermath of terrible crimes—but she's never faced a case quite as brutal as this. Each development is more heartbreaking than the last and the only lead is a collection of seemingly unrelated clues.

Available in hardcover from Berkley!